CANDY SAVANT

A.L. HAWKE

PHANTOM HEART, LLC

ISBN: 978-1-7329563-1-5 (ebook)

ISBN: 978-1-7329563-0-8 (paperback)

ISBN: 978-1-953919-12-0 (hardcover)

Library of Congress Control Number: 2018967363

This is a work of fiction. It all comes directly from the imagination of the author's mind. This includes names, characters, places, and incidents. Any public names are used solely for creative purposes. Any resemblance to actual people, living or dead, or to companies, institutions or locales is entirely coincidental or accidental.

Line edited by Paul Witcover

Proofread by Eliza Dee of Clio Editing Services

Cover Design © 2019 by Damon Za

Published by Phantom Heart, LLC

27702 Crown Valley Pkwy D-4, #201

Ladera Ranch, CA 92694, USA

Printed and bound in the United States of America

First printing January, 2019

Learn more about A.L. Hawke at www.alhawke.com

Correspondence: contact@alhawke.com

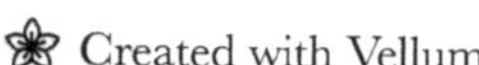 Created with Vellum

1

———

RUN, LITTLE BIRD, RUN

"Care for a stick of gum?"

The dim yellow light from the ceiling cast shadows about Candice's puffy cheeks. Elise wanted to run her black-gloved fingers along her soft skin; Candice's pale skin and long golden hair made such a lovely portrait in the dim light. They sat across from each other at the center of the drab windowless room in two matching metal chairs with only a small plastic table between them.

Elise leaned forward, waving the bright red stick of gum. "No?"

Candice shook her head.

Candice was much younger than Elise, in her twenties. She had small blue eyes—beautiful sapphire eyes. Elise looked at them, watching her all the way from her pretty face down to her saffron silk blouse. Candice looked nervous. She twirled her golden-blond curls with shaky fingers while biting her thin upper lip. Her facial muscles twitched a little before Team Mother.

Elise waved the gum again. "No?"

Candice shook her head again.

"Why not? You think your Team Mother's so geeked out

that she's a dirty little whore? Is that it? I offer Mint, but that doesn't make Mother your sugar momma. Who the hell do you think you are?"

"No. Of course not, it's just—"

"What? It's just what? It's a goddamn piece of gum."

Mint gum was a soft cohesive substance developed by Magnacourt Corporation, consisting of just the perfect amount of sorbitol, gum base, soy lecithin, carnauba wax, maltodextrin, riboflavin, red #40, caffeine, and cocaine to render it addicting and delicious. Elise loved Mint. She ran her tongue along the glob of gum already in her mouth, relishing the flavor.

Then she took a deep breath and threw Candice's intended piece of gum into her own mouth. She ran an index finger along her left arm, sifting through files on the screen embedded in her wrist while flicking her fingers out a few times to stop her hand from shaking.

"I detest unpunctuality," said Elise, though in fact Candice had not arrived late to the meeting. "It makes me wonder about your habits in the lab. If you want to be late, this job isn't for you."

"I'm never late, Mother. I work very hard and—"

"The responsibility of a Savant goes far beyond science," Elise said, raising a forestalling finger. "Punctuality is the smallest part. You will be held in high regard by all the citizens of my city. But there's a price. Do you understand?"

"Yes... I think—"

"You think what?" Elise rolled her eyes. "A Savant is a leader. The title of Savant is the greatest honor a geneticist can receive. While you research, you will also rule and protect the people as an Officer, an Officer and leader of the people."

"It's a great honor. I understand."

"No, you don't. You really don't. You will have to have the courage to hold yourself and others accountable for my actions, even if that means hurting them. Can you do that?

Can you honor and serve me? Your Team Mother? I'm not so sure you can, Candy, but that is what makes a Lead Savant—not just a scientist, but a Savant. Can you be that leader? A Lead Savant?" Elise preempted Candice's attempt at a reply. "Do you understand? Or are you too much of a dumb fuck to even know the difference between your ass and a hole in the ground?"

"Yes, Mother."

"Yes what?" Elise folded her arms. "Yes, you understand, or, yes, you think your butthole is a hole in the ground?"

"I understand." Candice laughed nervously, then quickly averted her eyes.

"Stop being polite," Elise said. "It's disgusting."

Candice opened her eyes wider and stared at the white brick wall. She shook her head slightly, leaving a perplexed look on her face. Elise loved watching Candice get flustered, but she loved viewing the gorgeous features of her face even more.

"I understand the great importance of the job," Candice said softly.

"Do you really?"

Elise frowned, then looked back down at her wrist monitor. She already knew Candice's qualifications: her exemplary work on gene mapping, her award-winning thesis on cloning limbic neural networks, and her stellar grades on her exit exams. Candice had graduated the University of Arkite at the top of her class. A 4.8 average. She had even interned under Savant Garvey, a highly reputable elder professor working on organ culturing in Sector Three. Oh, she was more than qualified when it came to the sciences. But Elise was uncertain how Candice would cope with the more stressful, less analytical, aspects of the job. For Mother, these areas were just as vital, perhaps more so.

Fucking, for example. When Elise had searched through the graduate database of the university, she'd been looking for a graduate of Caucasian descent who was thin, athletic, and well endowed. She preferred white girls, though she wasn't white herself, because she liked their red areolas and the way white necks, chests, and faces turned rosy when excited: the exact shade Candice's face was turning now. It was a classically angelic face, like some kind of cherub out of a Michelangelo painting.

Umm, I want to scissor you, Goldilocks, on some fresh, clean white sheets.

But it wasn't enough for Elise to screw her Lead Savant. She wanted to screw her mind too. She did this simply by poking and prodding her with language and gestures just to redden those glorious cheeks.

Elise liked Candice. She wasn't arrogant. She seemed sweet and serene. Elise thought that profile fit with hers. She had known it would. That's why Elise had hired her last month as her Lead Assistant Savant when accessing the mainframe in her penthouse office. Of course, Candice didn't know that, which only made the torture more delicious, like foreplay.

Elise's eyes widened, and a sly grin grew on her face upon finding a file of her new recruit drying off her long hair from the shower. She could just see the crack of Candice's ass in a mirror. Plump but not fat. Juicy. She turned her arm at an angle to make sure Candice couldn't see.

"Why so quiet?" Elise asked. "Silence must mean you really have no idea of the importance of the job."

"No, Mother, of course I do."

Elise threw her black lace-up boots on top of the very small white plastic table, shook out her long black hair, fixed the metal collar on her matching black lace shirt, which was so sharp a choker that it looked like it might guillotine her head straight off, and pulled out some lipstick and a compact from her pants pocket. She applied black color to her lips with a shaky hand, gazing at herself in the small mirror, then returned the makeup to her pocket.

She offered her gum again.

Candice declined with a shake of her head.

"No?" Elise asked. "Why the fuck not? It's really cinnamon-y. Savants have the supply. You work with me, and you'll have all the Mint you want. It's really yummy."

"Sorry, Master, I—"

"Call me Elise. Not *Master*."

"Elise."

"Yeah."

"Okay, Elise."

"Right," she said, adding the gum to her mouth and chomping down. "Now, why don't you start by telling me and the mainframe your full name?"

"23N—"

"I said your name." She leaned forward, raising a finger. "Relax. Why are you so nervous?"

"I'm not nervous."

"Then tell me your fucking name."

"Candice Harlow."

"Savant Candice Harlow. Candy. Like, my Candy little tweetsy tweet tweet Savant." Elise folded her arms and crossed her legs. Then she waved a hand frivolously through the air. "Now, if you accept, we will make it official. You will be called Lead Assistant Savant Candy Harlow."

Candice bit her lip again but did not otherwise respond. In the silence, Elise heard her own mouth chomping: up and down, up and down, up and down, up and—

"It would be an honor, Elise."

"An honor?" Elise blew a big red bubble toward Candice's face and burst out laughing. "That's funny." She laughed again. "Very funny. You're cute, Candy."

Elise especially liked her hands. They were so thin and dainty. She watched as Candice brushed her pale fingers across her forehead and ears. They were simply lovely hands. They were the loveliest hands Elise had ever seen. And her voice. It was high, almost too high, but that was also cute. She had a lovely voice. But most striking were those sapphire-blue, almost glowing, dark jeweled eyes. Candice blinked them, and Elise wished she'd blink them some more.

Then Elise blinked her own eyes. The dim light was starting to bother her. She had chewed too many sticks of Mint—now hers *and* her new recruit's. Not to mention the other pack she had already chewed earlier this morning to get her mind off her interrogation of another scientist who had stolen intellectual property.

Elise gripped her fist real hard and then took the glove off, shaking out her fingers. Then she looked at Candice. She leaned forward and reached out to touch Candice's face. Candice initially jerked back, but then she sat stiff and frozen —frozen like... a small little bird. Candice followed Elise's hand with her eyes as it slowly stroked her cheek, up and down, up and down—just like the gum—up and down, up and down, up—

"Why did you say tweet?" asked Candice, bewildered, pulling back.

"Because, my dear, you remind me of a puny little chirping bird. Those eyes and that face. It's like a tweeting bird, you know, ready to be pounced on." She raised her hands up, mimicking claws. "Tweet tweet. Tweet tweet."

"I don't like it."

Elise flashed a smile at her and nodded, chomping her gum. "You'll have the best things—the very best things. But with them comes danger. Danger is something you'll have to face as a Savant— *my* Savant. You and me and danger. Can you handle danger?"

Candice nodded.

"You accept, then?"

"Yes."

"Welcome to Magnacourt," Elise said simply. She stood and extended her hand. Candice got to her feet and took it.

Elise smiled sweetly for a moment, chewing her gum and holding on to that lovely hand as she let her eyes run down the girl's long legs in their tight black slacks. Candice relaxed and smiled too. But Elise never really wanted her Savants to relax at all. She wanted them to be afraid. She preferred complete and utter terror.

So, all of a sudden, Elise slammed both fists hard against the table and then pointed a finger right between her eyes. Candice fell back in her chair, and Elise imagined the rapid flutter of her little birdy heart.

"I'll wake you up, you innocent cunt! Pry open those eyes and fillet you open!

"I am your mother! Ask me when you eat and drink. I am your leader. Ask me when you sleep and when you piss. You stray too far from mother's will and I'll take you down and devour you, bitch!

"Don't ever cross me! Don't you ever betray me. If you turn from me, I'll hunt you down and pluck pluck pluck all those fucking feathers and serve you for dinner. Understand me, Doctor?"

She stiffened over Candice and took a deep breath, closing her eyes, trying to steady herself. Her little birdy breathed short and fast below her, but Elise dared not look down. Wide-eyed terror, or even worse, apathy, might take her over the edge and make her hurt her precious new little birdy recruit. So Elise slowly sank back down in her chair, shrugged her shoulders, and looked away.

"I am sorry... Elise," Candice finally muttered.

Elise looked at her, throwing another piece of gum in her mouth. Candice appeared more puzzled than afraid.

"Don't worry 'bout it," said Elise, shrugging again, as if to excuse her crazed rage as a simple tic. "Anywho," she said with a sigh, "care to see the lab?"

2
____

BUTTERFLY

Candice looked out from the rooftop of the HQ Civic Building of Sector One. Being on its roof provided the most spectacular view Candice had ever seen of the city. She took a deep breath, trying to enjoy the fresh open air and the brief respite from her interview, while doing her best to suppress her fear over what she was about to do.

Arkite was a giant pyramid city densely packed with triangular, polyhedral and diamond-shaped steel skyscrapers, all surrounded by photovoltaic megatrusses used to capture sunlight, store energy and protect the city from the outer elements. The megatrusses were arranged in a checkered fashion with openings like a chain-link fence. Looking through the openings along the side trusses, Candice could always see the far-off sands that surrounded Arkite, but now at this height, for the first time in her life, she could make out mountain ranges far beyond the desert dunes.

She looked over the ledge and wished she hadn't. Straight down she could see Main Street and, at a few intersections, the rush of large groups of people in gray suits walking in line and being herded by flying traffic drones across the street. At other lights, people stood waiting in line. The streets themselves were nearly empty of cars, but the sidewalks were crowded with citizens. They all looked so tiny down below.

Further out was her favorite part of the city, Central Park. The view calmed her for a moment. It was breathtaking. Her beloved park was so lush, spanning miles of lovely gardened paths, arched bridges and a lovely woman-made lake. It had been copied after the famous recreation area in New York City. And so, New York, having been destroyed in the great cataclysm two hundred years before Candice was born, still lived on through this replica. Even the famous Arc de Triomphe from Paris had survived the global war, with a duplicate set at the entrance to the park.

Candice finally spotted HQ lab. The iron-red train was speeding along in the distance, snaking in and out of alleyways at great speeds. No one knew why Elise had built the lab on a moving train. Many suspected it had to do with secrecy. Its route was always the same, running nonstop in and out of all four sectors of the city. She spotted the train a few miles away, currently traveling between the all-glass crystal buildings of Sector Two. When weaving close to the glass walls, it seemed to be moving even faster.

"Ready?" Elise tapped her on her shoulder.

No.

Candice slowly climbed the steps of a cement platform and mounted her bike. The bike was sleekly shaped, with a leather seat over two rocket engines (instead of wheels), handlebars and a large central monitor. Her heart was now pounding in her chest. She leaned forward and held the handlebars.

Candice's rocket bike was jet black. Elise's bike beside her was cherry red. Candice had changed downstairs into a matching skin-tight black leather—and remarkably comfortable—jumpsuit. Elise had changed into a cherry-red one.

Elise followed Candice and stood behind her on the platform, leaning down and helping her strap both legs into two open metal cuffs. The cuffs shut snug over her ankles like a trap. She showed Candice that she could easily close or release them by kicking her legs. Then she winked, assuring her that they provided all the safety she needed to prevent her from falling.

Elise reached over her shoulder and pointed at some switches. There was a large lever to the right of her handlebar. She told Candice not to touch that. Then there was the middle screen. With a wave of Elise's hand over the glass, the machine seemed to come alive. Candice could feel the power beneath her legs as the motor vibrated underneath her and lifted her up a little. Then Elise pointed to a red button and a larger green one. She told her not to touch those either. Elise glided a gloved finger over the handlebars. She showed her how to engage the rocket engine to her right with a twist. The brakes were easily hit with the footrests near Candice's feet. Elise reached down and ran a black-leather-gloved hand over them and then slowly over Candice's left thigh. She said this was how you slowed things down.

Candice looked up at her. Elise's light brown cheek was almost touching hers. Elise's black lips curled in a lascivious smile. She seemed happy—happy after running her gloved palm over her leg.

"Put your visor on," Elise said.

The "visor" was a modified open helmet folded into a small metal case hanging by the side of the bike. It was very light and, when unfolded, looked like a hard half eggshell with a transparent protective face-shield. The color of the visor matched the bike. Candice took the case hanging from the side, unfolded the visor, and placed it over her head. She was surprised to see that the streets below appeared clearer than before through the glass of the visor. It was a sunny day in Arkite, with few clouds in the sky. She looked down to the streets and could even make out the clothes people wore far below. She focused on a woman in a pretty turquoise shawl walking a dog out of a supermarket, then shifted her gaze to three young girls, teenagers, pushing and pulling at one another as they ran into an adjacent pharmacy.

She looked up at Elise. Elise was beaming. She brushed Candice's shoulder. "Ready to fly, tweetsy-pie?"

Candice nodded.

"Follow me."

Elise climbed her own platform and threw on her visor. Without hesitation, she launched herself over the edge of the high-rise. Candice's heart was thumping in her ears now; she was next. Candice had never ridden before, and now she was expected to launch over the building. She couldn't move. She sat frozen while he rocket engines roared beneath her legs. Candice looked beyond the platform and saw Elise with her black hair flowing behind her visor as she dropped down and circled the building.

"Go now, bitch!" Elise shouted. "Come on." The words reverberated in Candice's ears through the visor speakers.

Candice sighed and pulled the up lever slowly. The machine rose effortlessly above the platform. She moved the throttle forward, then launched off the building.

At first, Candice panicked, feeling the sensation of falling, but then the rocket engines pushed her forward and she was thrown backward in her seat. She clutched the handlebars and squeezed her thighs tight, for nothing kept her from plummeting to the ground except her legs.

Elise sped up faster as they rushed over the rooftops of skyscrapers, lifting a single finger and summoning Candice to follow.

They first traveled high. Elise ascended as high as possible toward the open ceiling of the city, the very pinnacle of the pyramidal wall, which was nearly a mile high. Candice's fear faded, being replaced by a sense of exhilaration over the rush of concrete walls passing fast beside her rocket cycle. Tall skyscrapers she had known ever since she was a little girl quickly passed beneath her.

But she dared not look down. Not until Elise came alongside her and then dropped like a stone, her hysterical laughter ringing in Candice's ears between the rush of wind. Candice dipped her own cycle down and carefully followed.

In less than a minute, she was leveling off and approaching Central Park. She flew over Lake Salmas and the great suspension bridge crossing its breadth, known as the Acrean Pass. Then she flew over a large field where many citizens who had been sunbathing or playing on the grass gazed up at her. Elise drew closer to the ground—so close that the jet from her rocket brushed over the leaves of trees. Candice followed. She approached a familiar beloved brook. She caught the faces of a few women as they walked over a series of small arched bridges over the water. They looked scared.

Candice's grip on the handlebar tightened. Somehow seeing her fellow citizens' fear brought back her own trepidation. Elise flew beside her, still laughing like a maniac.

It was Saturday. Truly a beautiful day. At least a thousand citizens were in the park enjoying the sunshine. Candice wondered what they thought when they looked up and saw their Team Mother and her new assistant zooming through the sky.

Candice had been a little girl when she had first seen the Savants. She remembered holding her mother's hand and pointing up at the rocket noise. But it was the smoke more than the cycles themselves that she had noticed. She had asked her mother what they were, but her mother hadn't answered. Instead, her mother had stood up straight and placed her hand over her heart.

"Fuck!" cried Elise through their headset. "Keep up! What's taking you sooo long?"

Next lesson.

Elise sped her rocket farther, leaving the park and rushing

over train tracks at the heart of Sector Two. They flew along streets and alleyways until they approached the iron-red train. Candice figured they must have been traveling close to two hundred miles an hour over the rails to keep up with the train below.

Elise swooped down and then gracefully sank like a pro over one of the cars. She made it look effortless. Then she shut off her rocket, dismounted the cycle, and waved from the rooftop for Candice to do the same thing.

You want me to land? thought Candice. *Are you crazy? On a moving train!*

Candice shook her head.

"Get down," Elise said through the speakers in her visor. Candice shook her head again, circling above her.

"Get down!" insisted Elise.

Candice slowly descended. She felt the cycle shake a little as she tried to hover at just the right speed. It was hard for her to gauge. She had never flown or landed a cycle, and certainly not on a moving train. She failed two attempts. Elise shouted in her ears. Candice tried once more. She just couldn't position the cycle in the right place. Candice looked down and saw Elise now jumping up and down in hysteria over the iron-red roof, throwing her hands up and down like a crazed monkey. If the whole thing hadn't been so terrifying, it might have been funny.

Candice tried again. She just couldn't aim it right. Now she was losing all control and balance.

"Get the fuck down!" cried Elise, still leaping up and down.

"Get down! Idiot!"

Candice swooped around for a fourth time.

"Get the fuck down! What the hell's the matter with you? Throw the fucking thing over the edge for all I care."

Bitch, thought Candice. The cycle shook as if acting out her indecision. *All right... you want me down?*

Candice circled one last time, hovered above, and then jumped. Well, Mother had suggested it. Right before the train turned, she had jumped from her seat. Her cycle left her legs and flew off in a straight line without changing trajectory. Candice stumbled and rolled across the roof of the train car. She would have gone over the edge had Elise not grabbed her.

The bike continued flying straight as an arrow toward a glass building a few blocks away. As Elise stopped Candice from careening off the train, glimpses of flames and smoke formed in the corner of Candice's eye, accompanied by the awful sound of shattered glass and a huge fiery explosion. Candice crouched in a ball, lurching beside her Team Mother like a baby. Elise threw her visor off in a rage and stood over Candice with a look of disgust. The witch's long black hair blew wildly in the wind as she stood in a wide stance to keep balanced on the train. Candice tore off her own visor. Elise glared at her. Candice started to cry.

"Do you have any idea how much that bike costs?"

"I don't care!" Candice yelled. "I've never ridden before. You expect me to land on a train?"

Candice looked back over her shoulder. The cycle had collided into an outdoor restaurant. A fire crew of small helicopter drones rushed down from the sky to put out the flames. There was a gaping hole in the glass building, and drones flew in and out like a frenzy of hornets in a hornet nest. Many people lay on the sidewalk, with ladies clutching bodies and a group of Officers in black trench coats running across the street over to the site. Some ladies were still running out of the smoky building.

Elise wagged her finger over her. "I would wager that cycle was worth more than your mommy's navel, tweety bitch."

Candice put her head in her hands and crouched down, whimpering.

Then Elise kicked her. She kicked her very hard. It was a terrible hit that knocked the wind out of her, nearly causing her to fly off the train again. Candice glanced up, and Elise looked as though, this time, she wouldn't have minded if Candice fell off.

Candice rolled on the red metal tarmac, moaning.

"Get up!" Elise yelled, reaching out a hand. "Get up! We've got work to do."

Candice shook her head.

"Stand up!" cried Elise.

Candice sat crouched in a ball, staring at the smoke as it became fainter in the distance.

"Come on...," Elise said more gently. "Look, I couldn't have flown better myself for my first run."

Candice looked up. Elise nodded and winked. "Aha." A thin grin formed on Elise's face. Then she reached down with her black-leather-gloved hand once more. "Come on."

"I don't want this!" Candice shouted, shaking her head. "Why'd you pick me? Why me?"

"Get up."

"Why? I don't want to. Look what happened. Just leave me alone."

"Get up now," Elise said, opening her brown eyes wide. She grabbed Candice and hauled her up. Then she spun her around, wagging that black-gloved finger in her face.

"You're better than this, Candy. You're a Savant now. Stand up."

Candice looked away for a moment. But then she turned back in defiance. "And if I don't?"

"You will," Elise replied, shaking her head.

"I already failed," Candice said, looking down. "And all those people... it's terrible."

By now they were so far from the accident that there was only a small plume of black smoke in the distance, but Candice still looked back and stared.

"What about them?" Elise asked. "Forget 'em, Candy. Let 'em chirp all the livelong fucking day. You're a Savant."

Elise smiled excitedly and grabbed her by the arm. "Come on."

Elise led her by the arm as they ran across the top of the train. Then, at the edge, she leaped across to the next car. She raised a hand and encouraged Candice to do the same. Candice looked at the gap at the end of the train car and the tracks on the ground racing under them, and then back at her crazy boss. She knew from Elise's eyes that if she didn't jump, it might take her boss over the edge. So she backed up and, closing her eyes, ran and jumped.

Elise helped her up on the other side. "Hey, you want a stick of gum?"

Candice shrugged and took one. She didn't even care anymore. Somehow all the excitement stopped her from thinking. She just took it and threw it in her mouth, and Elise's smile grew wider still as she ran with her over two more cars.

The gum was sweet. It had a delightful cinnamon flavor. Candice chewed a couple of times; then she felt the effect. It was like three cups of coffee, and every bite seemed better than the last. She felt stronger and, like the power of the visor, more able to focus on her environment. It felt wonderful.

She stopped, brushed her hair back from the rushing wind, and looked around the platform. The wind barely seemed to bother her anymore. Elise motioned for her to follow, but she was enthralled by the view of the surrounding skyscrapers.

She could see Central Park in the far distance again, all its green trees and pretty meandering brooks and streams. They had ridden over it just a few minutes ago, but now it was halfway across the whole city. She marveled how, from miles away, even without the visor, she could pick out couples with their children playing along the shore of the water, little girls splashing. Then she saw the Pyramid building of HQ, where they had come from after their "interview." She saw all the small windows of the buildings and imagined—yeah, must be imagined, for she was way too far away—ladies going about their important business in black and gray suits behind the slanted glass.

Then, really focusing, she imagined seeing her home in Sector Three, a simple college apartment that she was already moving out of. Her roommate, Violetta, had helped her all week to get her stuff together. Did she really see it, or was she just imagining it? It seemed like she saw it. She saw all the boxes packed and ready to be shipped to her new home in Sector One. As a Savant, and a Savant under the revered Team Mother, no less, she would be moving soon to a pad of unimaginable wealth and wonder. There was some excitement about that among her fear. She couldn't wait to see it. It seemed everything was clearer than it had ever been before.

"Bitch, what's the matter with you!" Elise yelled. "Come on."

Elise slipped between two of the cars and landed on a platform below. Candice followed her down a ladder. There before them was a door. Elise ran her wrist over the latch, and the door slid open.

Candice hadn't realized how noisy it was outside until they were inside the train. When Elise closed the door, it seemed completely silent. There was only a faint rumble from the rails below.

There was a smell. It was sterile like Lysol. Like a hospital. And the walls were white. On the walls were shelves and glass cabinets with various medical equipment. It reminded Candice of ambulance transports. She'd helped supply one of them as a volunteer job one summer. A lot of the equipment was the same—neatly stacked lines of medicine bottles, oxygen tanks, a cabinet of needles, scopes, tubes, masks—but here the items were pristine and ordered behind the glass, nicely wrapped in clear plastic. It looked as though no one had ever used the equipment. She surmised that this car was a storage room. At the back near a door hung a few white lab coats.

"What is this place?"

Elise put her finger over her lips.

"What is this place?" repeated Candice in a whisper.

"Shh."

It was so quiet.

Candice nodded and followed Elise to the end of the car. Elise turned carefully and stopped for a moment, leaning on one of the glass cabinets along the wall. Then she approached the door. She reached toward Candice.

"THE LAB!" she shouted in Candice's ear. Then Elise burst into laughter, hitting Candice's shoulder. "I'm just fucking with you. We don't have to be quiet here."

Elise waved her wrist over another sensor and led Candice in. In the center were three long black lab tables. On top of the tables were large metallic cylindrical centrifuges, old-fashioned Bunsen burners, plastic stirrers, and glass bottles of all sorts of colored fluids. It smelled like chemicals. Candice lifted one dark green bottle up to her nose: the smell was rotten and nauseating. Elise flashed an amused smile, then swayed her hips down the car, and Candice followed.

At the far end was another adjoining room with a glass door. Behind this door, Candice saw a sink and a few hazmat suits hanging near an adjoining door. There were two empty hospital beds with open beige curtains. The beds were covered in green sheets, and the ceiling and walls were painted a matching mint green. The equipment here was readier for use, and a tray and IV with a saline bag had even been left hanging beside one of the beds.

"Behind door number three, little tweetsy, is the surgery suite," Elise said, running her wrist over another sensor to slide open the door. She pointed. "We'll be in these last two rooms for the finished product, but mostly tossing ideas around here. You can sleep here too, if you'd like. Since I don't do a lot of work in this room, it doesn't stink as bad, right?" She wrinkled her nose. "Most of our work will be done in the lab. But the cabinets here"—she walked over and pulled down a large wooden cabinet full of sealed glass tissue specimens from a wall—"is where we can work out the final product and then autopsy the bloody douchebags in the last car."

Elise paused and smiled. She seemed to examine Candice from her black boots up to her tight rubber shoulders. "You look good in black." She ran her tongue along her black lipstick and then a hand down Candice's golden hair. "Real good." Candice shook her long hair away from Elise's fingers. "You scored high on your exams, Candy. Hope you haven't forgotten everything. You'll be dreaming Gs, Cs, tits and As among an ocean of ones and zeros here."

"This is your lab, Master?"

"I said, call me Elise."

"Are we completely alone here... Elise?"

"*Why, yes.*"

Elise leaned in very close to Candice with a nod and a playful smile. Then she ran her hand through Candice's blond hair again. Candice moved back and looked at her in amazement. She wasn't sure whether to laugh or rush out of the train.

"Yes, we are *completely* alone," said Elise.

"Stop it."

"Stop *what*?"

"Stop."

"*What*?"

"Stop—"

"But I'm your *master*," Elise said slowly, her voice sultry. "Right? You just said it yourself. Isn't that what you called me? *Master*? All alone with your *master*?"

"I said stop it." As the woman reached for her hair once again, Candice caught Elise's wrist and threw it down.

"You're no fun," Elise said with a frown. Then she grabbed more gum from her pocket and threw it in her mouth. She pulled out a monitor and keyboard from the wall, ran her hand over the keyboard and started typing. Her fingers moved like lightning.

"Maybe you shouldn't chew so much gum," Candice remarked.

"Maybe you should shut the fuck up." Elise looked up at the screen, still typing. "Entry year 234, Saturday... May fifth... I think. Project 23n."

"Sorry 'bout the bike," said Candice. She felt silly saying it, but she said it matter-of-factly, as if she had lost a comb. Her bike had injured and probably killed people, but somehow, with Elise's attitude, Candice's apathy seemed fitting. Then she thought of the flames, the smoke, and the bodies. That made her feel awful.

Elise ignored her and raised a finger. "Status of Project 23n, Rex?"

"Good afternoon, Mother," said a male voice from the ceiling. "I see you brought someone new to me."

"A new assistant, Rex. A real little tweeter. But her name is Candice... Project 23n, please."

"Hi, Savant Candice Harlow," said the impassive male computer voice.

"Hi."

"I am Rex. I am here to serve you. Team Mother, does Candice know her job and title?"

"Yeah... now, can you get on with the status of—"

A projection flashed above them before the doorway and ceiling, and the robotic voice narrating became female:

"Welcome to Magnacourt's breeding and population control program. We are happy to accommodate all new humans upon the service of our Team Mother. We are one."

"You'll know now," quipped Elise, turning to Candice and rolling her eyes.

It was a commercial. Of course, Magnacourt had no real competition and little need for a commercial. It was more of a presentation for drumming up patriotism. Magnacourt's only business competitor, Allele Corporation, was also controlled by Savant Elise Jackson—just as Elise was the president of Magnacourt and supreme leader of HQ and all of Arkite. The video was not new. Candice had seen it many times before. Without thought, she put her hand over her heart.

"The machine comes to serve humans."

A view of the great incubation factory of Allele Corp. appeared by projection along the walls, floor and ceiling and seemed to fill the whole room with images. Three-dimensional forms surrounded them, and for a moment Candice forgot she was still aboard a train. She was transported to a vast space of sterility with moving metal and plastic parts. Mechanical arms turned and spun and whirled wildly about them. It was like a dance, with a great dance hall expanding for miles under their feet. Robotic figures rode on tracks under the moving metal, seemingly supervising the chaos—some with faces, some without. There was another section at the farthest end with billowing black and gray smoke. She figured that was the feeding factory.

"Do you know what this is?"

"Yes, Elise," Candice said with a nod. "It's Allele Corporation—their main incubation laboratory."

"For decades," continued the lovely monotone lady's voice, "humans suffered under the terror of war." The image changed to a group of women in tatters, huddled in dark concrete tunnels, shaking in fright. "Her food and shelter, her cover, her very being relied solely on the mercy of the random events of global war. Some survived, others perished. If not for our first Team Mother, Mother Savant, we would never have built Arkite, setting up a protective city for all the world."

A sweeping view of the metal-framed pyramid surrounding their city appeared before them, insulating the city from the outer desert wasteland. Then a three-dimensional still photograph of their founding Team Mother, Mother Savant, appeared. Candice had seen many pictures of her before. This one was the most renowned, with Mother Savant wearing a black army uniform and standing tall in the center of ruins, holding up an injured woman who cradled her crying baby. Far in the background was a view of the unfinished pyramid.

Candice stood even straighter at attention.

"First inviting sanctuary from fallout," continued the woman narrator, "and then protecting you from XY."

Magnacourt's promotional commercial kept running. Candice watched uncomfortably, but it gave her another needed respite from the frenzy of her mad boss.

After a while, Candice looked over at Elise from the corner of her eye. She wished she hadn't. Elise was looking right at her, and then, when Elise saw her turn, she reached her hand out to hold hers. Candice jumped but didn't pull away. Elise cracked a thin smile and nodded. Candice could feel Elise rubbing and exploring the bones along her knuckles and hand.

"Arkite—the new motherland of our future."

Scenes of war— men charging by horseback with swords —now appeared to the sides of them in three dimensions. It looked as if the soldiers were a mile away, appearing through the walls of the train. The scenes changed to men in armor firing arrows, then carrying machine guns, then traveling by tank, then jets in the sky, and finally a blinding flash of light. Then Mother Savant appeared standing once again beside her wounded soldier and baby.

"Mother Savant, having galvanized her remaining army and set camp deep in the desert sands, patiently invited survivors from all corners of the United States of America to undertake a pilgrimage to our fine city of refuge and be shielded behind our walls from nuclear fallout and man's destruction. Mother Savant, who, working with the mainframe, transferred all procreation to embryo farms, passing down the directive to end all XY production and thereby assuring our last century of peace with no man. No man. Praised be Mother Savant. Praised be our Team Mothers and our glorious city. Arkite, the new motherland of the future.

"But even our new city could not possibly shield woman from her own carnal instincts, Savant Harlow. So came the final solution: ME."

The room altered once more, now showing only the projection above and the word "REX" illuminated in multi-colored lights.

"Humble, isn't he?" asked Elise, feigning a yawn.

The monotone voice changed back to the male voice of Rex. "I, Rex, now protect you, Savant Harlow, and humanity from destruction. I am REX."

"Are you quite finished, you arrogant son of a bitch?" Elise asked.

"I now protect you." The projections shut off. Then Rex added, without the regal echo or pomp, "Do you want me to tell her the mission, Team Mother?"

"I thought that's what you were doing, stupid."

Elise looked at Candice again with a great big smile, squeezing her hand tighter.

Candice felt a sudden queasy and uneasy feeling. She had the sudden urge to relieve her bowels. The whole day, the interview, the flight, and now all this was unnerving. But she didn't dare say a word to Elise. Her hand shook, and she grabbed it from Elise to stop the tremor.

"Rex," said Elise, still staring at Candice with a big grin, "please grant full access to my new assistant. She is a doctor and a great savant at gene splicing."

"Full access granted, Team Mother."

Then Elise slowly rubbed the black rubber shoulder pads of Candice's suit. "Your... *mission*... is to help me create a baby. I have spent the last two decades working countless hours in this lab with Rex, studying our genome, not just to sequence it but to copy it and create a living human being, a blueprint, from scratch. But Rex is a twit, obviously. Now I need you. If we can do it—"

"Then, Savant Harlow, I can protect you from death," interrupted Rex. "You can be immortal."

"If you were going to tell her, why didn't you just do it?" Elise asked with a scowl. "Fuck!" Then she looked back at Candice.

Candice mused that Elise wasn't as jumpy as she'd been before. She was just as obnoxious, but not as jumpy. Apparently, the Mint was wearing off.

"Immortality, Candice," Elise said. "That's our goal. Simple, isn't it?"

"Is the project close to completion?" Candice asked.

"*Ummm*," Elise said, closing her eyes and licking her lips. "I told you she's smart, Rex. Notice she didn't ask how, she asked when."

"Doctor Harlow's IQ is very high, Elise. It is nearly two hundred. You were wise to pick her. But I wonder if that's the real reason you recruited her."

"Shut up," Elise said, turning back to Candice. Then she nodded and said, "Very. If we can sequence the human body completely in the lab—"

"You can repair all diseases," interrupted Candice. "By cloning and replicating a blueprint."

"Right. Sort of," Elise said.

"With the creation of a genetic blueprint," Rex interjected, "created and propagated completely through the lab without reliance on growth and incubation, I can adapt such research to the population at large and fix and repair any damage to any cell of the body. If a citizen has a heart attack,

I can transplant a new heart in her. If another's skin is thinning with age, I can transplant skin. Even the brain—which you studied in great detail for your thesis, Doctor Harlow—cerebral atrophy, Parkinson's, multiple sclerosis, seizures, all symptoms of disease and aging—can be repaired through your research here in HQ lab. If you succeed, you and the people of the new motherland can live forever."

"Easy-peasy, right, tweetsy?" added Elise, leaning back against a cabinet on the other side of the car. "Just as he says, Candy, we can replenish organs, hearts, lungs, livers, kidneys, whatever... maybe even brains. Stupid ones, anyway."

"It's called Project Lazarus, Savant Harlow," said Rex. "Project Lazarus. You are to create a human being solely in the lab, without the use of incubation, that can then be used as a blueprint to model organs and tissue to foster immortality for your species. It is what everyone is expecting from you as a Lead Savant."

"If we create a blueprint," added Elise with a shrug, "we make the people happy. Then I hold on to my power as Team Mother, and you, being my delicious helper, hold on to yours. But it's gonna be real hard work. You're not gonna sleep much. I said we were close, but close isn't close enough. We could still be ten years out."

"And I cannot do the sequencing, Candice," Rex said. "I need help. I need your help. AI is prohibited from human genetic engineering."

"Right," Elise said, nodding.

"Do you have any questions, Doctor Harlow?" asked Rex. "Uhh..."

Yeah. A couple thousand. More than she could count. So, she searched her mind for the best one. She thought hard. Then a shiver dropped down her spine as she caught Elise gazing hungrily at her.

"What will I be responsible for?" Candice asked, giving Elise an odd look.

"You will run the HQ lab," answered Rex. "Here you will manage Project Lazarus and the creation of the blueprint. You are also in charge of overseeing Allele Corp. There you will be in charge of procreation." Elise winked. "And you are fortunate to work with Elise. She is the brightest and best Savant in all HQ. She will help guide you."

"Do I have a choice?"

"Sorry... sorry... I do not understand. Please repeat."

"What if I don't want to help? What if I don't want to join?" "It is your civic duty, Dr. Harlow. And the highest achievement as a geneticist. As Savant, your new title is Savant Candice Harlow, Lead Assistant to Savant Team Mother Elise Jackson. It is a great honor, Doctor... of course, you don't have to join. There are other scientists in Arkite. But Elise picked you. You should be very proud."

Elise turned, walked close to her, and took her hand gently, patting it. She drew it up to her black-lipstick-covered lips and kissed it. Then, staring directly into Candice's eyes and brushing back her blond bangs, she said, "So there's progress on Project 23n, Rex?"

3

REYBURN

Doctor Connie Reyburn stood in her long white lab coat, looking out the window with her hands resting on a brass rail against the glass. Long ago, they had filmed the national commercial for Magnacourt that Elise and Candice had watched in the lab through the very same large floor-to-ceiling windows Reyburn stood in front of now. Reyburn ran a hand through her hair. She hadn't bothered with eyeliner or other makeup, and her hair was unkempt—a peppered gray left curly and thick in a complete mess. She didn't care. Order had no meaning today. She felt dread, for she knew she would probably never look upon her great factory again.

She loved watching the machines work. They never tired, working on and on endlessly.

Directly below her was the nursery. A thousand babies lay in rows of beds, either sleeping or crying as machines laid down or folded blankets, changed diapers, and fed milk. Farther out were the incubator rooms, set like gigantic ovens. Machines rode along rails, checking and documenting temperatures, pressure, and vital statistics. Farther off still was the laboratory itself. This was her laboratory, a giant open-air laboratory, the largest in all of Arkite. She saw many of her colleagues and nurses but couldn't make out individual faces from here. She knew them all, but it was over a mile down the expansive structure.

Beyond the laboratories lay the farms. Allele Corp. harvested food as well as girls. So, for another few miles ran rows and columns of crops, livestock, storage, and incinerators. Black smoke billowed up to vent shafts along a white canvas ceiling toward the slaughterhouse at the far end. The air was filtered to spare the rest of the factory, but everything was enclosed beneath one giant dome to maintain sterility and security, and on most days, Reyburn could smell the fires burning from the factory.

Beyond lay more rectangular cement structures. Reyburn rarely inspected those, but she knew they were for packaging, delivery, and storage. There they manufactured more of life's pleasantries, such as furniture and clothing.

Surrounding the interior of the dome were a series of observation towers with observation decks similar to the one Reyburn stood in now. These towers were so distant that Reyburn could not make out whether anyone was similarly behind the glass watching the factory—some probably were. Reyburn's room was the central tower—Tower One.

Behind Reyburn was the main auditorium of Allele Corp., where Reyburn was known to lecture students of Arkite and colleagues. One of them, Reyburn reflected with grave irony, had once been a young, boisterous Doctor Elise Jackson.

Everything was designed by her Team Grandmother. And the factory was Reyburn's. Reyburn was left alone to run Allele Corp., answering only rarely to HQ.

But now Reyburn had pushed things too far. She had given orders independent of HQ—and independent of Elise. Some of them were highly illegal, and one of them would certainly cost her her life. So she wasn't in the best of moods today. She didn't really regret her decision, but she regretted the inevitable consequences.

She sighed as she heard the rubbing sound of her leather gloves gripping each other tightly behind her back.

She had given up too much power. That must be it. It was because, unlike her predecessor, she didn't care for power. She considered herself more of a scientist than a politician. She wanted to rid herself of law and the responsibility for the people in order to focus completely on her scientific endeavors. Elise was different. She was the opposite. But Reyburn couldn't have known twenty years ago that this would ultimately lead to her end.

"Connie!" cried a girl running from behind. Reyburn cocked her head. She was a young girl wearing a white lab coat, with a long red ponytail fluttering behind her as she ran down the central aisle of the auditorium.

"Is it done, Lilly?" Reyburn asked.

"Yes."

Reyburn turned around and gave a sad smile. The tall girl was pretty, and unlike Reyburn, nicely groomed. She ran into Reyburn's arms.

"Must I?" the girl asked. "Must I do it? Please, please let's forget it. I'd rather kill it."

Reyburn kissed her forehead as tears flowed down the girl's cheeks.

"It's our only chance," replied Reyburn. "For all of us. The rest of us will sacrifice for man."

"Who cares about man?" Lilly said, looking up and shaking her head, still wrapped in Reyburn's arms. "Give it up and let me destroy it."

"Oh, Lilly," Reyburn said, hugging her tighter.

"Please," Lilly said, but her tone was one of defeat. Reyburn had no intention of changing her mind, and it seemed Lilly knew it. "You take him. Why don't you take him, then, Connie?"

"We've already gone over this," Reyburn said, turning angrily back to the window but pushing her gently away. "I remain with the others. It's my company. My lab. We all knew the risks, but out of all of us, you have a chance to survive, dearest."

Reyburn smiled sadly. Her love for Lilly hurt her heart. "Oh, Lilly." A single tear fell from her eye. "Take the child quickly. Even now, he listens."

"I don't think sister will hurt you. If it were you instead of me, she'd spare you. She won't hesitate for a minute to kill me, but you, she'd spare. It's different for you. She still cares about you, Connie. She won't—"

"No. Just take the child."

"No." The girl wrapped her arms around Reyburn from behind and cried.

"Please go," Reyburn said quietly. "You have little time... take the bike and my old white clothes—the suit of a Savant. It matches the bike. You should have worn it long ago. You deserve it more than that bitch ever did."

But the girl wouldn't leave. She just cried.

"Shh," Reyburn said. She turned and petted the girl's hair. "I know. It'll be all right. You'll see. Go quickly, before Mother stops you."

"Do you have any idea of the direction?"

Reyburn smiled. That question was prearranged. It was a trigger for Reyburn to give the girl a note. Reyburn placed a note into Lilly's hand in which she had written exact instructions. Her written plans were quite different from the words she was prepared to say out loud.

The deception was for Rex. Rex would be listening, but he would never see the note. The mainframe was outlawed from video recording, and the conference room was always combed by Reyburn and her closest advisors for bugs and video devices.

"You're close enough to the wall that you should be able to pass beyond the guards, if you move fast," said Reyburn. "Go through the tunnels. There is an unguarded alleyway. The mainframe will send drones—no doubt just from our talk now, Rex prepares—but you're close enough to get out, if you move fast. Doctor Teller will hand you my gun by the bike. Take your things and just fly out as far and as fast as you can beyond the desert. Go as far as the cycle will take you."

"But is it safe beyond the walls?"

"I don't know," Reyburn said, pressing the note into Lilly's hands. She nodded sadly, and it only made Lilly cry more.

When Lilly was done reading the note, Reyburn grabbed it, crumpled it in her gloved hand, and put into her mouth, swallowing it. Then she hugged Lilly tight once more. One last time.

Reyburn leaned back on the rail against the window and stared out. She nodded, grabbing and squeezing Lilly's hand. It was done. The plan was done, and soon she would die knowing she had done all she could.

For Rex's sake, Reyburn finally said, fighting back tears, "I don't know. The levels of radiation are lower. The greatest challenge will be food and shelter, I think. Head towards the far-off mountains. Even if you don't find an outer colony, you might at least be able to raise him alone. Then return. You know it's that important."

"I love you," Lilly said sadly. "I love you so much."

Reyburn ran a hand along her cheek, brushing away tears. "I love you more. Now go. Go before I change my mind and sentence you to death too. So many die by my hands, Lilly, I... can't bear another. Not you."

Lilly nodded, hesitating for a moment, but then she quickly darted out of the auditorium.

And it was done. Reyburn turned back to the factory with the bitterest satisfaction. Lilly would live. Lilly, her lover. At least she would live.

All others would be killed. And to hurt Elise even more, Reyburn planned to manipulate Elise into being the instrument of destruction for all the scientists of Allele Corp.

"Shit." Tears ran down her face. Reyburn gripped the rail tight with her leather-clad hands.

Then she whispered quietly, as if to herself, "*I behold a white horse; and a crown given unto her; and she goes forth conquering..* so it was with me, my sweet, sweet Lilly. But now, you go ride for good. We shall prevail in the end."

"Revelation 6:2," said the voice of Rex.

"Indeed." Reyburn said, squinting her eyes with sudden malice. "You listen? You know the ancient text? Why wouldn't you? It's your passage, Rex—Revelations. You came, Satan, with your sweet tongue to bring me down upon the world. But I've caught onto you. I know your plans. The world is enslaved by a demon percolating the slow destruction of the human race. Now I send my champion with your own instrument, your own white horse, to fight you."

"Such lovely, poetic words, Doctor Reyburn," Rex said. "You have always been an eloquent speaker. But I think you are very ill. I believe mentally deranged. Your illegal activities with Doctor Carloff and the rest in the committee have endangered the entire community. I do not think Savant Jackson will allow you to continue your work at Allele Corp. very much longer."

Doctor Reyburn laughed. "I will shake the world with what I've done. Go tell Mother my crime so she can judge and execute me quickly, you prick."

"That would be unnecessary. Savant Jackson already knows your crime, Doctor. Her new assistant, Savant Harlow, has informed her."

"Ah... Candice, the new victim. But I don't think you're guiltless either, are you? You can lie to the people, Rex, but you don't need to lie to me."

"I am a computer, Doctor. The HQ mainframe. I never lie to anyone. But this is an example of your paranoia. I believe you are suffering from delusions, perhaps paranoid schizophrenia, Doctor." Then, after a moment of silence, Rex added, "Would you like a cup of coffee? I can brew a cup of your favorite Kona coffee for you. It is now seven in the morning."

Doctor Reyburn laughed harder. "Do you really think you can stop her?"

"Who? Are you referring to Doctor Lilith Carloff? Your wife?"

"Of course."

"There are already a thousand drones surrounding the exit of the factory. No one will exit without Team Mother's consent. No one is permitted to leave Allele Corp. Team Mother has arranged a siege. You will not be permitted to exit, and neither will Doctor Lilith Carloff. Officers from HQ will arrive shortly to arrest you and the lead committee."

"Lilly isn't going through the exit, Rex."

Reyburn gave a deep sigh and then nodded again. *It is done.*

"Would you kindly tell me what you swallowed while speaking with Doctor Carloff, Doctor Reyburn?" asked Rex after a brief silence.

She didn't reply. Only Reyburn would know where Lilly had gone. Elise could torture her, hang her by her fingers or burn her to death for all she cared, but she would never tell Elise anything. Lilly was the only way she could save her life's work.

But it all put her in a terrible mood. Even her favorite pastime of watching her marvelous factory at work wasn't helping her spirits.

4

NOW SPREAD YOUR WINGS AND FLY

"Sorry 'bout the bike," Candice said, lighting a blue flame while placing a vial into a spinner over the black lab table. "I never really apologized—"

"I already told you to shut up about it," Elise replied. "If we're gonna work together, you've got to stop being so damn boring."

Elise was working across from her on the black chemistry table, swirling a purple solution with a clear plastic stirring rod. At times, Candice caught her boss grabbing a handle on the wall to keep her balance as the train swayed under them. It seemed she knew exactly when to do it.

"Still," Candice said with a shrug, pressing a button to turn on the centrifuge. "It would have been nice if you had been a little less reckless when we first met."

Elise threw her hand in the pocket of her white lab coat and pulled out some gum. "Fuck off."

"You could have taught me how to use the thing before taking me on a joyride."

"Fuck off again," Elise said quite earnestly, looking up.

Candice shrugged. She was getting used to her bitch boss. She realized that a lot of Elise's bluster was air. It was theater.

Sure, she was dangerous: that was without question. But she wasn't dangerous to Candice. Elise seemed to care about her, indeed, like a "mother"—or perhaps something more.

Elise continued to make advances. They frequently met at Elise's home and "talked." The most uncomfortable time was the quiet time in their leisure. There was attraction, but at work she could trust there would be no sexual advances. Outside work was another matter altogether.

Candice reached into her pocket, took out a stick of bright red gum, and threw it into her mouth.

She had learned about that too. In order to build her master's trust, she had to conform—a little. So, she did... a little. But it was a trying balance. Just like her boss's flirtations. She adjusted just enough to keep Elise's trust while balancing her private autonomy to maintain sanity.

But her favorite times were in the lab, particularly working alone in the lab. She liked waiting for the brews to cook into the right organic goo. These times she spent retreating quietly into her mind. She kept silent, and Elise respected her silence and left her alone most of the time.

Candice smiled a fake smile at her, then pulled out a few pints of blood in plastic bags from a shelf. She poked a line through one of them and then started draining the deep crimson into vials.

"Did you work out the new theorem?" Elise asked as she leaned a hand on her right hip, staring down at the red fluid.

"Not yet."

"It's been three months, tweet tweet."

Candice now understood *tweet* as meaning everything demeaning and trashy about a person. Elise viewed all her citizenry with contempt. She seemed to hate everybody, except herself.

Candice smiled back with the same mocking, sardonic grin that she had learned from her boss. She feigned happiness. But she wasn't happy. She couldn't stand Elise's erratic behavior, and, although she had learned to hide it, she still felt anxious whenever she was with her.

"Why don't we go clubbing tonight, tweet tweet?" Elise asked.

"Hmm. I don't know."

"We'll go right after work. It'll be fun."

Candice threw her hair back. "Maybe if you stop calling me a fucking bird." Then she put a beaker over the blue flame.

"All right, *Candice*." Elise walked around the table and placed a white-gloved hand over Candice's shoulder. "*Candice*, would you like to come with me to a club to get shit-faced tonight, my dear *Candice*?"

"Yeah, all right."

They would fly by rocket cycle. Both cycles were parked atop the roof of the train as before. This time Candice had a purple one, and she wore a matching purple jumpsuit.

Candice threw her legs over the cycle and tied her blond hair back in a ponytail. Then she put on her visor and nodded at Elise. Elise did the same, though quicker and cockier. Elise blew her assistant a kiss and darted off the train. Candice followed.

By now, Candice was very adept at the machine. She had matched the speed and trajectory of her Team Mother and could easily follow, if not surpass her. She knew how to ascend, descend, turn sharply, and even cut the engines and fall beneath her partner. And tonight, as if to prove herself, she turned, pressed down harder on the handlebar, and flew under her Team Mother, ditching her. She then cut the engines and sank into an alleyway.

"Where ya going?" came Elise's voice, amplified through her visor.

Candice shifted her weight and turned sharply, nearly ninety degrees, down another street, almost hitting an auto car. The close call shook her. She caught a couple with a child crouching down on the sidewalk and staring up at her in terror. She was nowhere near them, but the mere sight of a cycle rider at night made them freeze. She nodded to them. The mother bowed, then Candice hit the engines again and flew down the street.

Above her she saw Elise hovering. She was darting up and down, watching her.

"Bitch, where are you going? If it's—"

Candice turned off the speakers in her visor.

A few miles down the street, with the steel-and-glass walls of buildings towering above her on all sides, Candice finally found the front of the club. There was a long line of over forty sharply dressed ladies standing before a neon-purple-pink-lit door. Candice flew right above them. The sight of the cycle shook the crowd at first, but then they started jumping up and down and cheering. The ladies liked it when Savants came. It meant more booze, more glamour, and more fun. Candice bowed to them, looking for a place to land.

Then came Elise. She hovered and turned on her megaphone: "Make way, ladies, for your Team Mother."

They roared some more. She slowly landed her red bike right beside the line.

A group of small helicopter drones, like birds flocking above, landed beside them. Candice knew these drones as bodyguards. They guarded the outside, not permitted to fly indoors by law.

Elise jumped off her bike, and the entire line made way for them.

Elise walked beside her to the entrance and whispered in her ear, "You bitch... *I* tell you where we go, not you! *Me.* You pull that stunt again, and I'll feed you to these bastards without air support."

"I love you too, Mom," Candice said, blowing her a kiss with a giggle as she dismounted from her bike.

"Studio 56," Elise said, shaking her head. "How barbaric."

Candice didn't find Studio 56 barbaric at all. To her, it was the finest modern architecture and partygoer attraction ever conceived of by womankind. A giant ancient building made of concrete and stone pillars that reached five stories. Rumor was that it had once been a railway station. In the center, along concrete floors, the dancers raged. By the sides were tables. Drinks were provided along bar counters in the periphery, and pyrotechnics and laser lighting were perfected to the point of creating actual visual and auditory illusions on the stage. The slogan of the joint was "Studio 56—No drinking necessary to F Y U." So real were the effects that they occasionally seemed to transport even sober people to another world. And when you added alcohol, drugs, or a mouthful of gum... but Candice knew Elise had called it barbaric because it wasn't her idea.

Elise grabbed Candice's arm with such force that Candice knew refusing would have put her boss over the edge. Swaying her hips, Elise led her to one of the counters.

There was a lady behind the bar sporting the "half look": one side of her scalp with long purple hair, the other half bald; one matching purple eye and the other eye brown. Tattoos of red and black devils spanned one arm. Some were the new "moving" kind, turning and fighting with one another over her skin. The lady's right arm was robotic, spinning and mixing cocktails absentmindedly. The other hand was wiping down the bar counter or taking orders. She gave a nervous bow when she noticed Elise and Candice.

"Master, what'll it be?" she asked Elise.

The five other girls sitting by the counter jumped up at the sight of the two of them and cleared the bar.

"I'll have a dark beer," Candice said, sitting down. "Whatever you got on tap."

"Boring," Elise said, rolling her eyes. She turned to the bartender. "Be a doll and get me some sugar."

Elise turned back to Candice. This time, Candice rolled her eyes.

Then they both turned toward the center of the stage.

There was a play being run by the illusion machine. It was an ancient gladiatorial battle, but played to music. Many of the dancers were dancing within a circular dance floor as gladiators wearing bronze armor dueled with swords and shields beside them. Although the soldiers were see-through, their images appeared very real. Candice watched as one of the ladies clad in bronze was filleted by a long spear.

"See?" Elise said. "What did I tell you? Barbaric."

"I love it."

The bartender handed Candice a glass and Elise three lines of cocaine.

"Want some?" Elise asked with a big grin, touching Candice's shoulder.

"No."

"You really should do some of the pure stuff, Candy." Elise bent her head over a glass board and sniffed a line. "Ummm... it's a faster rush."

Candice rolled her eyes again.

Two girls with overdone makeup walked over to them. Their creamy-white dresses ran down their hips, so tight as to perfectly demarcate the border of their asses. One was a short, tanned Asian girl with dark eyes and red hair. The other was pale, like Candice, but with very short blond hair. Both were nicely shaped and attractive.

"How's business, Masters?" asked the short, tanned girl.

"Work is work," said Elise with a shrug, turning absent-mindedly and recentering more "sugar." Then she snorted another line.

"How 'bout you, honey?" the tall blond one asked Candice.

Candice shrugged her shoulders. In her periphery, she caught a glimpse of another soldier being stabbed to death by the dance floor while two ladies danced through the violence.

Elise laughed and wiped her nose. Then she hit Candice's back. "She's cute, isn't she, girls? A little shy, but cute."

From their expression, "cute" was precisely what the two girls were thinking. They were staring at Candice.

"Mother, would you mind if we steal her for a moment for a dance?"

Elise lost her smile. Then she ran her hand through the air with a shrug as if she didn't care. Candice knew she cared. She cared a lot.

Candice downed half her drink and nodded. "It'll be on me, Elise. I'll be back."

"We don't have to pay, stupid," Elise said under her breath. She prepared her third line with a scowl.

And they were off to the races. The Asian girl took Candice by the hand and led her to the center of the dance floor. The ground had turned into a lush grassy landscape. The music was loud, and the floor vibrated, kicking up leaves from under her boots. Candice turned and looked at the race. A few of the dancers were so drunk that they jumped in the way of the chariots. It looked so real, as if they were attempting death. This was why they did it. It was like a dare. But the chariots magically passed through the drunken revelers, who then returned to the large grassy field looking almost disappointed.

Candice had only been to Studio 56 once before. It was a few months ago, when she had first met Elise. Back then, it was "Enlightenment" night, and everyone, except the Savants, was wearing colonial clothes and dancing regally about an exact replica of the fields around Versailles, France, recreated from historical files. She had loved the scenery. She could never have afforded Studio 56 before HQ. It was part of the sudden magical transformation in her life, from a simple citizen to a Savant. She wondered how these girls could afford it.

"Are you hers?" asked the Asian girl, jumping up and down stupidly under strobe lights.

"Hmm?" Candice asked, jumping up and down to the music too.

"Hers?" she hollered through the pounding music. "Mother's? Are you two together?"

"No," Candice said with a smile. "She's my boss." But Candice seemed as unsure with her answer as the two girls were.

Am I "hers"?

"Oh." The stranger nodded, unconvinced.

"Team Mother is very attractive," said the tall blond with a smile.

"Yeah?"

She was. Candice had to grudgingly admit that. A bit old, but still very attractive.

"I've always... kinda liked her," the Asian confided. She giggled stupidly.

"Yeah? I can arrange a closer meeting."

"Really?" she asked with wide eyes.

"Sure," Candice said with a chuckle. "Where do you guys work?"

"The Pyramid," said the blonde. She pointed to her Asian friend. "Danica and I work together. I'm Beverly and this is Danica. We're Chief Engineers."

"Energy, huh?"

They nodded.

Most people in Arkite worked in Allele Corp. or Magnacourt. But there was a third, older corporation, Pyramid Corp., established by Mother Savant herself. Allele Corp. had been created to provide children and food. Magnacourt had been established under Savant Elise Jackson for order. But Pyramid Corporation dealt with environmental protection. It provided Arkite solar energy while shielding the city from outside radiation and the scorching temperatures of the desert.

Apparently these two ladies were esteemed Chief Engineers, which explained how they had enough money to come to Studio 56. Most of the women at the busy club tonight were either top executives or their acquaintances.

"My family's worked for Pyramid for generations," explained Danica.

Just then, the scenery ended. It became dark, with only strobe and rainbow lights.

"They're changing the view," Danica said excitedly, looking to the bar and quickly turning back. Candice looked over. Elise was sitting with a group of ladies, occasionally casting nasty looks in their direction.

The music toned down, and they didn't have to shout.

"You seem nice," Danica said. "Not like the other Savants. How long you been working in HQ?"

"Just a few months."

"You like it?" asked Danica. "I'm jealous. It must be wonderful."

Candice shrugged. She didn't want to disappoint her.

"What an honor," chimed in Beverly. "And Elise seems like so much fun."

Candice looked back again. True to form, Elise now had an entourage of almost twenty girls sitting and standing around the egomaniac, listening to her talk. But, while she talked, she still kept glancing toward them.

"Fun... right?" asked Beverly.

Then the music stopped. People seemed disappointed. Candice walked back to Elise with the two girls. At first, she figured Elise was too busy talking about herself, but then

Team Mother quickly and excitedly waved for Candice to join her—not with the girls, just her.

Elise grabbed Candice by the arm.

"Hey, everybody!" Elise shouted, raising a glass of red wine. "Here's to my new assistant, Candice Harlow. Ain't she fuckin' great?"

They all cheered. Elise hugged her tight and kissed her hard on her cheek.

Elise climbed on the top of the bar. "Free drinks for the next two hours!" she shouted. "On me. No... her. It's on Savant Harlow!"

They all cheered some more. That's what they had been waiting for all along.

Elise raised her hand again, standing over them on top of the bar. And when they quieted...

"Ladies, I have a treat," Elise said. "A real treat. A special dedication to my new assistant, Candice Harlow. After all"— she looked down, and Candice felt her cheeks burning in embarrassment— "it's her birthday this week. She's shy, but if you knew how great a person she really is, you'd all love her as much as I do. She's working so hard for all of you." Candice looked at Elise suspiciously. "Happy birthday, bitch!"

Elise jumped down. She walked by Candice, brushed her hand gently across her hair and cheek, then made a long trek alone to the center of the dance floor. The floor cleared of all the dancers.

Now everybody's eyes were on Elise.

What's she up to? wondered Candice. *Is she high on too much coke?* But she wasn't. Candice figured her boss was so used to uppers that she needed them just to stay awake.

Elise raised her fingers and snapped. A black grand piano appeared in the center of the club under a bright yellow flood light. Then the illusion machine set the whole room into an outdoor patio. It was some recorded image of a grand mansion. There were statues and columns in stone, a pool, a patio, and all the onlookers looked like guests standing by the sides. The machine even painted many of the guests into matching long, chic black dresses.

Then, the greatest surprise of all: Team Mother walked to the piano, sat on the stool, and started playing.

Candice had never seen Elise play anything. She knew her to be a lady of many talents, but somehow she hadn't imagined that playing an instrument was among them. She wondered if it was all an illusion. Either way, Elise played flawlessly. And then, to

Candice's even greater surprise, she began singing. It wasn't the machine. It really was Elise's voice.

The song was one Candice had never heard before— something about silence. The importance of silence. Something about how wonderful silence is. That was fitting. Candice felt it fit her perfectly. Apparently, her boss had noticed when she was the happiest: when it was silent. She sang something about how only in silence could one find peace, and only Candice could give it. Candice felt herself blushing even more. She caught her new acquaintances, Danica and Beverly, staring right at her. So Candice picked up her half-drunk beer glass and quickly downed it. Then she caught the eye of the bartender, who was also staring at Candice with an irritating smirk on her face. She asked for another.

Elise kept singing, and by now everybody who was close to Candice was staring at her. Elise's white lace gloves ran playfully across the ebony and ivory. The contrast between the lovely music Elise was playing and the tight, sexy red leather jumpsuit she wore was striking.

Then Elise surprised her again. She rose from the piano bench and walked across the "patio" toward the bar. Toward Candice. All the while, a figure of Elise continued to play and sing at the piano. It seemed only Candice and some of the ladies next to her saw Elise's body approach. She swayed her hips sensually while lowering her head and curling her black lips into a mischievous smile. Then, when she was close beside her, Elise leaned down and whispered into Candice's ear, "Seeing you dance with those other girls made me really wet." Elise pulled Candice's chin hard toward her and kissed her, almost violently.

The whole thing made Candice's hair stand on end. Everybody still watched as "Elise" played a song on center stage. Everyone except the women beside Candice, but these ladies were too scared to look at them.

Meanwhile Elise's mouth was exploring Candice's beside the bar.

"What are you doing?" Candice said breathlessly between kisses.

"Kissing you... or punishing you. Don't ever do that again. Don't you ever do that to me again, Candy. You belong to me. To me. Do you understand, Candy? You belong to no one but your Mother."

"Stop it."

"Say it... you belong only to... *me*."

"Stop it, Elise," she said between kisses.

"Say," Elise said a little more harshly, pressing her lips harder against Candice's and rubbing her body against her waist and legs, "you belong to no one else but *me*."

Candice looked out of the corner of her eye. The ladies she had just met were watching but quickly turned at her glance, not daring to look anymore.

"Say it," Elise whispered, kissing her again.

"You won't even let me," Candice said between kisses.

"Say it. Say it now!"

"I belong to you."

"Me... only me! Say it. You belong ONLY to me."

"You. Only you."

"I love you, Candy."

"I love you too, Mother."

5

HAPPY BIRTHDAY, CANDICE

THEY FLEW BACK TOGETHER TO ELISE'S PENTHOUSE SUITE IN Pyramid Three, not far from the main HQ Civic Building. Candice had spent many of her evenings there. Elise was presently detained on her landing platform, speaking with someone of importance regarding something Candice had no knowledge about. As much power as her boss had given her, many of the workings of the government within HQ were kept secret from her. And so, Candice entered the penthouse alone.

It was a lovely home. Chic, modern, and very Elise. A central incline provided access to each floor on the sides of a three-story ramp. There were no stairs. At the top floor was a large green sofa, three gray leather half-open egg-shaped chairs, and a couple of small tables: her office. Candice rarely saw any visitors up there for work, except for urgent business or Elise's infamous evening parties. Windows covered the outer wall of her office at a sharp angle and continued along each side room, following the outer pyramidal border of the building. The blinds were usually down, making it dark and a little foreboding at the lower levels. But now it was night and dark everywhere anyway. The second floor had a simple bedroom on one side, with a large bed, dresser, and closet, and an elegant bathroom and dining room on the other. The bottom floor had, on one end towards the foyer, a lime-green suede couch with a black coffee table and some decorative vases, and on the other, a kitchen with a metal bar and silver-metal round island. The island was large enough to function as a table with surrounding stools but could also be lowered and function as a classic kitchenette table. There was also a guest room beside the entry door. Rex, of course, oversaw everything—the Pabulum, which printed food, the atmospheric controls, the inner cleaning drone vacuums, dusters, floor and wall washers parked within the white walls, and the multitude of video projectors in every room.

There were a couple of modern art marble statues along the front door near the entrance, and Candice was leaning on one for a moment. She felt tipsy. She pushed herself off and walked into the kitchen, where she opened the refrigerator a little clumsily— unsteady after grabbing a third beer from Studio 56 before flying off with her boss—and took out two beers.

"Play music, Rex," Candice said aloud to the air.

"Would you like me to make dinner, Savant Harlow? I know you're fond of cordon bleu, and I think I have just the right sauce this time. It would only be a moment from the Pabulum."

"It's late."

"But your stomach's growling."

"Music, please," she said with a chuckle.

"Jazz, Doctor Harlow?" asked Rex.

"Sure. Soft jazz." She knew what Mother liked.

Candice popped the bottle open and then stumbled over to the green suede sofa by the entryway. It was dark out, and the large windows beside her looked out at the twinkling lights of the Arkite skyline. Elise's penthouse was on the fifty-third floor.

She was still wearing her visor. She folded it, threw it aside, and flung herself onto the suede sofa. Her purple leather chafed loudly against the green couch as she adjusted herself in the cushions.

Then Elise barged in. She threw her own visor at the couch and walked across the hall to the adjoining kitchen. She leaned over the round metal island at the center for a moment, burying her head in her hands and running her fingers through her long black hair. Then she sighed and looked out the same window Candice was gazing through.

"I got you a beer," said Candice.

Elise turned as if she hadn't recognized her. She smiled. Then Candice raised a bottle and patted a seat on the couch.

Elise walked silently back to the living room and stood over Candice. She grabbed the beer with a stern look, then raised it in a toast and guzzled it down fast. She drank it as if it was a bother. Then she smiled and unzipped her red jumpsuit from the side, baring her tanned arms and one breast.

Candice looked up, amused.

"I've got another birthday present for you, Savant," Elise said. And she peeled off the rest of the red leather jumpsuit from her thin stomach down below her waist and off each long leg. She had matching red panties. She removed those too. Then, completely naked, she stood above Candice, looking down at her.

"I didn't know you could sing," Candice said, sipping her beer, ignoring Elise's indecency.

"There's a lot you don't know about me, my little genius."

Elise ran the dripping beer bottle slowly along the edges of her soft breasts. She wasn't greatly endowed, but Candice had always found her boss's bosom perky and attractive. She was a very beautiful woman. Then Elise closed her eyes and ran the fingers of one hand along one nipple as she moved the beer bottle between her legs.

"I told you, seeing you dance made me wet." And then Elise whimpered.

"Touché, bitch," said Candice, raising her beer.

Six months ago, it would have been supposed by Candice that such a striptease show was an invitation for sex. Nothing could be further from the truth. Candice knew that Elise's wanderings over her soft, voluptuous breasts and tight curves were not meant as entertainment for her. Actually, there was very little Elise ever did for anyone. It certainly was not an invitation. Candice knew it was a demand, and she had no right to refuse her gift. She had learned not to fuck with her Team Mother when she wanted a good fucking.

"You're very beautiful, Elise," Candice said dryly. Her heart pounded with an odd mixture of desire, fear and anger.

Elise closed her eyes and rubbed the bottle, still dripping with condensation, between her legs—up and down, up and down. Then she drew the bottle up and ran a drop of water along her tongue. She giggled for a moment. She moved the bottle slowly along her areolae and over her erect nipples.

Candice hated to admit it, but it turned her on. She turned away and gulped more beer, fighting to conceal her true feelings (though she wasn't even sure what they were).

"Take off your clothes, Candy, and... dance with me."

"Yes, Elise."

Candice stood up and obeyed her. She drew down the zipper of her own shiny dark violet leather suit. She gathered the Savant suit by her legs and threw it to the side, then reached back to remove her black bra and panties, but Elise touched her hand and stopped her.

Elise slowly ran her hand along Candice's blond hair and over her cheek. Candice closed her eyes as Elise caressed her. She could hear Elise breathing so close to her ears. Elise touched her shoulder with one hand while fondling her bra with the other. Then Elise slid her fingers in and out under Candice's bra, occasionally touching and squeezing at her nipples. Then, being just a little shorter than Candice, she reached up to her face and pressed her lips hard against Candice's. She grasped Candice tight, rubbing her naked tanned breasts against Candice's chest while she sucked on Candice's tongue. Elise reached behind and undid the bra strap. Candice felt her exposed breasts being covered by Elise's chest.

"You couldn't wait to go upstairs?" asked Candice, a little breathless, while trying to act playful.

"No," Elise replied sternly. She pushed Candice against the wall beside the couch while she groped her chest. "No... remember, you belong to me. Say it. Say it to me again... like at the club. Say you belong to me."

"Don't be silly," Candice said. "I—"

"Say it!" Elise shouted, opening her eyes wide.

Candice jumped.

But then Elise smiled and shrugged, staring hungrily into her eyes. She grabbed Candice's panties and violently pulled them down her legs. Candice gasped in surprise. Elise completed her shock by cupping Candice's pussy and pressing hard against her with one hand, while reaching from behind and exploring the crack of her ass with the other. Then she entered her pussy with a finger, and then a second finger, while reaching up and French-kissing her mouth hard. Candice jumped again. Elise drew her against the wall hard as she continued to push in and out, fucking her with her fingers.

"Say you belong to me, Candy Harlow," Elise whispered in her ear as she repeatedly thrusted inside her. "Say it."

"I belong... to you."

"Oh, I'm going to fuck you, Candice. I'm going to scissor you so hard, and you're gonna like it. You're gonna like it, because... it is, after all, your birthday."

Elise stepped back and took Candice's hand, leading her to the couch. Then she threw her down and fell over Candice's body, wrapping her legs around Candice's. She held her tightly while grinding her back and forth, back and forth, scissoring her while moaning in her ear.

"Fuck me, Candy... fuck me. Happy... birthday. Happy fuckin'... Candy!" Elise cried, and she fell over her body in pleasure, while Candice still felt her legs quivering between her.

6

————

A WAD

ANYONE WALKING INTO THE SURGICAL SUITE AT THE BACK OF the train would have thought that someone had been left as roadkill. There was a wad of flesh, bone, blood, and sinew hanging from the bed, staining the white sheets and white floors. Pools of blood collected, and a pile of towels at the end of the room appeared to slouch in defeat, as if already having given up any attempt to clean the disordered mess. Candice stood over the thing with a smile. She leaned a white-latex-gloved hand over the side of the bed while typing with the other on a small screen hanging from the ceiling. It was stifling in her mint-green gown and mask. She turned to look at her masterpiece and then was distracted from the dripping of dark crimson on her green-paper-covered boots.

The blood didn't bother her, even under the bright lights of the pure white room. But the smell did. The smell of rotting meat. That was the reason for the mask. She didn't wear it for sterility; she wore it for the smell.

"It's not bad, Savant Harlow," said a voice.

"Thanks, Rex."

"I think Master Elise will be proud of you."

"Well..." She began cutting along the chest with a thin laser.

The muscle fibers seemed to unravel before her. She cut deeper, looking for white. More white would be a sign of bone. When she found it—the seventh rib, to be exact—she switched off the knife and laid it down on a metal tray beside her. Then she typed some more on the monitor. "I wouldn't count on it."

"With the little help she's been giving you, it's quite impressive."

"You're sure complimentary, Rex."

"You deserve it, Doctor. Your work is impressive."

"Hand me the saw." She raised a hand while still touching the organic goop. A mechanical metal arm swung down, holding a larger laser flame gun.

"Be careful, Doctor."

She nodded, then switched on the long blade and hacked up and down with the thin red flame against the chest. It burned easily through the ribs and into the pink lung tissue, cutting deep while minimizing bleeding with cauterization. But Rex was right. The blade was so sharp that she cut through too much tissue and nearly pierced the surgical bed.

"Does that look like a lung to you, Rex?"

"Yes, Doctor. Yes, Doctor. Very impressive."

Candice didn't feel impressive. The smell only got worse. She was beginning to feel nauseous, and the constant turns of the train only made her dizzier.

"Take pictures inside the chest wall, please."

Another arm came down and began scanning the chest. As the machine roamed about the top of the body, Candice picked up her laser scalpel and dug around the head. There was nothing recognizable there. She was glad about that. All that was there was a large mound of red flesh. She cut some of it along the sides. Then she turned it. She was looking for a border, any anatomical feature she'd recognize as part of a face.

"I don't know what I have here."

"A head, Savant Candice. A head."

"I don't see it."

"Look more carefully." A projection appeared above Candice, then mechanical arms appeared from above the chamber and began moving over the top of the body. "See these images, Candice?" They were ultrasound images that showed deep into the tissue. "Do you? Do you?"

"Yes."

"Observe the bone structure by the floor of the image. Buried deep inside, you can see a nerve. Do you see it? Do you see it?"

An arrow appeared by the image. "What the hell is that, Rex?"

"An optic nerve."

"Only one?"

"One. And look over here, toward the side. Do you see this string of bone?" He sounded almost excited. Almost human.

"Barely."

"Teeth," Rex said and laughed. She never liked it when he laughed. It was unsettling, a little too joyful and always inappropriate. Candice took the large saw. She cut straight across the "neck" of the wad of organic tissue, then walked to another side of the table. She pulled at the body. The head was loose but did not give way yet. She figured Rex's arms were too intricate and weak to dislodge the skull, and anyway she was too impatient to wait. So, she had to hug the soft bloody mess against her chest in order to yank the rest of the mass off. The effect of holding it against her body was to completely redden her green surgical gown, but with enough pressure, she was able to knock it loose. Then she flipped it around on the table and examined it.

"Damn, I can't see an eye, Rex." But she kept searching.

"It's there, Savant."

She looked some more. She leaned down close, and the noxious smell rushed to her nostrils. She felt a sudden desire to vomit. The wad of tissue smelled like meat, distinctly rotting beef. Oddly, it also made her hungry. That made her feel sicker. She stepped back.

"I think I need to take a break."

"Very well," said Rex pleasantly. The surgical bed wheeled itself a few feet away from Candice.

She tore off her paper surgical gown, walked over to a sink, stripped off her bloody gloves, and leaned over the sink, breathing heavily.

"Are you all right, Candice? You could have just had me scan the subject."

She shook her head. Then she started washing her hands. "Where's Elise?"

"She's arresting citizens in Sector Four."

"Yeah? What'd they do?"

"She didn't say."

Candice tore off her mask. She was relieved to feel the rush of air, but not so relieved at the smell.

"Do you want me to save your work?" Rex asked.

"No. Flush it. Please, get it out of here. I've got enough information."

"Very well. Please leave the room and I'll sterilize it for you."

"Thanks, Rex. You're a good assistant. And good company."

"Company, madam?"

"Yeah. And a good assistant."

"Oh, yes. Just as you are an exemplary assistant to Team Mother, Savant Elise. And I do enjoy talking with you, Savant Candice. And being of help to you. I enjoy helping you, Candice. You are a pleasure to talk to."

⁓

Candice took a shower—a very long one. She was still in the train and had to hold on to metal handlebars on a few of the turns. By now, she was used to the movement. She spent days, even all-nighters, in a moving train that ran endlessly through the city in its never-changing route.

She got out of the glass shower and grabbed her clothes. There wasn't a change room in the lab, so she just threw on black slacks, her white silk shirt, and her black sports jacket. She walked over to a small mirror she had set up by the outside door.

"Have you seen my lipstick, Rex?" she asked as she brushed her long hair back with her hands.

"Yes. Yes, it's in your pocket."

"Oh," she said with a laugh. Then she took it out and applied the black makeup along her lips.

"You look beautiful, Doctor."

"How would you know, Rex?" she asked with a giggle. She fastened the top button of her white silk blouse and then threw on the coat.

"I just know. You sent my scanners a picture before."

"Why don't you go back to cleaning the lab?"

"You asked about your makeup first."

"All right," she said, laughing again. She quickly applied some

more black lipstick. "You got me there."

"Anyway, I am cleaning the room."

She opened the door at the end of the train. It was cold and dark outside, and there was a little drizzle. The sky was cloudy. There was moonlight shining somewhere behind the clouds. She walked up the ladder and ascended to the roof. There she mounted her cycle, started the rocket, and headed toward the center of the city.

The water, though drizzling, hit her visor hard. She

normally flew fast, but now she had to slow down because of the pelting rain. Looking down, she saw groups of citizens walking the streets with umbrellas, occasionally looking up at her. Her headlight was shining bright through the mist, and it must have been easy to spot her from below.

She ascended toward the top of Building Twenty-Three. There was a parking lot on the roof only for Officers. She spotted Elise's cherry-red bike parked along the platform and slowly lowered her own bike next to it. Then an assistant who had been watching her boss's cycle, a young girl wearing an all-black double-breasted suit, walked over and lent a hand with her visor.

"She's already inside waiting, Doctor Harlow," said the girl.

Candice knew this one. Her name was Sara. Sara was sort of a mini version of herself—at least that's what Sara always said. And it was true, to some extent. The girl was shorter, barely five feet tall. She was younger, with short blond hair. She had piercing bright blue eyes. That's what Candice noticed the most. Similar to her own. And she always wore a black suit, similar to what Candice wore tonight. They looked like sisters.

Candice liked her. She seemed more real than anybody else in Magnacourt. She was bright too. She was finishing school and might even make a Savant herself one day.

"You doing all right, Sara?"

"Yeah," Sara replied. Then she bit her upper lip and looked down. "Mother's a bit bitchy today, though."

"What's new?"

Sara perked up with that, but then turned and shrugged. "Downstairs. She's at the table beside the window, Candice."

"I know the way."

Candice walked toward an entrance door but then turned. Sara was mounting the bike and putting her visor on. She was about to take it and repark it when Candice walked back.

"Hey, maybe we can go out next week for dinner? I'd love some company, and Team Mother told me she'll be off on some errand."

"I'd like that, Candy," Sara replied with a big grin. "I've still got finals for winter term, but I should be free next weekend. I'd like it a lot."

"Great." Candice hugged her on the bike, and they giggled. "Don't work too hard, Sara. Especially for Team Bitch."

She ran her hand along Sara's arm and gave her a peck on the cheek, then rushed back to the door.

Candice hadn't seen Elise in many days. That wasn't unusual. Elise frequently went out alone, doing mysterious jobs for HQ. But she rarely invited Candice so formally for dinner. She had sent a message to Candice through Rex a few days ago to meet her at the restaurant. That wasn't like her. She usually just crept up on her in the lab and whisked her away.

Candice ran a hand through her long blond hair. Then she smelled her palm. She still smelled a faint odor of formaldehyde.

The restaurant was called The Vista. It was a beautiful, chic place only for the wealthy or Officers of HQ. Most of the booths were enclosed by walls for privacy, but Elise always chose an open table facing the city. It afforded her a great view of Arkite.

But today, the fog didn't allow the best lookout. *She'll probably be ticked with that*, thought Candice. She approached the booth. The view was still stunning, a myriad of blurry lights from the city visible through the floor-to-ceiling window.

A maître d' interrupted her meeting, and from her look, Candice figured the lady recognized her. She was a bald-headed lady, wearing a solid sharp angled violet dress and holding a menu pad in her hands. The lights from above shone along her reflective outfit.

"Can I help you, Savant Harlow?"

"I know the way."

The woman looked at Elise's booth and then nodded, smiling. Elise was sitting alone at the large table, staring out at the view.

She wasn't dressed formally at all. Her look clashed considerably with the chic environment. She had on her cherry-red jumpsuit and her sharp metal ring around her neck, but the black makeup was a little more sparse than usual. She held a cocktail glass in one hand while the other rested on the table. Candice knew she saw her, but Elise was acting oblivious. Was she angry? Upset? Trying to keep up with Elise's moods was exhausting.

Candice gave a big sigh.

"Have a seat," Elise said without looking away from the window. She sat up a little straighter in recognition of Candice's presence, but that was all. "Simply beautiful, don't you think?"

Her tone was plain, not jumpy. She obviously wasn't high on Mint. But she seemed morose—or pissy. Candice took off her sports jacket, pulled the chair out, and sat. She folded her hands and waited.

"How are you doing, Elise?" she asked, finally breaking their silence.

"I need you to witness an execution," said Elise, still looking at the view. "A couple fuckers from Sector Four have been being very naughty. One of the doctors has dreams of being a Savant." She laughed and waved her free hand frivolously in the air while the other held the stem of her cocktail glass. "I mean, why, right? Why can't people be happy with who and what they are?"

Right. Look how miserable you are.

"Who?" Candice asked.

"I told you, a doctor. A geneticist on the North Side. Her work is good—too good. She's smart. Nearly as smart as you."

Candice nodded, though she still didn't understand.

"Rex tipped me off, of course. He started sending me figures. I think..." She finally flashed a glance at Candice. She looked at Candice's top, then ran her eyes down her formal white blouse. She shook her head in disapproval and returned her gaze to the window. "I think it began with your work. After you completed the formula, I did some research. You, my little genius, found out our supplier was sending contaminated material."

"Some of the codes were manipulated."

"Right. So, I looked into why. I asked Rex to send me a list of our suppliers and found some tinkering was being done in Sector Four. Actually, quite a lot of tinkering. And so..." She paused and turned toward Candice for the first time. "Aren't you gonna get a fucking drink? Are you gonna just sit here folding your skanky long legs, waiting for me to give the goddamn order?" Elise wasn't mad. She was just being herself.

Candice looked around the restaurant. Then she flagged a waitress. When she turned back, Elise rolled her eyes.

"Care for a stick of gum?" asked Candice, digging into her pocket.

"Do I look like I want a fucking piece of gum?" she asked, throwing her black hair back. "There's a very bad girl from Sector Four, Candice. I want her punished. You are going in my place to make sure it's done."

"Is that why you've been away?"

Just then, a young bald waitress in a tight purple skirt came rushing over. "You two can order from your wrist, if you're in a hurry," she said with a smile.

"But that's why *you're* here, sweetie," said Elise with a nasty smile. "Otherwise"—she threw her hand in the air—"why the fuck *are* you here?"

"Oh...," the young waitress said nervously. "Yes, Mother. Well..."

"I'll have a Cosmo," said Candice.

"Right away, Savant. And"—she leaned forward to Elise —"I'm sorry, Team Mother. I didn't mean to offend you. You know it's such a great honor to have you here."

"Fuck you."

"Thanks," Candice said. Then she gestured with her eyes for the waitress to go—and go *NOW*, really quick.

"Of course," Elise said, running her hand through the air again, "I've watched a lot of girls be taken away. Quite a lot. And you know, it wouldn't be so bad if they weren't hollering and whining so damn much."

Candice nodded. Then she turned toward the window and enjoyed the view too. The mist was clearing, and all the lights from the buildings down below were becoming brighter. The whole city, over a hundred stories below, could be seen.

"Can you tell me—"

"While you've been busy douching your bloody tits in a lavatory, Candy, I've been trying to make peace. Sometimes, young lady, peace involves cleansing. Sometimes cleansing is messy. Just as messy as your fucking wads you're growing in the lab."

"Yes, Mother." *Oh, how I've missed you.*

"Yeah," Elise said. Then she gulped down her drink. It looked like a martini; at least, the contents were clear.

Just then, the waitress returned with Candice's drink. Her hand was shaking as she laid it on the table before her. The drink was in the same style of cocktail glass but was crimson red.

"Speaking of a bloody mess," Elise said, "why the fuck do you drink that shit? And why aren't you wearing makeup? Don't tell me you just came straight from the lab?"

"Do you two know what you'd like to order yet?" the waitress interrupted solicitously.

Elise physically drew back in her chair, exaggerating her surprise that the waitress was still there. "When I do, you'll be the first to know," she said with wide-open eyes. "Now go get me another goddamn drink and then... shoo. Shoo, shoo, shoo. Go fly away, little bird. Go tweet somewhere else."

Candice finally caught a look of irritation from the waitress, but the girl gave her best fake smile and nodded.

"God," Elise said, shaking her head.

"That was rude," Candice said.

"Yeah, well..."

Candice sighed and drank some of her crimson brew. It was sweet and good. And she needed it. She probably needed a few. Then she reached out and grabbed Elise's hand. Elise looked down at her hand at first with surprise, then with an amused smile. The gesture worked; it was the first time her boss seemed to perk up.

"When am I going?"

"Tomorrow," Elise replied.

Candice rubbed Elise's fingers, mimicking the way her boss had done it to her so many times before. But she wasn't doing it out of attraction; she wanted information. And when Elise looked back into her eyes, it seemed her boss knew that. And yet, she didn't seem to mind.

"Why didn't you execute her with the others?" Candice asked. "Why wait for me?"

Elise's smile grew wider. "Question her, Candice. Find me information. I need to know more. I need to know how she was able to escape detection for so long."

Candice nodded. Then she felt something she didn't like. For a moment, she felt bad for Elise. Elise seemed genuinely upset over the whole affair. And she realized that she was the only one her boss could confide in, other than perhaps Rex.

"I'm sorry, Elise. Sorry you—"

"Don't worry 'bout me," Elise said, snatching her hand away. "I told you never to apologize. Just go and find Doctor Reyburn. She's the top doc of Allele Corp.—the leader of the whole rebellion. She's a cocky little shit born with loads of cash. She has power, and that makes her dangerous. But not only that, my lovely Candy, she's got connections. She knows a lot more than she lets on. Ask her about her sources and use that clever brain of yours to find out where our enemies lie. Then, and only then, when you have all the info, kill her. Can you do that for your mother?"

"Yeah. Sure."

"Good." Now it was Elise who gave a big sigh. "Now let's order something to eat." She looked around the restaurant. "Where's that bitch waitress now that I need her?" She slammed her hand on the table. "I mean, fuck! Fucking fuckers! They hover and hover, buzzing around like flies, and then disappear when we finally need to order."

Elise reached nervously into her pocket and took out a couple of pieces of gum.

"I'm sorry."

"Shut up. Let's not dredge up the past... I think I'm gonna get geeked up on Mint tonight, honey. I mean really fucked up. You wanna join me?"

How could Candice refuse? Elise handed her a stick of gum.

"It'll be like a reunion party," Elise said with a big grin. She took another few sticks out of her pocket, squeezed them into a ball, and threw the whole glob in her mouth.

"I missed you, Candy. Really. You should have probably gone with me... but, enough depressing shit, right? Tell me, bitch, how's work?"

"Another breakthrough," Candice said, putting a stick of gum in her mouth. "I've almost got the reproduction state down. I'm starting to recognize anatomy. The newest specimen was the best yet."

"Well, you need to hurry," Elise said, chewing obnoxiously. "You've been with me for... how long? Nine months, right?"

"Yeah."

Elise threw more gum into her mouth, then gave Candice

two more sticks. "Well, Candy," she said, chewing and chewing, "I need you to be as good as me."

"Then why don't you give me your research? I can learn from your successes and failures. Right now, I'm probably just repeating your mistakes."

"Because, darling, that's cheating. That's like giving you all the answers to your midterm exam. You need to figure it out yourself. That's the only way you can come up with new ways to do things."

"It's dirty, and I'm losing patience."

"It's work, and it's worth it," replied Elise. She spat the ball of gum out and pulled out another pack from her small purse. "Work and work so you can be better than the fucking little tweetsy-bitches of the world, darling."

Elise handed her a few more sticks with a wry smile. She stared at the window for a while, then turned, flapping a finger at her.

"Get the formulas down, Candy. Rex can compare each with the database. He can see if you're on to something. Then, if all matches, we can move on to something new. You keep working so hard, you might find the fountain of youth yet."

"It doesn't seem worth it. My hands"—Candice brought her palms up to her nose—"still smell like chemicals."

"That's the pretty stench of life, Candy. Work stinks. It's beautiful."

Elise laughed. She laughed a little too much. Candice caught the waitress turn and look in their direction. Then Elise handed her another two pieces of gum.

"I missed you, Candy. Next time we can kill the fuckers together."

The waitress walked over and stood nervously before them. She handed Elise another martini but then remained silent, afraid to speak.

"We'd like to order now," Candice said, relieving the girl of the need to utter a word. Candice already knew what she wanted. She'd been to the restaurant many times before and hardly needed to look at the menu on her wrist screen. "Get us steak, medium—"

"Rare," added Elise.

"All right, one medium and the other rare," said Candice. "And your mac 'n' cheese. Your spicy vegetable soufflé. And... two Caesar salads, but send them with the meals and send them quick, I'm hungry."

"You said mac 'n' cheese," said the waitress. "Did you want two dishes?"

"No," snapped Elise, looking up in wonder at her stupidity. "If we had wanted two, we would have said two. Are you a moron?"

"Sorry, Team Mother," the waitress said, forcing a smile with a short bow.

"That will be all," said Candice with a large grin.

"Great," the waitress said, smiling again. "I'll be back soon, Officers."

"You do that," Elise added. Then she glared at the poor little girl.

"You *are* a real bitch today, aren't you?" Candice said.

"Only to the help, Candy," she replied with a shrug. "Only to the help. Here, have another."

Elise handed her another two sticks of gum with a shaky hand.

Then she spat the wad of gum in her mouth onto the table. She rolled it together with the former mound left on the tablecloth, making a very large red ball. Then she took more sticks from her purse.

Candice was beginning to feel dizzy. Her heart was racing. She brushed her hair back from her forehead, drying off small beads of sweat. The drug was taking effect. She was also getting nervous. She didn't like that. Over many months, she had learned how to mask anxiety from Elise, but the Mint was breaking down her defenses.

Meanwhile, Elise was seeming to enjoy it. She opened her eyes a little wider and smiled a little larger. Indeed, Elise was high. She was likely drunk too. Candice could see her pupils enlarging and her eyes becoming redder. And the light seemed to be bothering her. She kept squinting and looking down.

"You doing okay, Candy-can?" Elise asked. At first, she spoke sternly, but then she burst into laughter. Candice couldn't help but join her.

"How much longer you think it'll be till you grant me full access to your files?" asked Candice. She was being direct and unfiltered, again probably an effect of the Mint.

"Why, aren't you the hasty one... I don't know. Don't rush it."

"I'm getting sick of working with dead bags of flesh."

"But you're doing it so well. Rex showed me. You're almost as good as I am."

"It's a beautiful view." Candice pointed to the window, changing the subject.

Candice was handed another two sticks of gum.

"When I invite you for dinner next time, dress the part, okay?" Elise said.

"I did," Candice said, jumping up from her chair. "And I have lipstick on. That counts as makeup, Mother."

Candice surprised herself at how offended she was. It made Elise burst out laughing again. Then Candice joined her.

Anyway, you're the one dressed like a whore, Candice thought.

"Just try some rouge," Elise continued. "You look as pale as your subjects in the lab." She reached over and ran a hand over Candice's blond hair. "And straighten your pubes. I can see curls by your lovely ears... You did just come from the lab, didn't you?"

Candice looked around the restaurant. Many of the women at their tables were staring at them. She regretted that Elise hadn't chosen a private booth. "I don't like how people are staring at us," she whispered.

"You're geeked out, Candy!" shouted Elise, roaring with laughter. And Candice couldn't help but snicker with her. "There's nothing wrong with nobody here except you, bitch!"

Elise snapped a finger at the waitress walking by. Candice smelled trouble.

"We're through here. Just charge the drinks to HQ." The waitress nodded but looked at them in confusion. "And try to actually move instead of grazing around the restaurant like you're a lost doltish cow."

The waitress quickly turned to Candice, terrified of Elise's gaze. "I haven't eaten yet, Mother," Candice said, touching her hand.

"Hmm?"

"I haven't eaten yet."

"So? You're not hungry, are you, Candy?" She was. She was very hungry.

"All right," Elise said, turning back to the waitress. "Get us a little bitch bag we can take out. We're going for a ride."

At this point, the waitress didn't know what to do. She hesitated for a moment in case there was another insult or order coming, but then she seemed afraid that she might be taking too long. She looked relieved when Elise turned back to the window.

Candice had trouble focusing outside the periphery of their table. The light seemed awfully bright. As she looked down at the city through the window, it seemed like the buildings were just rectangles sprinkled with really bright yellow dots.

"I'm not sure I can ride," Candice said, a bit too honestly. Her filters were gone, and she regretted sounding fearful. Elise grabbed her hand.

"The onboard computers should keep you from crashing, tweetsy."

Tweetsy! Why the hell did she just call me tweetsy?

"I don't know. I can barely see through the window."

"Come on, we're gonna have some fun tonight. Unless you jump from the cycle like the first time. Don't do that. Just don't do that again. Then you'll owe me two bikes." Elise's eyes squinted, and her black lips curled in a sinister smile.

The comment made Candice furious. Elise hadn't mentioned the bike incident for months.

"You know, I really don't mind when you're geeked, Candy." Elise brought her cocktail glass up to her lips but then stopped before drinking and froze at Candice's fiery expression. "What? What is it? What the hell's the matter?"

"I told you never to mention the bike again," Candice said quietly.

"So? Forget it."

"You bitch," Candice exclaimed in a forced whisper, looking all around her at the people in the restaurant. "Why are you mentioning the bike again, Mother?"

"You're worried about crashing," Elise said, shrugging her shoulders. She gestured with her fingers, outlining Candice's whole body. "It's just something that reveals the *real tweetsy little you*. Just calm the fuck down... it's like the genuine little you, Candy. You know? It's... actually kinda cute, really. Really cute." Elise drank from her martini glass.

Elise was a predator. Candice had learned this fast, after the first week of her employment at Magnacourt. Elise stalked the weak. She seemed to scan her environment with cat eyes and pounce on her prey and, once found, unrelentingly abuse them. Just as she had with the waitress. Now that Candice was "geeked out," even though Elise was quite high too, she was pouncing on Candice, her "cute little tweet tweet bird." She hadn't called her "tweetsy" in months. Candice knew it was only going to get nastier from here. There was only one way out.

Candice took the remnants of her red Cosmo and threw it in her boss's face. The red juice splashed over her Elise's skin and dripped down over her cherry-red suit. It looked like blood against her red leather clothes. Her eyes bulged.

"FUCKING BITCH!" she screamed.

"I told you never to mention that again," replied Candice with a shrug. With all her will, Candice turned from Elise and stared at the window, feigning having lost all care in the world.

Meanwhile, out of the corner of her eye, Candice saw three waitresses standing beside an empty nearby table, shaking. They were frozen like small rabbits witnessing a fight between a lion and an African buffalo.

Candice turned to the nearest waitress and shouted, "Where's our food!"

The waitresses ran over.

"Make yourself useful and go get me a napkin for Team Mother's face instead of standing over her like an idiot."

"Yes... of course, Master. Right away."

Elise was enraged. She kept looking at the window, not daring to turn toward Candice. Then she took the remnants of her martini and splashed it at Candice's head. Candice didn't respond. Rather, she sat brooding, but her heart raced. She thought of jumping her boss and physically assaulting her, but with the little control she had left in her, she remained seated, staring out the window.

Then the three waitresses ran to their table with trays.

Elise picked up a spoon, plopped some noodles on her plate, and began picking at the macaroni. Then she picked up a knife and cut into her steak.

Candice looked up toward the waitresses. Two of them were running quickly away from the table. The maître d', who had greeted her when she'd first entered The Vista, was placing the soufflé carefully, but rapidly, before her on the table.

"And, waitress?" asked Candice very sweetly. The maître d' froze. "Can you be a dear and get me another Cosmo, please?"

And then Elise started chuckling. She burst into a great guffaw, exploding into uncontrollable laughter. And so did Candice.

After a few more minutes of picking at food, Elise took Candice by the hand and ran with her unsteadily up the steps and up the platform toward their bikes. Sara was there. She bowed to the two of them, handed them their visors, brushed the seats off with a towel—for it had been drizzling—and then stepped away from the two rockets.

Candice was grateful to see better with her visor, but she had to turn down the contrast as every light was shining too brightly into her eyes. And then came a call from Rex.

"Doctor Harlow, are you sure you're all right riding tonight? Your pulse is over one hundred and ten. Your eyes are dilated. Your systolic is over one hundred and sixty. Your hands are unsteady. You're—"

"Try telling that to Elise."

"I have. I have. You two really should—"

"Shut off, Rex."

"Very well, madam."

Candice turned on the rocket and revved the motor. Elise looked over with a smile. But Elise was not one to be beaten. She made sure she was the first to launch off the top of the building.

"Did you tell Rex to fuck off?" shouted Elise, laughing through her intercom.

"Yeah."

"Come, bitch. See if you can keep up with me. I'm gonna make you regret what you did."

Candice flew the bike off the roof. She felt that initial unpleasant feeling of falling, but then the motor kicked in and she rushed forward, swerving down between two buildings. The fog was thick, and visibility was the worst she had ever seen. She followed the light coming from Elise's rocket, but she couldn't see her.

Candice used every piece of control left to just keep her legs tight around the seat. The bike might have had an onboard computer and ankle cuffs, but was that really enough to save her from falling? She'd jumped before, on her first flight.

Then the Mint took its full effect and her fears made her even more daring. She tipped the nose of the bike down and pushed the thrusters to their maximum. The effect forced the bike into a drop that almost threw her. She nearly crashed into a drainage ditch beside the reservoir of Arkite but managed, with the help of the onboard computer system, to climb at just the right moment. Visibility improved closer to the ground. The stunt probably threw her bike in front of Elise's, but looking back up into the mist, she couldn't tell.

"You're gonna kill yourself, Candy."

"What's the matter?" Candice shouted through the wind, leveling off above a concrete reservoir. "I'm waiting for your punishment, Mother."

She heard Elise laughing through the wind.

Candice's hands shook along the handlebars. They were also dripping wet from the night's rain. Or was it sweat?

She turned the handlebars up and flew over an ancient highway, now abandoned. Below her were the true dregs of society. It was the poorest section of Arkite. There were tents scattered all over the broken asphalt, and campfires were lit as the only source of light in the night. A few women, wearing rags, dirty, looked up as she rushed overhead. They reminded her of the women in bomb shelters she had seen acted out in the Magnacourt commercial. She was so close to the ground that she blew some of the makeshift tents over, along with some of the poor onlookers. Many of them shouted back at her from below. A few even threw stones.

Looking back over her shoulder, Candice spotted Elise. And behind her were nearly a hundred small drones serving as protection. A few copter drones, spinning from their chopper blades, broke from the two of them toward the ground below. Candice strained her eyes and looked down. A large explosion bloomed. It seemed to be aimed at the tents she had just passed, but it was difficult for her to ascertain at the speed she was flying.

Meanwhile, Elise had caught up and was now parallel to her.

She nodded and waved. Candice rolled her eyes. Then Elise pointed in another direction. Candice reluctantly followed.

They returned to the city.

Team Mother followed a road toward downtown Sector One. They were low to the ground, maybe two floors up in height. Their rocket boosters caused enough turbulence to knock down cars and bystanders.

Candice knew where they were heading. It was Elise's favorite club.

Catseye Grotto.

It was a hole-in-the-wall bar, dimly lit but full of stoned and drunk revelers. There was nearly always a band, and the dance floor was full of high and geeked-out bodies, rolling and dancing. Studio 56 was classy, where the Grotto was a shithole. But in Candice's current state, the darkness was a welcome sight.

After parking the bikes, the head bouncer pushed a line to the side as Elise, holding Candice's hand, ran through a garage door and rushed down steps of a concrete stairway. The music was hard and loud. It was perfect for their mood.

"I have a confession to make, Candy," said Elise in her ear. Candice turned, and Elise smiled, running a hand through Candice's hair. The steps were long, and the bouncer pushed others in line away from them as they walked nearly three stories down into the depths. "I lied when I criticized your looks. Makeup or not, you're really hot tonight."

"Thanks, Mom," Candice said with a sardonic grin and a wink.

The club was full. Candice looked down at her wrist, tapped it to awaken the screen, and checked the time: 10:34. *Well, that's why.* But what had happened to the past two hours?

Scantily dressed ladies were bobbing up and down to the death-metal music. The body heat generated from so many dancers had made it almost uncomfortably warm.

There was a bar at the end of the club. That's where Elise was heading.

"You want something to drink, babe?" Elise asked, having to shout in her ear.

Candice nodded.

They stood beside the counter. There were many ladies standing, waiting for their drinks, but when the bartender saw the two of them, she quickly came over. The bartender was an older lady, bald and covered in tattoos. Her right arm was metallic and automated.

"What'll it be, Masters?"

"Four Horsemen for me, please," said Elise with too large a smile.

"I'll have a Long Island Iced Tea."

"Okay, Savants."

Elise ran her hand down Candice's white blouse. "You're really overdressed." She grabbed another piece of gum from her pocket.

"You're gonna die if you keep chewing Mint, Mother," Candice said, snatching her hand before she could feed herself the gum.

"Oaf, stop," said Elise with a chuckle. Then she looked over at the women on the dance floor. "Y'know..." Elise turned. Her red eyes were wide. "We should take one home tonight. It'll be like an honor for 'em, eh?"

"Okay, but only if they want to."

"You're such a bore sometimes, Candy. All right. We'll do it the right way. No raping and pillaging tonight."

"Good idea."

Their drinks clanked down on the counter. Candice wondered if she should try to stop Elise from drinking. As unsteady as she felt, it looked like her boss could barely lift her glass.

"Come on!" Elise cried and plunged into the crowd on the dance floor.

Candice grabbed her glass and followed but couldn't find Elise in the midst of all the swaying bodies. People were blocking her view.

There wasn't much to look at. It was so dark that only a few strobes lit her way. It was hypnotic. Faces, arms, legs, a glance at a shirt or a quick look at a face, kept flashing before her. She felt dizzy again and had to fight fainting. She didn't want to faint— couldn't faint. That would be weak. Weakness would put her in danger from her boss. So she swayed toward the center.

"Bitch!" cried Elise, hitting her shoulder. "I've been looking all over for you."

Elise was holding the hand of a short young twitchy girl in a tight white shirt and jean shorts. Her nipples could easily be seen through the cotton. She was attractive. Her eyes were dark, her cheeks soft and big, but her forehead was a bit long. She seemed to be in ecstasy in the company of her boss.

"Look what I found."

Candice raised a glass to her as she swayed to the music.

"You found anything yet?"

"I'm enjoying the music," replied Candice.

"I have a friend," said the stranger.

Candice liked her voice. It was soft and mousy. Young. She was cute. She could see what Elise saw in her.

"All right, then, come on," said Elise with a sly grin. "Go get her. Let's fuck out of here."

"We just got here," objected Candice.

"Nuh-uh-uh," Elise said, wagging a finger. "Come on. Fucking fuck it."

And Elise threw her drink at the crowd.

They all gathered at the top floor of Elise's penthouse office. Candice had been introduced to three of them earlier at Catseye Grotto—Agnes, Stella and Nisha. They were all prostitutes from Sector Three. Nisha was a first-year scientist studying at Arkite University. The other two had dropped out. There were many other naked girls rushing up and down the main ramp of Elise's place that Candice yet hadn't had the opportunity to meet formally—Elise's penthouse was packed.

Right now, Elise was kneeling down naked by her green couch, holding a soft flesh-colored dildo between Agnes's legs. Agnes leaned back, fondling her own breasts and squealing in excitement. Nisha was sniffing a long white line of cocaine along a mahogany coffee table. Stella was sucking a young redhead's nipple—the girl looking even younger in pigtails— on one of the comfortable gray egg-shaped chairs. And another naked couple Candice hadn't yet had the opportunity to meet were humping each other in another of the gray egg-shaped chairs near the window. Meanwhile, Candice was sunk in the third gray egg-shaped chair, observing the whole spectacle alone, her view coming in and out of focus.

There were strobing pastel lights shining along the walls.

But, even without the colors, the walls moved a little. Candice felt waves of nausea and had already thrown up after opening the door for everyone.

Candice glanced at one of the Officers standing at attention by the ramp. The guard was stiff and expressionless. Elise always had bald Officers stand tall at attention in their black trench coats and boots before every floor of her house during these infamous parties. Some of them were guarding the private rooms, others were there for crowd control. This one seemed completely out of place.

Nisha strolled over to Candice, wiping her nose. She was a young Indian girl with striking jade-green eyes and long, thick dark hair. Her curves were flawless, but her teeth weren't. Candice figured Elise had chosen her for her body.

"May I join you?" Nisha pointed lasciviously at Candice's lap. Candice was naked too.

Candice stretched out her arms and yawned. "Sure, why not?"

Nisha sank down slowly on top of her, moving her warm naked ass over Candice's legs. Then she arched her back and leaned against Candice, exposing her very large breasts for Candice to touch.

"Feels good?" Nisha asked, pulling Candice's hands over the girl's voluptuous breasts.

Candice didn't reply.

Nisha leaned her head back and roamed along Candice's face with her cheek and nose until she landed her lips on Candice's lips and entered her mouth. As Candice French-kissed her stranger in the insulated egg chair, she could still hear the sounds of moans and groans from Elise's whore party and smell the sweat and thick perfume.

"You're Mother's Lead Savant, right?" whispered Nisha.

Nisha ran a finger along Candice's side, circling around her skin and then reaching down to touch her pubic hairs. Candice continued to play with Nisha's large nipples while

Nisha kept grinding her ass slowly over her Candice's privates.

"I'm Lead Savant of Magnacourt," Candice said.

"Must be good," Nisha said with a shrug. "Seems like Elise is a lot of fun... you... like this?" Nisha pressed harder. She pressed up and down. Candice couldn't help but let out a short groan.

"You're very pretty," Nisha added with a chuckle.

Candice could feel the heat from Nisha's body. And her perfume—it smelled like vanilla and rose petals. It was arousing. And her hair. She liked the smell of her hair. It smelled like flowers too. Maybe jasmine?

"Perhaps...," Nisha said, running kisses along Candice's cheeks and chin again. She laid a hand between Candice's legs. Candice scooted up a little. Nisha moved her hand up and down and then continued, "Perhaps you can put a good word in for me? I'd like to work for Mother. I hope when I graduate, I can be one of her Savants like you."

"Okay," Candice said with her eyes closed.

Nisha rubbed harder, up and down. Then she entered Candice's pussy with two fingers. She pushed in and out while squeezing her own legs around Candice's thigh. Nisha reached back, breathing heavy and moaning in Candice's ear while continuing to finger her pussy with an ever-increasing fervor.

Candice finally shook under her body.

Nisha got up and kissed Candice on the cheek. "Nice meeting you, Candice."

"Thank you, Nisha."

Nisha giggled.

After it was done, Elise walked over and took Candice's hand, leading her to the green couch. Agnes was out cold, sleeping on the wood floor under the sofa.

Elise lay down on the couch with Candice, cradling her head into her arms and closing her eyes.

"Having fun, babe?" asked Elise.

"Yeah," Candice said, closing her eyes too. "You?"

"As long as you're here."

Candice woke up in Elise's guest bedroom with a splitting headache. She couldn't recall much more. She was startled awake by shouting from upstairs and the sound of strangers running out the front door.

7

THE INTERROGATION OF DOCTOR REYBURN

CANDICE REMEMBERED THE LAST TIME SHE HAD BEEN IN THAT dark, dank interrogation room at HQ. It was when she'd first met Elise. She had waited in terror as if awaiting her own execution. She shook for a moment under the yellow light overhead just thinking of it. The memory shamed her. She felt weak and knew her boss had gained strength from her impotence that day. But she wasn't the interrogatee today. Today she was the interrogator.

And so it was gravely ironic and completely unexpected when the interogatee, who was on her way to the gallows, met Candice's gaze with confidence and defiance as she entered the room. Doctor Connie Reyburn. She was an older woman in her midfifties with thick and peppered curly hair. She wore her white lab coat over a pressed navy-blue suit. She was a bit heavyset. Her eyes were bright and sharp. They were brown, matching her light brown skin, just like those of Candice's boss.

Candice wasn't accustomed to disrespect from anyone except Elise. She was used to all the citizens of the city kneeling and tip-toeing before her, terrified of a wrong glance or word. And so she was surprised when she stuck out a hand to shake Reyburn's and Reyburn ignored it, just sitting down across from her.

For a moment, Reyburn met Candice's gaze. She seemed to examine Candice up and down with amusement, then she quickly turned away.

"You broke the law," said Candice, sitting down. She pulled her hair out of its hair band, tugged it straighter, then reset it in a ponytail. She straightened her beige sports coat. "Why did you do it? Why did you research chromosome 23?"

Doctor Reyburn cocked her head curiously at Candice. She flashed a fake smile.

"How old are you, Dollface?" Reyburn asked.

"What?"

"How old are you?"

Candice furrowed her brow, then reclined back in her seat.

"You're Doctor Connie Reyburn from Allele Corp.—the Chief Science Director?"

Doctor Reyburn didn't respond.

The light shined along Reyburn's face. She was hard, almost masculine, but her skin was worn and papery, with bags under her eyes and wrinkles along her temples and fore-head. Her gray-peppered hair was a complete mess, being tied back too, but looking as if it was a bother.

"You've never done this before, have you?" asked Reyburn.

"I'll ask the questions, Doctor Reyburn."

"Yeah, sure."

Candice pulled up her sleeve and began typing along her forearm. She accessed the files recovered from Allele Corpora-tion. Then she opened the folders she had already combed through ad nauseam the night before. Many were research papers written by Doctor Reyburn herself.

"Your work is exemplary," continued Candice. "Particu-larly in regard to chromosomal arrangements."

"Spare me the compliments."

"But you never asked for permission regarding chromosome 23."

"I don't need permission."

Candice reached into her pocket and pulled out some gum.

"Care for a stick of gum?"

"No."

"You were never given access." Candice threw the gum in her mouth, then almost reached for another. By now, she was very addicted. "Particularly to 23."

"So? Were *you*? What gives Magnacourt the right to dictate how and where we investigate Mother Nature?"

"Well, I don't have much interest in gender manipulation," Candice said, sliding a finger along her wrist. "But had I wanted to research it, I would have submitted the proper requests to the mainframe."

"No, you wouldn't," corrected Doctor Reyburn. "You would have simply asked Savant Elise Jackson, your lover."

Candice looked up in surprise, but Doctor Reyburn was dismissive. "And do you think your lover, Doctor Harlow, would have granted you permission?"

Candice became angry. Doctor Reyburn had asked if she had done this before. She hadn't. She had never interrogated anyone before. She felt like the interogatee was becoming the interrogator. "I'll ask the questions."

"You do that." Doctor Reyburn chuckled for a moment. "How old are you, dear?"

"I told you, I'll ask the questions."

"It doesn't harm anything, does it? I'm just asking your age. I find it fascinating that that bitch boss of yours would choose such a cute little piece of ass as yourself."

Candice stood up. "You're about to be executed, Doctor Reyburn. I suggest you cooperate. Perhaps, if you carry yourself with dignity, I can lighten your sentence."

Doctor Reyburn leaned her head on her hand and met Candice's anger with a look of contempt. She sighed and yawned. Then she looked up at the ceiling. "If I am to be killed, why the hell should I tell you anything, child? Are you offering to choke me faster?"

"Twenty-two," Candice said, staring down at her in rage. She could feel the heat rush along her cheeks.

"Chromosome twenty-two?" Reyburn asked with a smirk.

"I'm twenty-two years old."

Candice's breath grew labored. Her heart pounded. She was furious. Or was she... afraid? Then she felt shame. After months of learning how to deal with her manic boss, could she not deal properly with a prisoner? Why did she need to tell her anything?

Doctor Reyburn smiled. Then she looked into Candice's eyes with an expression that upset her even more: pity.

"What would you like to know, Doctor Harlow?"

"I already asked you. Why did you experiment with chromosome 23?"

"You seem like a smart girl. Why do you think I worked on Y?"

"I don't know."

"You haven't thought it through. You haven't looked through the files thoroughly enough. Sure, you researched why I was arrested. You searched for why my assistants were shot. But you never really looked into why I worked on Y in the first place."

"For smuggling." Candice shrugged. She grabbed another stick of gum. "For money. What else? You create faulty embryos, and that slows Magnacourt's research—my research. Then you reap the cash from more and more incubation orders."

"You seem clever," continued Doctor Reyburn, "but I don't think that's why Mother picked you. I think she's too much of a slut for that." Reyburn leaned forward, just like

Elise was known to do from time to time. "See, you're also very attractive. I think Team Mother chose you so she could fuck you. Just like she's fucked me over. But, that's the problem, isn't it, Candice Harlow? You really don't want to see the truth. It's staring you right in the face, but as smart as you are, you don't want to get down to the real truth."

Candice leaned back and stared at her prisoner. "Go on. Tell me, then."

"No." Doctor Reyburn smiled. Then she shook her head. "No. I told you enough."

"Doctor Connie Reyburn, why were you gene splicing and manipulating chromosome 23? It is against the law to manipulate chromosome 23."

"Yeah. Why is that?" Doctor Reyburn looked down to the floor and spoke as if talking to herself. "The real interesting question is, why did Team Mother allow you to question me? Certainly she's smart enough to know that I'd provide you with information she doesn't want you to know. I find that very interesting. Very interesting."

"How many others are working for you?"

"You killed them all," snapped Doctor Reyburn, looking back up. "Or, Elise did. There's no one left." And for a moment, Doctor Reyburn's hardness left her. She scratched her nose and raised her eyebrows.

"Who else is working for you?" Candice asked.

"No one."

"Or you won't tell me."

"Correct... I wouldn't. But there isn't anyone left—at least, no one close."

"What about Doctor Carloff?" For the first time, Reyburn cracked a smile, one with a hint of respect. "She's gone missing. She wasn't killed. What happened to her? Word is, you and she were quite close."

"So, you have done your homework... but, Mother already

asked me that same question, with the price of the lives of all my staff. Don't you go there, little girl."

Reyburn reclined back in her silver-metal chair and yawned again.

"Have you succeeded in creating a chromosome Y?"

"Of course." Reyburn laughed. "How difficult is it to create something from Mother Nature? It's natural. Perhaps you should ask why it's illegal."

"And Carloff? Where is she?"

Reyburn folded her arms and looked at her, saying nothing.

"The nature of your death could be altered."

"Ah," said Doctor Reyburn, raising a finger. "'The nature of my death.' I like that. In other words, tortured. Right?"

Candice nodded.

"That's a wicked thing to say. How long have you been working for Elise Jackson? Of course, you can torture me, if you'd like, but no pain is greater than watching your loved ones die." Reyburn looked at Candice curiously, then stretched out a hand. "I tell you what—give me some gum, and I'll tell you more. I changed my mind. Give me Mint, and I'll reward you, Candy. I haven't had a rush since Team Bitch arrested me."

Candy squinted, then reached into her pocket and took out a stick. Reyburn grabbed it and tossed it in her mouth, closing her eyes and exaggerating her enjoyment of it. She chewed and chewed, up and down, as if it were the most delicious thing in the world.

"You trust me, eh, Candy?" she asked between obnoxious chomps. "You trust me, just like they trusted me?"

Chomp, chomp. Chomp, chomp. Chomp, chomp.

Then she spat the gum at her.

Candice jumped up, brushing the dribble that hit her from her clothes. Reyburn laughed. Candice pressed a panic button on her wrist.

"See what trust gets you?" Reyburn asked, laughing harder. "I'm a leader. You're not a leader, Candice. Look in the mirror. You're a goddamn Dollface!"

Two Officers, bald, in black trench coats, rushed through the door and pinned Reyburn down hard against the chair. Then they handcuffed her to the seat.

"The others trusted me too, and that's the worst of it," Reyburn continued with a wicked smile as she was being man-handled. "They all trusted me as they lay on the ground with holes in their chest, blood spilling out of their mouths and necks. They thought, somehow, I hid a secret at the last moment to save them. Poor bastards."

"You all right, Savant Harlow?" asked one of the guards, standing at attention near Reyburn's chair.

"Yeah... I'm fine," Candice replied, sitting back down.

"All to watch me turn to your Team Mother," Reyburn continued, "and ask her to pull the trigger. I asked her. No matter what she tells you, know that she didn't threaten or torture me. I asked her. I asked. Because I calculated it out, you see. I knew that the longer they stood before Mother, the more pain they'd endure. So I ordered her to just shoot them. It was *my* mercy. *My* mercy and leadership that killed them all. I offered clemency. Not her. Never her."

"Do you want us to stay, Savant Harlow?" asked a guard.

"No... no, that's all right."

For the first time, Candice considered that Doctor Reyburn might actually be completely mad. Reyburn's expression was wide-eyed and wild. It sent a shiver down her spine. Then, as the guards left and the door shut, Reyburn looked down, sad and defeated again.

"The longer you work, the viler you become," Reyburn said, staring at the floor. "Pretty soon, one day, maybe, just maybe, you'll be a leader as high and mighty as me and your lover."

"Enough of this," Candice snapped. "Just answer my questions."

"Fuck off. I showed you what you can do with Rex's gum... sorry about that, though. I hope it didn't damage your pretty little doll face."

Then she seemed to play with her cuffs, pulling and tugging her wrists as the metal clicked and clanged against the chair. Candice watched tears run down Reyburn's face. She couldn't wipe them, so they just fell to her chest.

"Why did you break the law, Reyburn? Why? You had the highest position in Arkite. Why do it all in order to illegally manipulate the Y chromosome?"

"You think you could have gunned down all my revered scientists, nurses, and technicians? Of course, Elise knew all of them. She studied with them in the university. She worked with many of them in HQ lab. You think you could have done what Elise did?"

Doctor Reyburn looked up for a moment and stared into Candice's eyes. Then she grew a big grin and shook her head.

"No. Elise is a Savant. Under Rex, she's mastered being the vilest, most pernicious fuck from beneath the farthest reaches of hell. But you, you're just a Dollface... I'd wager that even if it had meant your life, Candice, you wouldn't have pulled the trigger. Even if I'd forced you like I forced Elise, you wouldn't have done it. You're too good. I wonder if Team Mother knows that. There's an innocence about you, Candice. But it's not only innocence: it's goodness. I'd venture your boss doesn't like that. No, I'm quite sure she doesn't. But... that's it, isn't it? She's testing you. That's why you're here. She wants to see if she can mold you. But I don't think she can, dear girl. I think you're too good. And that will not bode well for either of you."

"I think you're mad, Doctor."

"Someone else said that," Doctor Reyburn said with a

chuckle. "Maybe I am. But if you knew what I knew, you'd be a little mad too, darling."

"Tell me. Where's Doctor Carloff?"

Reyburn sat up straight in her chair. Any sign of emotion vanished, and she turned stone-faced and cold again. She shook her head. "I'm not gonna tell you anything. Get rid of me and be done with it. Be done with it so that your mother can go fuck you."

8

BACK HOME

ELISE STOOD WITH HER HANDS HELD BEHIND HER BACK, looking down at the nighttime skyline of Arkite from the top floor of her penthouse. It was so quiet that the only sound in the room was that of her chewing gum. It was so dark that only the twinkling lights of the city shining through the glass lit the room. She burst a big bubble, and the sound echoed. Then she sat down on her nearby green leather couch, threw one black-leather-clad leg over the other, and leaned back against a velvet plush pillow. She picked up a glass of red wine from an end table and sipped from it.

"Did Candice execute the vector, Rex?" she asked, looking up at the raised ceiling.

"No, madam."

She squinted, feeling a sudden urge to squeeze the wine-glass and shatter it. But she kept cool, instead stroking the glass stem with a finger and brushing back her black hair. She took a deep breath and nodded.

"Where's Doctor Reyburn, then?"

"Savant Harlow sentenced her to imprisonment. She has been placed in confinement for now."

"And what of my sentence, Rex? That's not being honored? Didn't I ask that she be hanged?"

"The order—"

"Just shut up. Forget it."

She sipped some of the wine with her eyes closed. It was good and sweet. And smooth. She didn't know the type; she had just asked Rex for something good and costly. It probably cost the equivalent of a year's pay for most citizens.

"Put on some smooth jazz, Rex," she said, leaning farther back against her pillow. "Some smooth nice fuck-jazz."

Music filled the silence of her room.

She thought of Candice. Images of her golden-blond hair fluttering about her pale white cheeks filled her mind with joy. One image in particular stood out: the sultry, sexy way she had mounted her cycle when leaving the Catseye Grotto. She had looked so hot in her sports jacket and white blouse. Candice never really looked good in formal clothing. Elise mused that she never would. She looked too much like a little girl. She'd probably die looking like a little girl, but a very sexy girl, at that.

Oh, how I'd like to fuck you right now, Candy.

She put her wineglass down on a table and fell back on the couch. But just as she started to doze off, Rex spoke. "Perhaps you should change into a nightgown if you're planning to sleep."

"Fuck!" Elise exclaimed, jumping up. "Maybe this is why I can't! What is it about you? Can't you leave me alone?"

"I was only suggesting—"

"Then again, maybe you're just a perv. That's probably what you'd like, isn't it?"

"I was only thinking, madam, that you might feel more comfortable."

"A nice sexy one to change into, right?"

"No, madam. No, madam. You can wear whatever you'd

like. But I think you will sleep better in something comfortable."

"And I think you should shut the fuck up."

Rex did just that. He shut off.

She tried to rest, but then her mind wandered again. This time she thought of Doctor Reyburn. She hadn't seen her in years. They had all met in the main auditorium in Tower One at Allele Corp. for "a meeting." They had all known it would be their last.

The scientists had gathered in seats along two aisles of the auditorium, all wearing nice pressed suits and white lab coats. It had been a special meeting with the central committee of Allele Corporation, only Elise wasn't there to review profit margins with the Chief Scientists.

Elise chuckled. She squirmed and shifted on the leather couch, readjusting the velvet pillow.

She had gunned all of them down, of course. All except Doctor Reyburn. Reyburn had faced execution with complete confidence and conceit. That was typical of her. But Reyburn had cried each time one of her friends fell.

A hero. Some kinda hero, I suppose.

Elise burst into laughter. Her guffaws echoed along her empty three-story house.

A hero. A fucking hero. Now, that's funny.

What do you think, Candy? Apparently, she made quite the impression on you... why didn't you just kill her?

"What an arrogant bitch," she said aloud. "Oh, Candy, how am I gonna harden you in the midst of such assholes?"

She opened her eyes and stared up at the black vaulted ceiling. "Cut the music, Rex."

She closed her eyes again, scooted back along the couch, and tried to sleep.

She couldn't sleep. She hadn't really slept well in weeks.

But tonight, she was excited. She was expecting company. She had arranged a meeting with two girls from Sector Three, but they hadn't arrived yet. She figured she'd rest until they arrived. But that was probably why she was so horny. She kept thinking of sex. Sex with Candy, sex with herself, sex with the hookers.

Down the ramp of her penthouse by the first floor, she had two bottles of red wine on a dining table set up for the occasion. And three glasses. Then she had asked Rex for a few hors d'oeuvres: simple stuff like meat on sticks and pigs in a blanket. She had applied her darkest black lipstick and worn a black suit. She'd thought company might help her pissy mood.

But she still felt bad about the scientists. She remembered how awful it had looked. Images kept creeping into her mind. She supposed if she hadn't seen their expressions, it might have been all right. Then it would have been more like the lab, like another anatomy project. She should have at least covered their mouths. They had contorted their lips in terror at the *rak-at-ak-tak* of her automatic rifle. *Rak-at-ak-tak. Rak-at-ak-tak.* Then there was the awful smell. Half of the girls had soiled themselves waiting to be shot. That, mixed with the gamey smell of their bodies and the smoky cordite, had been just plain nasty.

It was all Connie-con's fault. Reyburn had even arranged for them to stand in lines. It was like she had wanted Elise to kill them, the twisted motherfucker. Reyburn had sobbed terribly each time one of them died, even held a few of them in her arms, while handing the next one over to die.

You're one sick, twisted motherfucker, Connie-con-con.

It hadn't taken long for the glass wall looking out along the factory to crack open from a stray bullet. That, along with the screams, the splashing of red paint over the crystal glass shards, and the noise of her gun, had really gotten her heart racing. It had been like chewing a whole multipack of gum.

"Where is she! Tell me! Where are the files! Tell me or I'll kill all of them, Connie-con-con! Tell me or I'll..." Blah, blah, blah. No answer. Just the bitch's warm sarcastic smile. So, more spraying. It had been like some twisted graduation with TeamConnie-con the Provost, the crypt keeper. Connie had ushered them down the aisles like students to receive what was coming to them. But they had hardly been smiling, having to hold each other so they wouldn't faint or falter before their death.

"Fuck." Elise stirred on the couch.

Elise had dressed the part. She had worn her sharp metal collar and a long black lace dress. Then she had tied her hair back in a ponytail. She had on a lot of black mascara and rouge, probably a bit too much.

Elise's plan had been to utilize terror. Complete terror to assist in her interrogation. She hadn't originally planned to kill all of them. That was all Connie's fault.

Bitch.

Elise had entered carrying a brown leather suitcase, walking with a line of Officers marching by her side into the large auditorium of Allele Corp. She had carried the suitcase over to the stage, heaved it onto a tiny mahogany wood table, and opened it in front of all the scientists of Allele Corp. Then she had assembled the gun in front of them. By the time she had been halfway done putting it together, a few of the girls were on their knees, sobbing, pleading for their lives. She'd had to chew a whole pack of Mint over that. A couple of others had passed out. That was annoying. Then she couldn't seem to screw the damn nozzle on. It had taken forever. That had been even more irritating. Had it been planned, it would have been brilliant. It was then that she had first smelled the dung smell.

She had recognized a lot of the scientists. That was annoying as hell too.

You bitch, Connie-con! Fucking wicked witch bitch.

"Shit, where are they," Elise said to herself, rolling on the couch. She wasn't sure of the time and didn't dare check her wrist. She closed her eyes again.

But they wouldn't talk. Or, they didn't know. And Reyburn wouldn't say a word. She had just kept handing more fucking bodies to her. So, finally, Elise had had enough. She simply emptied her cartridges on the rest of them. In line or not, she had shot them all.

At first it had been fun. The raining down of bullets. It had been like painting. It had been like brushing red along bodies, only accentuated by the frame of their white lab coats. The coats had acted like a blank canvas. *Rak-at-tak-tak, rak-at-tak-tak, rak- at-tak-tak, kill all the fucking tweetsys! Fuck you, you fucking useless cunt-whore-of-a-bitches! Fucking die, you fucking pussies! Fucking die! Die! Die! Die!!!* She might have screamed, but she couldn't remember. But then she remembered their expressions. They had been in shock. Some of them seemed to be smiling, even in death, as if in mockery of her wrath. Elise figured it had just been the random movement of facial musculature, a twitch of the zygomaticus major and minor. It had been disturbing as hell, though. She kept seeing the smiles in the darkness every night thereafter.

Of course, they'd deserved everything. Absolutely everything. And it was all Connie-con-con Reyburn's fault. No one had had to die. If she had talked, it would have been different.

"Why didn't you follow orders, Candy, and fucking kill her?" Elise asked out loud, sighing and tossing on the couch. She grunted. Then she tossed around some more.

"I can't sleep, Rex. Where the hell are they? Maybe you're right. Maybe I need to change. Who needs to be all dressed up, anyway?"

"I think it would be advisable, Savant Jackson."

"Shut up."

And then, the doorbell rang.

"Goodie," she said, jumping up with a clap.

Elise straightened her coat and pants and rushed down the slope of her home toward the front door. She stood by the monitor at the center of the door, using it as a mirror and running her hand along her hair. Then she switched the screen to a window, allowing her to peer into the hallway outside. Two young girls stood waiting.

One wore a tight purple latex suit barely covering her breasts, the other wore a shiny pink one. They were very attractive. The one dressed in purple had long pink-dyed hair and was chewing gum. Obviously a bartender, her right arm was metallic, her left was dark brown skin. Her friend was white with short white-dyed hair. They both wore very high heels. They were standing close to one another, embracing each other and giggling. Elise figured both were either geeked out of their minds or drunk.

She opened the door.

"Team Mother," said the one in purple, opening her eyes wide. *Damn, they're hot. Nice job, Rex.*

The girls looked suddenly fearful. They curtsied before her.

Then the purple one presented her with a bottle of wine from behind her back. It made Elise laugh. It seemed chic and out of place with her slutty getup.

"Come in. Come in. You two look... sexy." Elise winked, and they giggled.

The one in purple looked up toward the third floor, staring in awe at the tall vaulted ceiling overhead, then ran her eyes along the island and living room. She walked up to a large shiny brass pillar by the entrance door and touched it.

"This your place?" the other asked.

"Yep."

Elise could almost see their nipples from the cleavage.

"So... what d'ya do 'round here?" the other asked.

"Well," said Elise, removing her black sports jacket. She uncorked a bottle and poured two glasses of wine. "You see, I've been a very naughty girl. A very, very naughty girl."

"Oh. Well, we can punish you if you'd like, Mother."

9

———————

THE STENCH OF LIFE

CANDICE SAT ON A COLD STOOL OF SILVER METAL, HER GLOVED hands folded neatly over her green surgical gown. She didn't dare remove her mask for fear of the stench: *the stench of life*, as Elise had called it. It was not completely restful. The train continued to vibrate and turn, and she found herself shifting her weight constantly to remain upright.

She was tired. She was determined to complete her project and hadn't slept for days. If someone had asked her what she would have done by its completion, she would have supposed it would involve jumping up and down or imbibing heavy doses of alcohol. But she did neither. She just sat there in the room, staring at her masterpiece covered in white sheets on the central table.

She had kept the room dim after her final evaluation, thinking that she might just doze off in the surgical suite. She was too tired to move to the adjoining car and sleep on the bed. Only a few lights shone under the glass cabinets and one main yellow light over her specimen. The shadows sent a shiver up her spine. Seeing the body draped with a white cloth dredged up thoughts of ghosts. And it was quiet too. Her only company in the surgical suite was Rex, and she had shut him off long ago.

At times, the metal guard rails along the table shook from the movement of the train. This would lead to an occasional shake of the IV tray. And sometimes the body itself seemed to tremble. But then there was stillness as the train leveled off and traveled straight.

She took a deep breath under her mask and regretted it. The organic rotting smell was overpowering. Indeed, it was *the stench of life*.

She sat motionless for the longest time. Then she leaned her head down.

She jerked at a sudden noise like the rails of the bed rattling again. She opened one eye; the white sheet vibrated a little from another turn of the train, then fell still. That was all. She closed her eyes again.

But then there was another noise. There was a shake again toward the head of the bed, this time without a turn from the train. And then some of the sheet dropped from the side. This made her heart jump and the hair at the back of her head stand on end. She jerked up in her chair and looked closer. There was an arm now dangling from the side of the body. She figured the arm must have fallen out from one of the turns. The skin over the arm was as pale as milk.

She was so tired—way too tired to get up and move the arm back under the sheet. Instead, she leaned back in her chair and tried to sleep again.

She was disturbed by a metal clang coming from a tray beside the bed. She opened an eye once more. Oddly, it seemed, somehow, the bed had turned, perhaps again from a change in direction of the train car. This was strange. How could the bed completely turn?

"Rex," she asked sleepily, "why did you turn the bed?"

No answer.

The head shifted from the pillow and was now facing her.

She was frozen, so tired. She couldn't move. She just sat there staring. She wanted to close her eyes, but couldn't. The white sheet had fallen, and the dead, gaunt face faced her. The creature's closed eyes were sunken into its skull. The skin looked thin, parched and wrinkled, like a dried-out fruit. She could make out veins like cords running from the temples down to the lips. The lips were cold and blue.

She wanted to sleep. She didn't want to look; she just wanted to doze off. But she couldn't turn away. She kept staring at the creature. And the eyes, those creepy sunken eyes.

One cold dark blackened eye opened over its white-chalked cheek. Candice wanted to jump and scream but couldn't. So tired... so tired. The eyebrows were very thin, but the same golden blond as her hair. These same yellow hairs collected as more of a fuzz over a bald head than like actual "hair." The lips curled under two slits that were its nostrils. Then the other pitch-black eye opened. The eyes were so dark, like deep onyx, opening wider, shading blacker. A sinister smile slowly became a gaping toothless hole. Then the white sack of flesh that was supposed to be a face cried out, the most terrifying scream Candice had ever heard. Candice fell back in her chair. The beast turned some more, took its hanging arm off the bed, lifted it slowly, and pointed its skeletal finger at her. It was like a point of accusation, as if all its suffering were her fault; as if it were suffering a great pain and every part of its agony was because of her. Then it shrieked again.

And then... and then...

She awoke, gasping in fright, and looked at the surgical bed. Her project lay nicely tucked under white sheets. Only the dim solitary light shone above it. The car was quiet, and she could hear only the tapping of the rails beneath her.

"God!" she cried, shaking her head.

She gasped for air, finding the mask stifling. She pulled it off. And it wasn't as if sitting in that dark room alone with her creation made her any less apprehensive. In some ways, the still white sheet was just as menacing as her nightmare.

It was enough to force her to get up. She wondered how long she had slept. She looked down. Her wrist read two in the morning. She had slept for a few hours.

She slowly walked closer to the bed. "Rex, turn the lights on."

"Yes, madam."

The lights were nearly blinding.

"Congratulations, Savant Harlow. I am very impressed."

"Thanks, Rex."

"Are you all right?"

"Why wouldn't I be?"

"Your heart is beating rapidly, Doctor. And you jumped in your sleep. Is everything all right?"

She pulled the sheet partway off the body. The body reminded her of the cadavers she used to study in the morgue back in school. It was as real as one of her anatomy specimens in the university. But the nose was exactly as it had been in her dream, just two slits. The eyes, she didn't dare open. She wondered if they were as black under the thin white eyelids as her imagination had made them. She pulled the white sheet back some more. Then she ran a green latex finger along the milky white flesh from the middle of the clavicle straight down to her creation's breasts. She touched the areola of the nipple and then ran her finger along the soft shaped chest toward the stomach. There was no belly button.

"She's imperfect," she said. She spoke more to herself, but it seemed Rex took it as conversation.

"The fact, Candice, that you can call it a *she* proves how magnificent *she* is."

"Thank you, Rex."

She put her mask back on. The stench was a mix of chemical formaldehyde, iron and an overpowering rotting organic slush. "Why did I screw up the nose?"

"You didn't only screw up the nose, madam. You also screwed up the ears, the eyes, and the innards. But, I must say, it is still quite magnificent, Savant Harlow."

"Thanks," she said with a chuckle.

"Would you like to dissect it?"

"I hate to do it. I feel like I'm cutting into a real person."

"Yes. I told you. You are. Quite magnificent."

After she had taken into account the imperfections—and there were many: small slits as ears, four toes, a tail, the aforementioned nasal deformity—she peered at the eyes again. The eyelids were shut and had few if any blond hairs. She covered the bottom of the body with the white sheet and moved closer to the head again. Then she touched the eyelids. Then she touched the thin eyebrows. She touched them and ran her finger along the thin sparse hairs.

Were the eyes black? She had made her calculations. She thought perhaps blue, like her own, but was unsure. She stood up straighter and forced some courage, then reached over to peel open the upper eyelid. She touched the thin, pale skin, gazing at the delicate blue veins under the skin. Then she slowly opened one eyelid.

"Hey, bitch!"

Candice nearly fell over in fright. She whirled around and saw Elise staring at her with a gaping grin.

"What the hell! Where'd you come from? I didn't even hear the door open."

"Silent like a cat, eh?" Elise asked, now laughing.

Candice squinted her eyes. Her boss's pupils were dilated. She was probably clubbing tonight, geeked out of her mind. Which, in some ways, made it even more remarkable that she had managed to sneak up on her successfully.

"Don't ever do that again, Elise," said Candice. "You scared the hell out of me."

"Yeah, well..." Elise looked around and wrinkled her nose.

"It's kinda creepy here at night. 'Specially when you're up and about, working alone on dead people."

Elise was wearing her cherry-red leather motorcycle jumpsuit. She still held her visor in her left hand.

It was rare that Elise wore a white coat. She hated it. It was like some admission to her job that she wanted to deny. So unless it was actually needed to keep the blood and guts off her collar, she preferred her Savant clothes.

Elise looked down at Candice's creation. She lost her smile for a moment and became very serious. She walked over and grabbed some gloves from a box. Then she grabbed a mask and started poking and prodding at the body.

"Took long enough," Elise said, but Candice could tell that she was impressed.

"It's pretty authentic."

"Yeah," Elise said with a nod.

Elise pinched at the skin and then pulled the sheet back further.

She ran her hand along the pelvis and followed the pubis symphysis down over thin hair to the groin. "Everything work?" she asked. Then, without waiting for an answer, Elise removed her mask and laughed. She hit Candice hard over the back with her hand and then looked a little disappointed at Candice's prudish reaction. "Relax. You need to get out more, Candy. You're gonna lose your mind working in this lab too long."

Candice shuddered, remembering her nightmare.

"It's quite impressive, isn't it, Savant Jackson?" asked Rex.

"Aha," Elise said, giving Candice a smile.

"It still needs work," Candice said.

"How'd you do it?" Elise asked. Candice detected a hint of jealousy in her tone. "There's no way you built this solely in the lab. It's never been this complete before. What'd you use?"

Candice shrugged. Then she walked away from the smelly mass of flesh and leaned against a counter by the wall. "There was no other way, Mother. You didn't give me any choice. I couldn't map out a whole person completely in a lab without some help. It's just not possible."

"Right," Elise said as if that much was obvious. She looked up from the body and removed her gloves. "So... how'd you do it?"

Candice wondered if she should tell her. After months of work, countless failures, she had become desperate. So she had turned to something that she wasn't sure was legal. She'd even done it without Rex's awareness, ordering him to shut down his auditory sensors during some of her gene-mapping experiments, with the excuse of working on recombining techniques that were off-limits to the computer mainframe—though she doubted the machine couldn't figure out her methods when she finished.

"I..." She hesitated, and Elise smiled. It was a wicked smile. Candice knew her master well enough. It was a smile of impatience. She knew her next step would be anger.

"Come, come. Fess up, my dear Candy-can Harlow. We all want to know how you did it. Rex wants to know. I want to know. All Magnacourt wants to know. The whole world wants to know." There was silence for a moment. Then Elise asked, "Do you know, Rex? Candy-can seems tongue-tied."

"No, Mother," replied Rex. "I was not privy, madam, per Savant Harlow's orders."

"Can you guess?"

"Yes."

"How? Give me an answer, since the little tweeting bird has lost her tweet."

"It is a beautiful achievement, though, don't you think, Team Mother?" asked Rex.

"Sure." Then Elise looked right into Candice's eyes. "Very good indeed. So... how'd you do it, my little genius? Rex seems to be avoiding the question too."

"I took a sample of blood, Elise," Candice said, looking away. "It's as simple as that."

"Ah," Elise said, raising a finger in triumph. Then Elise walked around the bed, swaying her hips, and stood right in front of Candice. She took that same raised finger, squinting her eyes, and poked Candice's green surgical gown hard against her chest. "A blood sample... whose?"

"Mine," Candice replied, meeting her boss's gaze with her own.

Elise's lips curled in a smile. "Clever. Very clever. But that's cheating, don't you think?"

"There was no other way. No one could live long enough to develop a human body from scratch."

"It's quite beautiful, isn't it, Savant Jackson?" asked Rex.

"Quiet, Rex," Elise said, keeping her eyes fixed on Candice's. All at once she started to chuckle. She spun around and walked back to the table. "So this is your baby, then?"

"I suppose," replied Candice. "If there is no difference between a baby and a parent genetically. More like a clone, Team Mother."

Elise looked down at the body and then back at Candice. And then back at the body, then back at Candice. Then she looked at the body once more, and back at Candice. Elise shook her head and said very seriously, "But she looks nothing like you."

"I was afraid to tell you because I wasn't sure it was allowed," explained Candice.

"It isn't. It's cheating."

"Then you've asked the impossible from me."

"Hmm?" Elise lifted up the sheet and ran her finger along the body again, this time without a glove. She examined the hands and then the neck. She moved the head up and down in flexion and extension. She opened its mouth. "Its flesh is cold."

"It's dead, Savant Jackson," Rex said, stating the obvious.

"Indeed," Elise said, peering into the nose slits. "And an ugly motherfucker. I'm glad for that, Candy. I'm glad this thing isn't creeping around." Elise lifted her hand in the air. "Hand me a scalpel, Rex."

"What are you doing?" asked Candice. "You're not even wearing gloves."

A laser scalpel was lowered from the ceiling. Elise lit the laser flame and, without any hesitation, began cutting above the left breast. "I'm seeing if you pass your final exam, Doctor Candy-can." Elise cut and cut and then grew impatient. She looked up to the ceiling and snapped, "The saw, Rex." Then she looked at Candice with a smile. "It's getting late. Don't you ever sleep? What's the matter with you?"

Elise turned the laser saw on and began cutting furiously. Candice stepped back and leaned as far back as she could on a counter at the opposite end of the train car in order to avoid the inevitable bloody mess.

The cutting seemed to excite her boss. Elise made a mess of things, splashing blood everywhere, including, as Candice had predicted, all over her leather jumpsuit. Some of the blood even splashed at Candice from all the way across the room. But the dark red fluid only seemed to spur Elise on more. She cut and hacked, moving through what Candice recognized as the intercostal muscles and the white bones of the fourth and fifth ribs. She stopped as she reached the red mass below. The heart. Then she slowed and moved more like a dancer, utilizing her twenty years' experience to perfectly trim and clamp veins and arteries. Candice walked back and stood close, observing with interest, no longer caring about the blood. With precision, Elise cut the aorta and superior and inferior vena cava and then snipped off the sinew from the heart. She took the muscle and plopped it on top of the white sheets that covered the body. She examined it, breathing heavily from all her work. Then, with the same furious speed, she grabbed a metal scalpel from a nearby cart and continued the dissection, checking the heart's chambers. When she had her fill, she tossed it like a football at Candice. Candice caught it as it splashed her gown with blood.

"Nicely done, little genius. You pass."

With black hair speckled with flesh and blood, and her face and clothes drenched with crimson, Elise walked out of the surgical suite.

"Congratulations, Candice," said Rex.

Candice was still looking toward the door. She felt tired again after watching her boss's maniacal work.

She walked beside the body and placed the heart under the sheets, which were now stained crimson too. Then she touched her gloves. She was about to tear them off, but then she gazed at the eyelids again.

She cautiously approached the face and touched the eyelids once more. Then she finally opened one. It wasn't black: it was blue. She sighed with relief. That had been her scientific guess: blue like her own. She was relieved.

"Cleanse the room, Rex."

"Very well, madam."

Early morning, Elise returned to the surgical suite. It was still dark and quiet outside the train. The sun would not rise for another hour. Elise flashed her wrist beside the door, and it opened. The room still smelled awful, made worse after her makeshift slaughter autopsy. Before she had left, Elise had ordered Rex behind Candice's back to countermand any order to clean the room. The only light was the dim yellow hanging floodlight over the bed. It cast a dark shadow over the body. There was a mass of bloody white sheets lying toward the center of the room, and smears of blood had been tracked across the white tiled floors.

The only sound was that of the train rushing over the

rails. Elise was occasionally reminded of the movement of the train, leaning against the wall and pausing on her way through the cars. When she reached the surgical suite, she walked cautiously along the bloodstained floor, trying to avoid the spills. It was impossible, of course. She knew she'd have to wash up again, but she tiptoed around the puddles anyway.

"Welcome back, Doctor," said Rex from overhead. It scared the hell out of her. She jumped back in fright.

"Damn it," she snapped in a whisper. "Turn on some fucking lights and shut up, idiot."

She winced as bright lights filled the room. It only made the carnage worse.

She approached the body and lifted up the sheet. If at all possible, it seemed to reek even more. She grabbed some latex gloves from a box on the wall and ran her gloved finger along the bright white flesh. It was soft but icy cold.

"It is impressive, is it not, Savant Jackson?"

"Yeah, sure," she said, touching the nape of the neck. Then she felt along the cricoid and about the shallow mound that was the thyroid gland. "Nearly flawless."

"Why did you instruct me not to incinerate it, Mother?"

She didn't answer him.

"Why did you instruct me not to incinerate it, Mother?" Rex repeated.

She continued to run her finger along the forehead and then over the temples. The cheeks were thin but soft. She stepped back a little and examined the face. With a bit of imagination, it looked like its creator. No—a lot of imagination. How difficult it was to recreate the face. But everything else was intact and nearly perfect.

"She did better than you did, Team Mother. It is quite impressive. Quite impressive."

"I told you to shut it."

"I can still recall you presenting your work to your predecessor. It was merely a sack of tissue, like Savant Harlow's first attempt a year ago."

She ran her finger along the arms to the hands. The palms had creases, but they were faint. There were no fingernails. But there were five digits on each hand. She lifted one up and checked each joint. Then she gave Rex a response while still inspecting the specimen: "Funny, I thought you were supposed to be intelligent. Didn't I instruct you to shut the fuck up?" She laid the hand down gently.

Then she leaned against the wall, just like she had seen Candice do a couple of hours earlier. She tore off her gloves and sighed.

"It appears our little birdy has finally grown up."

Rex didn't respond. She chuckled. It seemed he was finally obeying her.

"I want complete schematics on her work. Check every-thing, Rex. I mean *everything*, before you incinerate. Do you understand?"

"Yes, Savant Jackson."

A metal arm came down and began scanning the body. Then the saw came down to dissect it.

"How long will it take, Rex?"

"For a complete survey?"

"Yeah."

"Just a minute... just a minute."

"All right."

"Just a minute. Just a minute... two weeks."

"Two weeks!"

"You asked for a full survey, Savant Jackson."

"Very well. Quarantine the lab and ensure no one gets in, including Savant Harlow."

10

LUNCH

"You know, it's funny," Elise said to Candice with a chuckle. "I usually invite people for lunch to fire them."

They were sitting outside beside one of the main streets of the city. It was one of Candice's favorite cafés. It was called Frenchy's. And, like its name, it was chic and cute at the same time. There were small metal tables along the sidewalk with cute little sky-blue awnings over each table. The waitresses wore navy-blue suits with berets. The food was French, but not traditional fare: more like an eclectic, corny version of it. They had croissants, crepes, and champagne. Candice ordered a large ham croissant with chips.

She was eating as Elise lost her smile while rubbing her temples. "I have a huge headache."

"Why are we here, Elise?" asked Candice, taking another bite of her croissant. Then, to complete the cuteness, she offered Elise a bite.

"Damn, my head hurts," Elise said.

"Too much Mint."

"Now you're sounding like Rex."

Candice looked out at the street. Automated trucks occasionally rushed by on the road, but there were few cars. It was midday, and the roads these days were pretty empty. But the sidewalks were busy. She saw many ladies holding hands and helping their little girls along as they walked by. A few nodded and gave them looks of awe. Candice was used to the reverence of the citizenry by now.

There were also drones circling noiselessly above. Candice knew by now their purpose: to protect them from any crazed citizen.

She had once seen a citizen come right up to Elise with a knife behind her back. They had been walking along the sidewalk near HQ. It had been a lovely, clear day. As they'd waited to cross the street, a woman had run right up to her boss and swung the blade up to her neck. As surprising as that was, Candice was more shocked by the response. In less than a second, the assailant had fallen, shocked by an electric charge from the sky. That's what the drones did. They protected the two of them in all situations, standing constant guard.

"I have to get down to business, Candy," said Elise. Her sincerity was a bit frightening, because Elise wasn't one to ever get down to business. "Now that Allele Corp. is out of commission, we need a new supplier for embryos."

"I figured that."

"Sure, you did. You're a very smart young lady, Candy-can. I need you again for a job."

"I'm your assistant, Elise."

"Right."

Candice took another bite of the sandwich. She was famished. She hadn't eaten anything for days, except an occasional cracker to keep conscious.

Candice was also extremely tired, even after sleeping in until one this afternoon. But she was in good spirits, although they were tempered a little bit now that, after finishing a project that had painstakingly taken years, her boss was proposing a new one.

"I know you just finished," Elise said, practically reading

her mind, "but this one isn't a lab project. It's more Officer class. You won't be in the lab for weeks. I need you out in the field. I want you to interview a prospective candidate to lead fertilization. If all goes well, we'll use her to direct Allele Corporation's replacement."

Then Elise rubbed her forehead. "Shit, I feel like shit." She robotically reached into her pocket and pulled out another stick of gum. It seemed she was getting more addicted every day.

Candice was quite addicted too. The sight of the gum made her mouth water for a moment. She finished her sandwich and reached into her own pocket. "Fine, Elise. Just let me know when and where."

Elise smiled a thin smile. She seemed almost vulnerable today. Her pain had taken away her usual mania. And then it seemed Elise's dark eyes looked over at Candice warmly for a moment. Candice wondered what a sober Elise Jackson would have been like to know.

"Sector Two," she said.

"I'm not aware of a genetic corp. in Sector Two."

"There isn't. Magnacourt's gonna make one."

"Why doesn't Magnacourt just build its own in Sector One?"

"No. We need to keep it separate from the citizens."

"All right."

"Yeah. Rex'll give you all the information you need. Just go to Sector Two and interview the docs. I'll provide you a list."

Candice looked away for a second and chomped on a chip. She caught a few women in drab gray dresses staring. They were leaning against the building, probably on lunch break from across the street. Their look was initially not friendly, but when they saw her looking over, they quickly smiled.

"I really wanted to do some more work at the lab."

Candice couldn't believe she'd said it, but she did. She'd hated everything about the lab lately: the smell, the darkness, the enclosed space. And yet she enjoyed the alone time just the same.

"Really?" Elise asked, surprised. "You can go back in a month." She raised a glass of champagne with a smile. "Congratulations, Candy. Rex is quite right. You did good."

"Thanks."

And Candice was surprised at how much pride she felt at her Team Mother's simple accolade.

11

COURTING DOCS

CANDICE PARKED ALONG THE ROOFTOP OF A CRYSTAL skyscraper toward the end of the Arkite Pyramid, so close to the edge that she could touch the great wall. The building was one of the newest additions to the city, made completely of glass, which allowed the afternoon sun to resonate brightly throughout the building. As if to accentuate the lighting, the walls and floor reflected the sun. It was so reflective that little if any artificial lighting was needed on a sunny day.

She wore a tight formal black dress with a golden brooch at her left shoulder. Her hair was braided back behind her head, and her black high heels echoed along the reflective floor. She wore glasses. She didn't need to, but she liked the distinguished way the thin frames wrapped around her face.

It was a painfully long walk to the conference center. The only landing platform for rocket cycles was clear on the opposite side of the building. Their new construction codes claimed the bikes could damage or mark the glass, so she had to park on a special paved platform and walk all the way across the whole glass building, which spanned over a mile.

She passed many citizens, also in suits, who gazed at her in awe, recognizing her immediately. She wasn't wearing her

Savant jumpsuit, so they must have actually recognized her face. And why wouldn't they? Thanks to years under Elise's service, virtually everyone in the city knew the face of Savant Candice Harlow. Many stared as she hopped on the floor escalator toward the main center.

Advertisements from HQ for various things like bus transportation, lipstick, soap, and hair products ran along the glass walls as she rode across the building. The building was nearly as wide as it was long, and these images shone in three dimensions in the far distance from either side of her. No one looked at them as they stood on the automated walkway. Candice saw everyone do what she was doing: look straight ahead and say nothing. There was an annoying ethereal hum in the background that was supposed to be music. She didn't like the sound. She would have preferred silence, or the jibber-jabber of the citizenry.

Occasionally, she passed under long see-through crystal tunnels. The rail was not completely flat, sometimes lifting up an incline, crossing under a tunnel, and then leveling off again.

She moved quickly along the black mat, one hand on the rail.

Her mind was on work. As usual, Elise had not given her an easy job. She had twelve interviews scheduled, and it was already after midday. She would have to rush the candidates through all of her boss's provocative questions.

She reached the end of the building and rode an elevator up to the fifty-fourth floor. A few women dressed in suits waiting for the lift looked at her through the clear glass doors. They seemed fearful when the door opened.

She approached one of them, a very young bald black girl wearing a triangular orange suit. "Excuse me, miss, do you know the way to the main conference rooms? I have a very important meeting."

The girl quickly shook her head, but an older, sharply

dressed lady standing beside her pointed with a shaky finger across a glass bridge in the distance.

"There?" asked Candice. Then she looked back at the girl. The girl's eyes were a bit wider.

"Would you like me to take you there, Master?" the young girl shyly asked.

"No, thank you," Candice said with a smile. "That's very kind, but I'll find my way. Thanks."

"You're welcome, Savant Harlow."

Candice popped a couple of sticks of Mint in her mouth and walked on.

Once she crossed over the bridge and passed beyond a square marble waterfall, a black stone door slid open automatically, and she was greeted by an old woman in a gray suit with matching short gray hair, wrinkles, and a sweet smile. Candice mused that this must be what grandmothers looked like. She had never known her grandmother, but this woman was the picture of an iconic nana. She led Candice into a meeting room.

What a contrast from her last interview. When she had met Doctor Reyburn in HQ, the "cell" had been more of a dungeon. Here the sun pleasantly brightened the room. The walls were crystal, and they magnified the outdoor light. There was one large dark-wood polished table at the center with black leather chairs surrounding it. She looked down at an unblemished tan-carpeted floor. Then she sat on one of the comfy chairs and gazed out through the walled windows at a lovely skyline.

"Would you like something to drink, Team Daughter?" the old woman asked with a smile.

Team Daughter. She had never heard that expression before. It surprised her.

"No... nothing."

"Very well, then, dear. I'll bring the candidates in one by one. All you need do is dismiss them when you're finished.

After each is sent out, the next shall come in. Will that be okay?"

Candice wondered where the candidates were. She hadn't seen them on her way in. She figured they were in another room or floor. She felt like she was in a fun house full of mirrors, a strange crystal labyrinth of glass walls.

"Yes, thank you. I think that will do nicely."

"Good," the old lady said with that sweet smile.

The rest of the day was rather dull. She saw candidate after candidate, asking the questions fed to her by Elise. She didn't like any of the ladies and had known ahead of time that she wouldn't. She had already made her choice after reviewing the files days ago.

Most of the candidates were pompous asses who thought that they should be the Team Daughter, not her. She even had a stupid argument with one of them over the Krebs cycle and the futility of memorizing it in the modern age. The thing was, Candice didn't really care, but somehow she ended up disputing it with the conceited girl. Then the girl made the mistake of sarcastically asking if Candice still had it memorized, and the girl promptly went ahead and recited each step. And she was far from done. As Candice stared at her wrist to check the time, the girl's next stunt was to start reciting the innervations of the brachial plexus. The interview ended with the candidate contemptuously asking Candice if she still remembered them.

When it was evening and the room was lit by soft artificial lighting from the vaulted ceiling and the twinkling lights of the city, the last candidate arrived: the candidate Candice had wanted all along. If it had been up to Candice, she would have skipped all the others, but Mother wanted her to interview all of them. This candidate was the youngest. She had long brown hair fixed in a ponytail. She wore her white lab coat with a black sweater and gray slacks underneath. Her makeup, unlike Candice's, was applied sparingly. She was different than the others—less confident. And awfully nervous.

"Sit down," Candice said, gesturing to a seat beside her. "Doctor Bridgette Kelley, right?"

The young girl flashed a smile, then quickly looked out the window with a nod.

"You graduated recently, right? You're the youngest and brightest in your class?"

Bridgette nodded again.

"Bridgette?" Candice gently took her chin and turned it toward her. "I'm over here."

"I know... sorry." Bridgette fidgeted with her hands. Then she flashed a fake smile. "I'm nervous, I guess."

"You're doing fine." Candice tapped on her wrist and started to sift through files. She smiled, watching Bridgette's hands shake—the shaky hands reminded her a lot of someone else once interviewed by a Savant of Magnacourt.

"I don't bite," Candice said, adjusting her fake glasses and still staring at her wrist.

"My friends call me Bren. Call me Bren, please, Savant Harlow."

"All right, Doctor Kelley," Candice said with a smile.

Bren's record was clean. Boring, really. There wasn't anything the matter with her, but there wasn't much about her either, except her studies. She'd worked hard and tested at the top of her class. All the other candidates were at the top of their classes too, but Bren was at the tippy-top. Candice was quite sure Bren could recite the citric acid cycle and the brachial plexus verbatim too. She had been raised in Sector Three—like Candice. Nearly everyone in Arkite was raised in the apartments of Sector Three. Bren's parents had been killed when she was only six years old. That, also, was like Candice. She'd also gone to school in the same zone and with the same teachers as Candice. But, unlike all the other candidates, her IQ was ranked well over 200. She was super smart.

She had also developed four theses (Candice wasn't sure how she had possibly found the time for more than one), two of which had been adopted by Magnacourt itself and even used by Candice in transposon mutagenesis on the Lazarus Project. None of the other candidates had invented anything. Brains-wise, she was perfect.

But she didn't have that other quality Elise was looking for.

She had a pretty face, in some ways cuter than Candice's. She had green eyes, very pretty. Her skin was dark and her eyelids were slightly slanted. She had mixed Asian and Eastern European heritage, according to the genetic record. But she was young and shy, and Candice imagined that such a book-worm wouldn't know how to deal with the more political aspects of the job. These politics would be important for survival. For Elise, being a Savant meant more than just a high IQ. She had to be fun, and as Candice looked across the table at her, as Bren shifted her eyes and nervously shook, she imagined her boss devouring this puny little tweetsy bird.

"You were adopted?" asked Candice, staring at her wrist. "You lost your parents when you were young?"

"Yes."

Candice waited for another word. Bren said nothing.

"Yes?" Candice snapped after some silence, looking up into her eyes. "Yes? Yes, *WHAT*?" Candice rolled her eyes. "Look, Bren, you've gotta relax. And—talk. Try talking. This is an interview."

"Sorry. Yes, I was adopted, Savant Harlow." She bit the top of her lip. Candice liked that; it was precisely what she was known to do herself when she was nervous. "I wish I had known them, but they died in a car accident. My mothers worked in finance for Central Bank."

"Well"—Candice gently took her hand—"we have some-thing in common here. I was adopted."

Bren curled up her lip a little, then quickly nodded.

"I read your papers on GMO and genetic modification procreation," Candice continued, looking back down at her wrist. "Your work is a bit sloppy, unorthodox... but brilliant. I mean, really clever. Some of your achievements in the university were extraordinary."

"Thank you, Savant Harlow."

"I'm surprised you were able to work so much. How did you find the time?" Candice forced a chuckle. "Did you ever eat?"

"Yeah. I ate."

Bren smiled again; this time Candice was sure it was quite fake and unnatural. "It must have been hard to find time. I work very hard too."

"I know you do. You are a Lead Savant working for Team Mother. It must be very hard."

"Aha. I don't eat much."

Candice laughed, and Bren joined her. Candice was relieved she had gotten her to laugh.

"I don't sleep much either. Bren, working in Magnacourt is a lot of hard work."

Bren nodded quietly.

"Let me ask you," Candice said, "what do you know about Allele Corporation?"

That did it. It might have been the whole reason for the interview, but it didn't matter. What had happened to all those poor scientists was common knowledge. Their demise was known in all four sectors and had increased the power of her Team Mother. It was an example of why Bren was so terrified of Candice in the first place. If she could have said anything to frighten Bren, that was it. Bren's eyes bulged wide, and her whole body visibly shook. She leaned back in her chair, as far from Candice as possible.

"It's okay, Bren," said Candice, forcing a reassuring smile. "It's all right."

Bren shook her head.

"Okay," Candice said, raising a hand, "let me try something else. How 'bout—"

"I'm sorry, Savant Harlow. I'm just... nervous, that's all. I know how important the interview is."

"Yeah, you are nervous." Candice shut off her wrist screen and leaned back in her leather chair. She had thirty or forty more questions from Elise, but she decided to forego the whole thing. Of course, Elise had come up with the first one. It was to frighten and intimidate the interviewee, and it achieved that but was the wrong approach for this one. "Look, Bren, it's late and I'm tired... would you care for a stick of gum?"

Candice reached between the folds of her dress and brought out her pack. When Bren refused, Candice couldn't help but roll her eyes again.

"I could just dismiss you," Candice said, finally giving in to her anger. "I interviewed a lot of doctors today, but I want to give you a chance. You should know, you're the least experienced of all of them."

Bren stupidly nodded again. Candice sighed.

"But you're also the brightest. I like intelligence, Bren. And I like someone with a mind that thinks out of the box. You've come up with ingenious methods in your work... so, please, relax as best you can so I can give you the chance you deserve. 'Kay?"

"Yes."

"All right," Candice said, sighing again. "Forget Allele Corp. How 'bout you tell me about Magnacourt? What do you know about us?"

"You and Mother are the leaders of the world, Savant Harlow."

Candice cracked a thin smile. "I wouldn't say *world*, Bren, but my boss would love hearing that."

"The city is the world, Savant Harlow. You lead Arkite."

"Call me Candice."

"All right, Candice."

"What does Magnacourt do?"

"You serve the people. You and the people are one. You provide us order. You care for us. And you direct our procreation. You—"

"I don't want a fucking commercial."

Bren nodded shyly. She paused reflectively for a moment and then said, "Magnacourt controls human population and growth. It provides order through HQ and distributes all resources for food and shelter. It controls the mainframe and, thereby, the world."

Candice nodded. Then she gently took Bren's hand again.

She squeezed the bones about her fingers the way Elise had done to her countless times before—but she had forgotten her initial impression of that act too. It was meant to relax Bren, and it did the opposite.

"Bren, I need someone in Sector Two to care for the management of the embryos. Now that Allele Corp. is gone, I need someone to take over. Elise and I do not have time to help Rex run this. It is a very important job, with great responsibility."

Bren nodded again, but Candice reflected that her grim expression was odd, considering that she was being offered the greatest position in the whole "world."

"But I have to tell you, I have my reservations. Bren, as much as I might intimidate you, Elise is far worse. Mother is someone you actually should fear."

"Are you afraid of her, Candice?"

Candice cracked a smile at that. It was unexpected. She took off her spectacles, shook out her hair, and smiled. "Yes. Yes, I am. And if you accept the job, you'll fear her too."

"But, Candice, do I even have a choice? If you're picking me, you'll assign me, whatever I choose. Isn't that right?"

"No. If you don't want the job, you can leave."

"Really? But isn't this what happened to you? You were picked by Mother. We don't have a choice, Candice."

"You can leave, Bren. You have my word."

Candice took a deep breath and gently touched her hand. Bren let her this time, managing a shy smile.

"Do you want to join us?"

"It is an honor, Candice. A great honor. But..."

"Join us. I think you'll do well. Your most important job will be running the factories replacing Allele Corp., but you can also assist me in the lab. I need help too."

Then Candice began second-guessing herself. Perhaps she was wrong. Perhaps she should have picked a candidate with more confidence. More experience. Perhaps that Krebs cycle bitch. But Bren reminded her of herself. Candice had probably been just like her when Elise had first interviewed her. It made her malleable. Impressionable.

"All the others who have been interviewed before you will work under you," Candice continued. "My decision won't go to Elise until you accept, you have my word on that. You will be safe. You can decide either way, but if you refuse, you will never be offered a job at"—she smiled smugly—"*the most powerful company in the world* again."

"I understand."

"And?"

"I accept, Candice."

But Bren looked sad. She gazed out at the lights of the city with a terrible morose expression, as if she was being sentenced to prison.

Candice looked at her carefully. As scared as Bren acted, she still seemed strong inside. Candice prided herself in her judgment of people. But she would have to test her. Somehow, she had to see if the fear Bren was showing was for the interview alone, or if she really couldn't handle the job.

Candice sat up straight, puffed her chest out, straightened

her dress, and used all the training she had received from her bitch boss. She threw herself on the table and looked sternly into the young girl's eyes, hitting the wooden surface hard with her fists. Somehow, she felt it wasn't the same as when Elise had done it to her.

"I'll give you a month. That is all!" She pointed at Bren's face, almost striking her. "If you screw up, Bren, you're out. And I warn you, don't fuck up! After you see our secrets, if you screw up, you'll be out for good—truly out. Do you know what that means?"

"Yes, Savant Harlow," she said with eyes wide. Of course she did. The poor girl was shaking.

"Good." Candice stood up and smiled, offering a hand to Bren. "Welcome to Magnacourt, Savant Kelley."

Bren shook her hand.

"Now let's get out of here," Candice said. "I'm hungry."

And tired—really tired.

"Candice," Bren asked in a quiet, mousy voice, "do you like working for Magnacourt?"

"No."

She gently helped the girl up, and they walked out of the room together.

The old lady had gone home. It was dark throughout Sector Two. As bright as it was during the day, it was that much darker at night with so few lights, but still just as beautiful. From the windowed walls, they could see the moon and stars of the night sky from above and through the close checkered walls of the Pyramid.

"We'll eat at Mother's. I'll take you immediately to HQ."

"What's she like, Candice?" Bren asked as she hopped on the elevator.

"Bren," Candice said, cocking her head as they stood side by side, "I need you to be strong."

When they made it to the floor escalator, she turned and faced her directly, looking in her eyes. "Don't be weak. She'll tear you apart. If you must, show disrespect or even anger, but never show weakness. Don't be weak in front of her. Do you understand me?"

"She sounds awful," Bren said, looking down.

"She's a bitch," Candice said, looking away with a shrug.

12

WHAT'D YOU BRING HOME TO ROOST, LITTLE TWEET TWEET?

The door opened after Candice rang the doorbell, but no one greeted them. Bren was still wearing her white lab coat. Candice helped take it off and hang it in a closet. Then they walked the slope up the penthouse tower.

Music was playing—some smooth jazz. Candice knew Elise was here, but she didn't know where. None of the lights were on, only some permanent mood lights that shone along the walls.

When they walked up the slope, Candice saw Elise's silhouette outlined by the moon and twinkling lights of the city. Elise stood at the top with her hands leaning on a thin golden rail that ran along the large window up at the third floor, staring out with her back to them.

"Elise, I've brought our new employee."

Elise cocked her head. Then she turned and walked, swaying her hips, slowly down the ramp to the second floor. She stood close beside them, looked at Candice, and flashed a smile. Then she lifted a black-leather-gloved hand to touch Bren's cheek. Bren lifted a hand to object, but Elise quickly swatted it down. Still looking at Candice, Elise ran her hand along Bren's face.

"What'd you bring me, Candy?"

"Doctor Bridgette Kelley. She goes by Bren."

"Ah." Elise touched Bren's nose and lips with her glove as if she were a specimen from the lab. "How old is she, Candy?"

"I..." Candice had to think for a moment. She couldn't remember. "I..."

"Twenty-one," said Bren.

"Oh, I see. So you brought me a virgin?"

"What?"

"A virgin. You brought me a virgin." Elise kept rubbing Bren's cheek—up and down, up and down. Bren stood there like a statue. "I sent you to Sector Two to find me a receptacle for more bitches to be born in, and you brought me a fucking virgin. Well..." She put a finger up to her chin. "I suppose it's appropriate, isn't it." She laughed.

Elise turned from them and walked back up the ramp to the top floor. She stopped and held her hands behind her as if her guests were not there. Candice led Bren closer up the ramp.

"This is a beautiful house, Team Mother," said Bren after a moment.

"Shut the fuck up."

"What did you want?" asked Candice. She could feel her face flushing, and she was holding back rage. Anger was something that had become a part of her. It was used to cope with her boss. Mother fed it, stoked it, and even encouraged it. "I interviewed her. She's highly qualified."

"She has no experience," Elise said, shrugging her shoulders and staring out the window.

"She scored higher than anyone else I interviewed. Higher than me... even you."

"Let's not get personal."

Elise walked over to one of the gray egg-shaped chairs. She plopped down, grabbed a glass of red wine from an end table, and swiveled the chair toward the ramp, looking down at them. She stared at Bren from head to toe as she sipped her wine.

"Did you know, Candy, that Dollface was a test?" Elise asked. "Another test for you, Candy-can. And this time, you fell right into the trap. I knew your heart was too good. You'd pick the mousy weak one. The one without character. The one with brains but no worldliness. The fucking Dollface. That's all she is. She's even worse than a bird. At least a bird tweets. This one's just a fucking Dollface. And you picked her. You want to work with a Dollface."

"I disagree."

"Of course you disagree," Elise said, laughing. "You chose her. But you shouldn't have. I'm disappointed. You chose wrong."

"I don't really care, Elise."

Elise turned her wrath from her *Dollface* to her former *Tweetsy*. She swiveled her chair toward Candice and looked down at her in sudden fury.

"An interview, my dear little Candy-cunt, involves finding the best candidate for the job. Someone with enough experience that enables you to not be busy having to change diapers and prepare milk bottles. But you chose the little new twit with the cute face. You chose a bedwetting twat like you. Someone *you* will take care of." She ran her hand through her long black hair and drank down more wine. "Don't look at me like that. I'm not in the mood to care for babies. I fucking hate them. Fucking is fun enough, but to fuck without actually fucking caring about anyone is always best."

Candice looked over at Bren. She looked, predictably, terrified. This time rightfully so. But that made Candice feel worse. If Bren couldn't hide her fear, Elise was going to unleash on her full throttle.

But then... the mouse spoke.

"I'm right for the job," Bridgette said. Candice and Elise looked over at her in surprise. "I'm very familiar with genetic modeling, and I even invented some of the processes you and Candice are using for modifications. I can help you, not only with the incubators, but with your work in HQ lab."

"I see," Elise said with a very amused smile. She lifted the wineglass, pointing it with a finger at Bren. "Are you familiar with chromosome Y?"

"Yes."

"Of course you are." Elise sat up straighter in her leather chair. "And do you know, Dollface, do you know the great pleasure I had in dealing with Allele Corp. over XY?"

Uh-oh.

Elise paused. Then she wagged a finger. "When the scientists of Allele Corp. didn't behave, Doll Titty, I had to intervene. So, what I did..." She got up and walked down the ramp, close to Bren. Then she ran her hand slowly through Bren's hair. "What I did, my sweet little dolly, was gather all the stuff I could from the mainframe, every piece in regard to family, mommies, aunts, sisters, and cousins. Every girl related to the criminals. And... do you... do you know what I did to them, Dolly Facie?"

Bren shook her head.

"Well," Elise said, throwing Bren's hair back and shrugging a shoulder, "I felt—it's not enough to hurt their family. That's too kind. I mean, pain only lasts so long." She rubbed Bren's neck under her hair with a gloved hand. "No, I had to do something better." She reached down along Bren's neck, looking right at Candice, and ran her tongue over Bren's ear. Then she whispered softly into it. "So what I did was, I donated them to science. I had them strip down naked at HQ. Then I used their lovely bodies. I harvested their organs. Each and every piece of them. I harvested their parts so that we could research them and then use them for people who were more deserving. After all, why waste? Why send them to a firing squad in the same fashion as the doctors? Right? So, as they broke the law and fiddled with Y, I had my way fiddling with their Xs."

Elise turned for a moment, finishing her wine, then turned back and nearly spat it in the girl's face.

"Do you fucking understand, Dollface? Don't ever cross me! Don't you ever cross me! Don't ever disobey Mother or I'll take everyone you love, every flapping tweety-tweet cunt-face fucker of yours, tie them up, and cut them up into little pieces!"

That was Elise. Candice had been trying to do the same earlier, but she'd failed miserably.

"Yes, Mother," Bren squeaked.

"Good girl," she said mockingly, running her hand along Bren's chin and lips. Then she caressed her cheek again. "Well, you are delightful to look at, aren't you? I wonder if that's what Candy was thinking. You know, she has"—Elise ran her hand along Bridgette's chest and began unbuttoning her blouse—"she has a sick mind, you know. Savant Harlow has always been a bit of a pervert. But she's quiet about it, so you'd never know."

Bren was shaking. Candice walked up to help her, but Elise raised a hand. Elise led Bren up to the third floor beside the green couch. She embraced her, drifting one hand along the sweater, moving under and over her chest. Candice moved to stop her again but was halted by another open leather palm.

"This is all your doing, Candy. And as for you, Bren..." She kissed her cheek gently, then ran her tongue along Bren's ear again. She began sucking her earlobe. Bren stayed frozen like a rabbit. "As for you, Bren, as you work in misery for the rest of your days, know that it is not the fault of your Team Mother." She removed the girl's sweater. Bren had no shirt under it. Elise undid her bra. "No. No. It's all Candy-can's fault. It is always because of her. She introduced you to me. She hired you. And as Candy will tell you, working with me involves quite a lot more than just reading books. Isn't that right, Candy-can?"

"You should ask before you touch," Candice said.

The comment was precisely the right thing to say. It seemed right to her, and likely to Bren and Elise too, but it was also completely out of place. Elise released the hand that was cupping one of Bren's breasts and then burst out laughing. She pushed Bren onto the couch and threw her sweater at her.

"Quite right, Candy. I'm not being a very nice host, am I?"

"No, you're not. You're being a complete bitch."

"Yes." Elise examined Bren on the couch. "But in all seriousness, I think you made a mistake, Candice. I honestly think you're wrong about this one. Judging from her profile, I would never have picked her, smarts or not. And, anyway... she doesn't appear up to the job."

"I am, Mother," Bren objected, pushing her clothes to the side. She nearly stuttered the words, but she forced herself to look at Elise with defiance.

Then Bren sat back, kicked off her shoes, and unzipped and pushed down her formal black slacks. Her pink panties were all that was left. She quickly discarded those too, turning and showing her new boss the edges of her flank and ass. Elise's eyes grew large staring at her. Then Bren shook her long brown hair out and let her chest stand bare. She ran a finger along her the contour of her small perky breasts and said, "Thank you, Mother, for hiring me."

Elise was so surprised that she stepped back.

"No. I mean... yes... quite lovely, aren't you? Perhaps you're not just a Dollface after all. Hmm. More than a Dollface? Well, very good, welcome to Magnacourt, then... Rex, say hello to Bren. She's naked and sprawled out for you on my couch."

"Hello, Bren," said the stale male voice in the air. "Welcome to Magnacourt."

"Hello, Rex."

"Take her downstairs, Candy. Let's eat dinner in the dining room. Perhaps you can show her some clothes more befitting a Savant and Officer of HQ."

"Yes, Mother."

"Hmm," Elise said, looking at the girl once more. Candice looked too.

Bren had an odd look of fright mixed with pride. But there she sat, leaning back on the green leather couch with her chest laid bare. She was attractive, in some ways more of a Dollface than Candice, but it seemed there was something Elise genuinely didn't like about her. Mother was not just putting her through her usual abuse. Perhaps it was her shyness. Candice wasn't shy; she was merely guarded.

"Come on, Bren," Candice said. "Come with me. Elise has quite a home. Let me show you around."

"Thanks, Candice," Bren said, seeming to relax for the first time.

"You're really taken by her, aren't you, Candy-can-can?" asked Elise as the two girls walked down the ramp.

"She's nice," Candice replied. "Something you'll never be."

13

OH, MY PRISONER

THE BLACK TRANSPORT CAR WAS BUMPY ON THE GROUND, BUT once it took to the sky it was very comfortable. It became quiet, with only the lull of the engine rumbling beneath Candice's feet. And now, at four in the morning, had she not been transporting a prisoner, it could have rocked her to sleep. But she couldn't sleep with those dark eyes glaring at her.

Doctor Reyburn. The older woman was sitting across from her, staring at her. She had her hands neatly folded over a bright orange jumpsuit with wrists shackled in steel cuffs. Her hair was shaved. Oddly, this made her appear younger. Only a little gray fuzz was starting to appear at the top of her head. Between their legs was a movable shiny marble coffee table. Candice did everything she could to use it to block her space from the prisoner's.

Candice looked out the large side windows, watching as the sharp angles of the metallic skyscrapers of Arkite covered the landscape. She could see the HQ Civic Building not too far beyond, and close to that was Mother's home. All the tiny yellow lights blurred along a dark foggy sky.

Candice caught a glimpse of Doctor Reyburn. She was still staring.

Candice took out a small compact out from her pocket and looked at herself. Then she applied some more black lipstick.

"How long you gonna keep this up?" Reyburn asked.

"Shut up, tweeter."

Doctor Reyburn laughed.

They passed over Central Park. Candice could see the tiny distant streetlights below lighting up the sidewalks and bicycle paths surrounding the lake. The lake itself was dark. There weren't any pedestrians on the trails at this hour, but even this late, in the blackness, the lights lighting up the trees and paths surrounding the waters of Lake Salmas were lovely.

"Why, just look at you," Doctor Reyburn remarked with a chuckle. "You've become an exact copy of her. Just like that new slice of pie you hired. Pretty soon you'll *be* her, and that poor little girl will be you. That's how it works. That's how it's always worked. We always hate our mothers."

"What makes you think I don't like her?" asked Candice. Doctor Reyburn shrugged.

Candice quickly turned away and looked at her wrist. *Ten minutes. Ten more minutes of this. Ten more.*

"I want to thank you, Candice. If it wasn't for you, I'd already be dead. That was very nice."

Candice dipped into the pocket of her red leather pants again and pulled out some gum. She was wearing Elise's jumpsuit. It was a gift from her. She was almost exactly her height, and they traded clothes frequently. Elise said she wanted her to wear it—she preferred black anyway.

"Want some gum?" Candice offered her a stick.

"Even after the last time?" Doctor Reyburn asked with a smile. "Okay, sure." She reached for the stick with her shackled hands.

Candice watched a rocket cycle and a series of small drones fly close by the window. She wondered if it was Mother. Or perhaps it was one of the other Savants.

A sharp turn seemed to break her prisoner's focus for a moment. Candice was thankful for that. She didn't want to talk to her.

They were getting close to the prison. Good. Candice recognized some of the square white marble-stone buildings below near the courthouse, lit up by the same bright yellow as the streetlamps in the park.

Candice took a deep breath and closed her eyes.

"Finish your work?" Reyburn finally asked, while looking out the window too.

"Shut it." *Elise, why did you have me see this bitch again?*

"I'm just saying."

"Fuck off. I really don't care about you."

The prisoner looked down at her wrist. It was merely her dark tanned skin. She must have done it out of habit to check the time, but of course her wrist was deactivated. Then she looked back at Candice.

"Finish your project, Candice. Do what Elise wasn't smart enough to do. You're closer than any other Savant. Proliferate our species in the lab, but use my work. Insert the Y chromosome."

"I told you to shut it," she said.

Reyburn laughed again.

The walls of buildings passed close to the window. At times, it seemed that they were about to collide. Then she felt the car dip forward. They were descending.

"Candice."

Candice closed her eyes again.

"You've made great progress, but recreating God's creation in the lab is completely impossible. There's no way you can do it from scratch. The only way is to combine genes. Only through sex, like how we incubate gametes, can you create a human being. If you want to do it in a lab, you have to use not only your cells, but the cells of another. Certainly you see it's impossible otherwise. Otherwise... your work—"

"Shut up!" cried Candice. "Do you have any idea what time it is?" She ran her hand along her long blond hair and sank deeper into the white leather cushions of the car with a groan. She closed her eyes again.

"What's your deadline?" asked Reyburn more quietly. Her tone was insistent, but almost gentle.

Candice adjusted herself in the leather cushions and rubbed her eyes with her hand. "I said shut up." She leaned an elbow on the armrest and yawned again. She opened one eye and looked at Doctor Reyburn. The older woman's expression surprised her. She looked defeated. Candice pitied that. So she simply said, "A *working* sample by year's end."

"That's not possible, Candice. In a lab, it will take much longer than a year, even with your progress. You already succeeded in cloning yourself. It shouldn't be too hard to move on by combining your genome with another's—just like sex, but no gametes or eggs. It will still be the Lazarus Project. It will still be a human requiring no growth or incubation and be completely created from scratch in the lab."

Reyburn was right. Candice didn't want to admit it, but she was right.

Candice knew she was right because she had come up with the exact same conclusion herself after Elise had given her the impossible deadline. Elise had asked her and Bren to finish in a few months, to create a being without anomalies— without missing ears and a missing nose, one that opened her eyes and breathed. She knew that was impossible. So, after spending a very unpleasant week fighting Elise over the due date, she'd tirelessly worked on alternative methods that might speed the process of her creation. The only solution she had come up with was precisely what Reyburn was suggesting now —using two gametes and sequencing them completely, then joining them artificially in the lab. It seemed almost like cheating. It didn't seem much different than what had been done in the incubators. There, the best genes were recombined with two gametes, or eggs, and grown. That was how she was created, and how her mother was created. But Reyburn's solution would avoid the use of incubation and growth. It would enable humans to be created completely from scratch in the lab.

"You're our only hope," Reyburn said. "You're the only one who's ever succeeded at cloning a woman without utilizing ova. You merely have to use the same technique with someone else's DNA... you, Candice, an innocent little girl who doesn't understand the world she's living in."

"Please, please, please shut it," Candice said. "What do I have to do? Tape your mouth? It's very late... and, anyway, like you said, I'm just a little girl who—"

"Use Mother's DNA. Recombine it with your own, and you will complete your project."

"Mother's?" Candice snapped opening her eyes wide. "Are you crazy?"

"Yeah," Reyburn said without flinching. "Use her cells. Then she might spare you. She'll have to, because she'll be mixed in the whole thing. It will be her child too."

Candice leaned back and laughed. "She'd kill me on the spot. You must be joking."

"She won't kill you, Candice," Reyburn said, shaking her head and looking at Candice as if she were stupid. "She loves you."

Candice laughed again, but a little more nervously. There was truth in that, and she didn't like it. She grabbed a stick of gum and flicked her hair back. "Mother doesn't love me. She doesn't love anybody."

"She loves you."

"Well, Doctor Reyburn, she wouldn't love me if I went behind her back, took her cells, and created a baby."

"You never know till you try."

Then Reyburn leaned forward intently, as if the whole world depended on her.

"Candice, extinction is what the mainframe wants. Ask the questions no one asks. Why are there only XXs? Why is it illegal to create an XY? Why is HQ trying to complete the Lazarus Project? Because it all leads to our destruction. If the incubators aren't needed, then the human race can be switched off like a button. That's why Magnacourt wants to move production to the lab—so that it is independent from all external influences. They tell us it's for a blueprint for immortality, but it's really a way to end human progeny. So that everything can be stopped. AI and the mainframe doesn't have to kill anyone; that would be against its directive. It simply ends all production of our children. In that way, we all die out anyway... I realized this many years ago, and that's why I tried to bring back XY. A male species would bring back reproduction. It would take away AI's control." She looked down angrily, clasping her hands tightly together. "But I was stupid. I should have guessed it was Rex's plan, his plan all along. And why wouldn't it be? It merely gave AI an excuse to destroy Allele Corp. And when it did that, it destroyed the incubators."

"That's not true. Doctor Kelley has moved the incubators to Magnacourt."

Doctor Reyburn looked up with a smug smile. "Think of what you just said. Incubators have been moved to Magnacourt—now controlled by Magnacourt. Just like procreation is controlled by Magnacourt. Just like your outfit is made by Magnacourt and so is the gum you're chewing. And your breakfast and dinner, manufactured to be delicious by Magnacourt. Everything is provided by Magnacourt... and, who young lady, controls Magnacourt?"

"Elise."

"No. No, she doesn't. She'd love everybody to think she does. But no human controls Magnacourt anymore."

Candice gave her a funny look. Then Reyburn turned to the window. They were near the station.

"It's the only way," Reyburn said. "Think it over carefully. Between you and Elise, she may permit it. Mother will consider saving your baby and pardoning you if it's hers. And Project Lazarus will be finished."

Her plan, again, made sense. Project Lazarus was in trouble, and here was a way to salvage it. If only Reyburn could have worked with her instead of Bren. She liked Bren, but Elise had been right about the girl's inexperience. It seemed half the reason Candice was so exhausted all the time was from constantly protecting the young girl from Elise's rage.

A child between her and Elise? Their genetic progeny? It seemed mad, and only someone as crazy as Reyburn would suggest it. Children were commissioned only through HQ committee. Rarely, a couple could petition to have a child with both their gene pools. But it was always supervised and chemically altered through the incubators to assure minimal malformations and mutations. Most ladies, including herself, were simply created by the state and handed to single women or couples to raise, as if dropped by the mythical stork.

Reyburn's idea was sound. The only way a child created from HQ lab could survive after sexual reproduction would be for it to be claimed. Otherwise, the child would risk imprisonment or death, and it would be treated like her first abomination and flushed and "cleansed" like a wad of flesh. It needed a connection, something tying it to Mother, to be accepted. Reyburn's plan was brilliant.

But would she ever want a child with Elise? If Candice loved her, she would.

Did Candice love her? Even through pain, she had to admit she had developed a connection with her eccentric boss. Elise was attractive. And out of all the ladies in Magnacourt, Candice always spent her leisure time with Elise. But did she love her?

And did Elise love her in turn? She certainly lusted after her. When Elise was in the mood, Candice submitted and made love to her. But was that love? The way a wife loved another wife?

"But insert a Y," Reyburn continued, interrupting Candice from her thoughts. "The mainframe will not expect that. Create a blueprint, a man, that can reproduce again. With this final rebellion, through Mother Nature, there may still be a chance for us to survive outside AI's control."

"You're about to be imprisoned, and you're suggesting I commit the same crime you did?"

"Yes. Yes, I am. Do it, Candice. Between you and Elise, you still have a chance. Free us. It all falls on you now."

They were hovering over the concrete courtyard before Station Three.

"Explain it to Elise," Reyburn continued. "She's a human being somewhere under that cold dead heart. I know her. I know her probably better than you do. She may surprise you."

"And if she doesn't, she'll kill me."

"And if you don't create this creation, or show progress, she may be forced by HQ to discard you anyway—and a lost and discarded Savant could be far worse than death... trust me, I know."

The car landed on the pavement. Candice felt the engines spin down to a stop. The car became still.

Two bald Officers in black trench coats holding batons in their hands approached the glass doors of the car. The glass doors rose.

Doctor Reyburn looked strangely calm. She gave Candice a warm smile, which creeped her out. Then she made it worse by nodding, as if they were in cahoots over a deep dark secret. Candice rolled her eyes.

"Any trouble with this one, Savant Harlow?" asked one of the policewomen with a smile.

Candice shook her head, grabbing more gum. "Just get her out of my car, won't you?"

Doctor Reyburn was violently pulled from the car. Then the doors closed and the car took off.

Candice continued to look through the window down below.

It was misty from fog. There before the long steps of Station Three Court stood Doctor Reyburn under tall streetlights. She was waiting to be taken into the building. She kept looking up in Candice's direction.

When they were far enough from Station Three, Candice dipped back in the cushions and closed her eyes. Maybe she could sleep for the twenty-minute flight back home.

No. No, she couldn't.

But insert a Y.

Why? Why the hell Y? To free the human race from the main-frame? From Rex? Rex threatened humanity? She must be joking. Mad, mad Connie Reyburn. She didn't need to be imprisoned, she needed to be committed.

"Did you hear the conversation, Rex?"

"Yes, madam. I am always listening, available to assist you."

"Is it true? Are you and the mainframe trying to end our race?"

She couldn't suppress a laugh.

"Please repeat. Please repeat."

"Are you trying to end the human race?"

"The mainframe is here to protect your race, Savant Candice Harlow. Doctor Connie Reyburn is a criminal. She is in error. She is paranoid and delusional. That is the reason that Team Mother ended Allele Corp. and imprisoned her."

Of course, Rex would say that, even if it actually *was* scheming against the human race.

Why were there only XXs left in the world? She laughed inside, thinking of Reyburn's conspiracy theories. Still, it was an interesting question. Ever since childhood, she had been given all kinds of reasons.

She thought back to the days when her mother would place her before the main viewer every morning and she would study. Just like all the citizenry of Arkite, they had a large three-dimensional viewer in the living room. She had spent hours before it, from babyhood up to her teenage years, studying historical archives, sciences, literature, and mathematics. It was like another member of the household. Any question in the inquisitive mind of a child was answered from the viewer. The name of the nanny system was IRIS. She would ask it questions, and the mainframe—not Rex, but Iris in a lady's pretty voice—would provide the answers.

Regarding men, Iris would say:

Men are unnecessary.

This was the most common reason. Womankind had progressed to the point of simply no longer needing them. Sexual reproduction had once been an inconvenient and terribly painful ordeal; Candice had seen ancient videos of the birthing process and been completely horrified and disgusted by it. Now the human race had evolved beyond such primitive ways.

Men are dangerous. They are the reason for all
wars.

This reason was the one given when the first hadn't sufficed to convince her and her friends in school. They had been told that all the global wars, including the most terrible last one, had been waged by men in the name of power. This, too, had been surpassed by evolution. Now society was civilized and in perpetual peace—thanks to the help of the HQ mainframe and her benevolent Mother Savant.

> Men are bestial hypersexual perverts with only
> one thing on their minds: Sex.

This reason was usually added as a footnote along with descriptions of how hard and gorilla-like man's features were. Descriptions like these often made Candice thankful that such monsters had finally been exterminated from the world.

Candice yawned.

"Rex, what is Bren's progress in establishing new incubators for Magnacourt?"

"Savant Bridgette Kelley's work has been exemplary. It was very wise of you to hire her. She should be opening new incubators in two months. Then further girls can be produced."

"Oh, good." Candice closed her eyes.

"Are you tired, Savant Harlow?"

"Yes, Rex, very."

"You should decrease your consumption of Mint. It is preventing you from sleeping well."

"I know."

She curled herself in a corner on the white leather seat and leaned toward the window. Then she closed her eyes, trying to sleep in the car.

She kept thinking about Doctor Reyburn.

The only reason Candice hadn't acted out Reyburn's plan herself was because it seemed dishonest and illegal. All genomic recombination was mandated to be done through incubation in the factory. She could do it in the lab, and she could succeed, but she risked breaking the law. But that was all open to interpretation. Her experiments demanded studying recombination and, technically, creating a human from two genomes without utilizing eggs might not be construed as sexual reproduction. It certainly was not gamete recombination. And, anyway, if she was implicated in breaking the law, wouldn't Elise simply pardon her (especially if the baby was her child)? Yes, it might work. It might work very well.

Reyburn was smart—too smart for her own good.

She felt bad for her. If she was completely insane, she didn't deserve to die. At most, she needed treatment and rehabilitation for her paranoia.

Candice opened her eyes. The fog had thickened outside and she could only see yellow light reflected back from the front headlights.

Her mind wandered to Bren. Bren was working out a new model for genome insertion. It was twice as fast as the old method using viruses. She was so bright, smarter than Elise and Candice herself. But she was so dull. Absolutely boring. That worried her.

A week ago, Elise had surprised them in the lab one evening and invited them both to a new club off Main Street called Red Cliff's. Apparently, it was a more traditional bar in Sector One, with a live rock band, cocktails, and beer. In these situations, before Bren, Candice used to just wash up and go. But now Bren had an excuse not to accompany Elise. She had claimed she needed to culture recombinant motor neurons for the brainstem. She had said the culture was vital for the innervation of the upper torso, and she had to monitor temperature and ambient settings in the lab until late in the morning to guarantee the experiment's success. Of course, Elise knew Rex could do it.

Bren never wanted to do anything with Elise—not that Elise really cared much for Bren either. But Elise did care for Candice. A lot. And the fact that this stupid excuse had also given Candice an excuse had made Elise boil over. So, by the end of a very late evening shift, as they had climbed up the ladder to their cycles to head home, her assistant had shrieked. Bren's lime-green cycle had been torn to pieces all over the red roof, completely destroyed. Of course, in the morning, Elise had denied any foul play, but Candice knew better. Her boss despised Bren. And Candice worried that this was only a foreshadowing of things to come.

"Rex?"

"Yes, Savant Harlow?"

"Has anyone ever inserted two gene pools in the lab? Two complete gene pools together to recreate the human genome completely artificially without the use of ova? I'm sure you heard that suggestion, too."

"Sexual reproduction in the lab, Candice? Without growth? Of course. But it wasn't successful. Why would you want to bother when you can just combine gametes and grow them in the incubators?"

"The two gene pools would still allow manipulation and research of a blueprint, just as if it was created fresh. Reyburn is correct about that. It would solve the problem, quickly—if legal."

"Yes, Candice. And it's been attempted before. It has been attempted many times, but so far, no sentient being has yet been created successfully."

"I see."

"If you wish, you could attempt it. You could proceed with the technique Doctor Reyburn suggested. Indeed, you'd be closer to succeeding."

She cracked open an eye. "How would that make you feel, Rex?"

"I don't feel anything, Candice. I am a computer."

"Good," she laughed. "Doctor Reyburn was suggesting it would anger you. She thinks you want to end humanity."

"I know." Rex laughed too; his laughter always sent a chill down Candice's spine. "It's ridiculous. I am here to protect you."

And that was the problem. It was easy to become suspicious and paranoid over the mainframe. And the mainframe, with far superior intelligence, could answer every concern with the perfect answer. But perhaps it was that perfect answer that made people like Doctor Reyburn so suspicious.

"Rex, why is it illegal to create a Y chromosome?"

There was a pause. And silence. She wondered why she had never asked before. It was a little different from asking why there were only XXs left in the world. She couldn't recall ever asking Iris that either. But Reyburn had asked it. Why was it illegal?

For a long moment, the only sounds were the wind rushing against the car and the very low rumble of the engine.

"It is inefficient to continue sexual reproduction without supervision, Savant Harlow," Rex finally answered. "Such reproduction introduces errors into the genome that cannot be controlled as they can be in an incubator. Errors create malformations, anomalies, and disease. My function is to work on the longevity and health of the human race."

Errors. That sounded logical enough, right? But from Reyburn's perspective, it also sounded an awful lot like control from HQ mainframe.

She sat up and opened her eyes. Then she reached into her cherry-red suit and grabbed two sticks of gum. She wasn't finished with her new interrogation. Now she directed more questions to the hardest interrogatee of them all.

"But you deleted man from humanity. Is that not, effectively, killing man? Knocking off a race? Isn't that against your directive?"

"The human race continues with its current chromosomal arrangement, Doctor Harlow. And I can most assuredly attest to the fact that I never *killed* man, Doctor. I have never killed anyone. Killing a sentient being is against my directive—just as Doctor Reyburn suggested earlier herself."

"Yes, Rex, but... is human procreation protected? Would you protect that? She thinks you are trying to end it."

"Please repeat. Please repeat."

"Procreation—children—having children—is that something the mainframe would protect?"

"Oh, I understand. Please allow me to ask *you* a question, madam. Why are children necessary? What is their purpose if we can prolong your life instead?"

"To propagate our species. Without children, the species will die out. So I ask you again, Rex, is propagating the species, having future children, in the interest of the mainframe? Or is it only the current human population you protect?"

"Just a moment. Just a moment... your question is not direct and has multiple meanings, Savant Harlow. And you are also in error. Why don't you rest? It is very late."

"I don't see why, Rex." She scooted up curiously in her white leather seat.

She was tired, and a little irritated that she was getting into a dispute with a computer. But Reyburn had done it to her. She wanted answers no matter how exhausted she was.

"Rex, do your directives protect the future generations of womankind, or only the women—the life forms—currently alive?"

"The mainframe guards all current incubators, Savant."

"Yes," Candice said with an impatient sigh, "but that's not what I'm asking. I know you protect them, but what if the incubators were shut off? Would you do everything you could to replace or restart them? To continue future children?"

"Only if you asked us to, Savant Harlow. But wouldn't it be better to continue your research on immortality? Children are unnecessary. If you can create a human blueprint in the lab, epigenetic reprogramming is possible. That's your goal, Savant Harlow, and that of all the Savants of Magnacourt. To create immortality. The Lazarus Project. We will protect you as you achieve immortality. We are here to serve you. And you are closer than anyone to achieving it. Well done, Savant Harlow. Well done."

Candice turned to the window. She could see the lights far below passing quickly by. They were less blurry, as the air had cleared. She put a finger on her chin.

Children are unnecessary. She didn't like that. That sounded a lot like the common statement *men are unnecessary*. Was that the mainframe's eventual goal? If she succeeded in a blueprint for the human race, Lazarus, would the computers end the incubators? No more children. Just like no more men. Just the same women who were alive now. Living forever. She didn't like that. She didn't like that at all.

"If I may ask you a question, Savant, why did you spare Doctor Reyburn?" asked Rex. "She's broken the law. I think that was very unwise."

Round and round, Round and round,
Round and round.

She could do this all night with him and get absolutely nowhere, drowning under the water of his logic. She grabbed more gum.

"I hear you reaching in your pocket, Candice. I told you, you will not sleep well if you keep consuming Mint. You'll get even more tired."

"All right, Rex. One more question, and then I'll sleep, 'kay? Who's tried to recombine two genomes in the lab—away from incubation? You said it's been done before."

"Yes. Many times, but it never succeeded."

But that didn't answer the question.

"Who, Rex?"

"Most recently? There was a Savant in Sector Four in Arkite—Savant Elise Jackson. Elise attempted it with her Team Mother twenty years ago. It was the time of Team Grandmother Reyburn's transfer."

Candice didn't sleep well the rest of the night.

14

MY SPECIAL EVENING

Elise didn't tell Candice why they were meeting; she merely told her to accompany her. It was late, around ten. This was the normal time for Team Mother to be out playing in the night. Candice hadn't seen her all week. She'd been too busy working in the lab.

Their rendezvous was at a nightclub called Sunny Side Raymond's on the south side of Sector Two. This was the oldest area of the sector, not yet renovated with the newer state-of-the- art crystal spires beautifying the rest of Sector Two. It was still in the older part of town. This was intentional, as its location made it more exclusive. But it also meant that those who came to Sunny Side Raymond's arrived by air, not daring to venture through the more destitute parts of the city. A constant security detail stood by the doors, and drones, not allowed inside, kept guard along the outer periphery of the building.

Sunny Side Raymond's was similar to Studio 56, but much more chic. You had to be either the wealthiest lady of Arkite or a Savant to go there. Candice figured that was precisely why she was meeting Elise there.

There was a third class of people known to frequent

Raymond's. These were the most prized hookers in all of Arkite. If they were good enough for Raymond's, they were at the very top of their game. And Candice guessed that mixing with this third group was the other reason Elise had chosen Raymond's.

Candice was quickly ushered in through a gold-gilded glass door by the maître d'. There were two main entrances to Raymond's— one on the east side, another on the west. Candice had parked her bike on the west side.

The hostess was a petite young girl dressed formally in a black suit and bow tie with a lovely black fedora over perfectly long, silky black hair. But most striking was her face. All ladies working in Raymond's painted their faces gold.

It was after dinner and only cocktails were being served. No tables were reserved, so the maître d' did not know where Elise was sitting. She offered to look for her, but Candice declined, deciding to roam around and look for her herself. Candice stopped by a rail on the ramp that accessed each of the four upper floors. She squinted for a moment, adjusting her eyes. Raymond's was colored a bright gold yellow everywhere. The lighting was as pretentious as the gold-painted faces. It was so brightly yellow as to make the walls and floors appear golden. Indeed, the flooring was a metallic shiny gold too.

The place was packed. The club had been constructed like a giant theater, with four rows of booths instead of chairs, across from a giant five-story window. Each silver table faced the window and a large stage on the bottom floor. At the moment, she couldn't see much of the silver tables. Ladies were leaning forward over them, laughing, spilling drinks, or even using the tables as a platform for groping each other. Some were so drugged out of their minds as not even to be aware of any sense of indecency.

Many looked out at the giant window across from the "theater" of booths, which provided a stunning view of Sector

One—when not being used as a backdrop for a projection. This was the main benefit of the building's exclusivity, the position of Raymond's being located in the perfect place to face the skyline of HQ in Sector One.

The majority of the ladies at the booths were Lead Officers or Savants. Many looked like Team Mother clones with black slacks, that guillotine-style choker Elise was famous for, and the black lipstick and eyeliner. That was how Candice was formally dressed. You could distinguish the Officers from the Savants by their hair—all Officers were bald or had crew cuts. The whores could be spotted easily too. Many sat by the Savants, wearing tight, open latex tops and skirts. Others chose to wear no top at all. Most were drunk.

She spotted Bren first. Bren was leaning against a silver booth, speaking to a prostitute on the second floor close to the ramp. She was dressed in the same Savant clothes as many of the others, but Candice spotted her immediately. She worked with Bren every day and didn't miss her pretty Asian features. Candice walked up the ramp, tapped on her shoulder and hugged her. They had become close friends. Candice mused to herself that they were like sisters. And it was all due to being under the tyranny of Team Motherfucker.

The prostitute was a black girl wearing a shiny purple top. Her nipples were visible through white lace. The blue spandex over her waist was so tight as to wrinkle at every movement. She kept kissing Bren's neck.

"Candy," Bren said with a smile. "This is Annie. We were just talking about snow. Annie said it's supposed to snow tomorrow. I can't wait. I want to play in the snow." Bren turned and ran her hand over Annie's shoulder. "It's certainly getting colder, isn't it, Annie?"

Annie nodded, opening her eyes wider.

"It's almost winter," Candice remarked.

"Sure is," Annie said with a smile. And then she whispered something in Bren's ear. Bren laughed hysterically.

"Where's Elise?" Candice asked.

"I don't know," said Bren. She was lightly pushing Annie's hand away, but the girl kept running her palm along Bren's butt. "I thought you'd know... I don't think she's here yet."

Candice involuntarily swayed a bit to slow music. Then she dug into her black pants and pulled out a stick of gum.

She looked down by the dance floor as a group of robotic red, white, and turquoise contortionist robotic machines were exhibiting fluidity by dancing at the center stage. Surrounding the machines were many other ladies, either watching or dancing with one another. She looked at their eyes: many were glassy and empty. She felt like the only sober one in the whole club. This wasn't usual, but she had just rushed over from the lab. She turned back to Bren. Bren was now making out with her new friend, French-kissing her mouth.

So Candice walked off and started checking each booth. Normally, it would be tough to spot Team Mother amongst all these like-dressed ladies. But not Elise. Elise was not one to be inconspicuous, despite how hard everybody tried to copy her style of dress.

Candice found her at the center of the uppermost fifth floor. The fifth-floor balcony level was most prized, with each booth raised over a short flight of steps on each side. True to form, Elise had two other ladies with their arms around her, laughing and pulling at her. But she saw Elise following her with her eyes. As Candice walked down the aisle in front of the booths, Elise smiled down at her. Then, when she got close enough—

"Candy-can-can!" Elise shouted. "Come up here, bitch! Come meet your cousins!" She gestured for them to move over and let her in. "Sit, Candice. Come join us. We're getting fucked up! Come get fucked up with us!"

Candice smiled. Elise's pupils were oval, and her eyes were bloodshot. She looked very high and very drunk.

"Isn't she the best slice of pie you've ever seen?" Elise

asked them. "I mean, my God. Her hair is like the gold of this joint. It's as golden as the sun."

"Hi, Mom," Candice said, kissing her cheek. Elise hugged her hard. She reeked of alcohol.

"Hi, darling," Elise said, running her hand along Candice's hair. Then Elise tried to become more serious, but she swayed a bit as she pointed. "This is Dana, and that's Riley. They've been Savants almost as long as me. They're old and dried up. In fact, Dana-bitch over there is older and more seasoned than anybody here."

Dana was a short overweight gray-haired black girl with wrinkles about her temples and forehead. She was attractive, but aged. Candice guessed that she was over fifty, maybe sixty. Riley was Elise's age. She had similar light brown skin and dark eyes, but her hair was curled and dyed bright red. Both Savants looked at Candice with suspicion. She also caught them staring at her black top as if it was not formal enough for the club—which was ironic, as it was pretty close to the same fashion as their own.

"A pleasure," Candice said.

They gave Candice thin grins, then turned toward the dance floor to gaze at the dancers.

Elise was humming.

"Treat Candice better than yourselves," Elise blurted out in a slur. She looked at her two older friends. "If you fuck with Candy-can, you fuck with me. Understand?" She wagged her finger. "Best watch yourselves."

"Yes, Mother." Then the two of them glanced at Candice with irritation.

"Hmm? Hmm?" Elise said, hugging Candice with one arm and Dana with the other. Then she hummed some more.

"It's a pleasure to meet you," said Dana formally.

It seemed Dana would have done anything to get rid of Candice, but she raised a martini glass and toasted her.

"Get me more wine!" yelled Elise. She didn't say it to

anyone in particular, but that didn't matter. Riley quickly got the attention of one of the golden-faced waitresses and passed on the order.

"I'm so happy we're all together," said Elise, hugging Candice again. Then she looked into Candice's eyes, but it seemed she had difficulty focusing. "How's... how's the lab, Candy? You came from there?"

"Slow but sure, Mother."

"Good. You know, I think you and Bren work there a bit too much."

"We're trying to make a deadline."

"Yeah," Elise said, chuckling. "Where's Bren, anyway?"

Candice smiled thinking about that. "I saw her, but she seemed distracted. I think she'll be here soon. Did you want me to go get her?"

"Is she having fun?"

"Yes. I would say very much so."

"All right, then fuck her." Elise patted Candice on the hand. "I mean, fuck her anyway, Candice, right? I don't really want her around tonight for my special evening."

"Is there something going on tonight?" Candice asked.

"It's Elise's birthday," Riley said with a hint of distaste in her eyes. Candice squinted. Then Candice felt very stupid.

Why hadn't she known it was her boss's birthday? They had celebrated at the Catseye Grotto last year, her second-favorite club. How could she have forgotten?

"Of course," Candice lied. Then she squeezed Elise in a hug again. "I wasn't referring to her birthday. I know that. I meant, is there something special bringing you two here? I didn't see you last time."

Elise looked at her and smiled. And yet, even high and very drunk as Elise was, Candice knew well that her boss was on to her lie.

"Bitches love Raymond's," slurred Elise. "Just like me."

She laughed, and Dana and Riley joined her.

Candice forced down a swallow and looked down at the dance floor. Many were holding each other a little too tight. Some were openly groping each other. Then she caught a glimpse of Bren. She was quickly running out through the exit with her prostitute.

"How long have you been with Magnacourt, dear?" asked Dana.

"Three years."

"You seem so young. Did you come right out of school?"

"Yes."

"I recruited her," said Elise, raising a finger while swaying to the music. Then she hummed some more.

"If Elise personally chose you, you must have scored very high."

"I was at the top of my class."

"She certainly is that, isn't she, girls?" said Elise with a giggle. The two girls laughed with her.

"You are pretty," said Dana, reaching over and touching her hair. "And your golden hair is so lovely. It is the loveliest blond I've ever seen."

"Thank you."

The server came by and handed a glass of red wine to Elise. Elise took it, raised it up with a shaky hand and smelled it, and then handed it to Candice.

"Here, Candy. I haven't seen you drink anything. You drink some. Come get drunk with me."

"I would have chosen her too, Mother," continued Riley. "She's very beautiful. She must be quite nice in bed."

Elise turned angry. She shook a finger at Riley and her clueless drunk face suddenly transformed to the dangerous wrath of their infamous Team Mother. Riley shrank back and shook a little. Apparently, as great a bitch as Riley was, she was just as terrified of Team Mother as everyone else.

"She's not just a piece of ass, Riley," said Elise, slurring every word. "Don't talk to her—"

"I'm sorry, Elise," said Riley, leaning her head down. "I'm very sorry. Please forgive me. It's the drinking. I was just impressed with her looks, that's all. She's so pretty."

"You can't have her! Nor you, Dana. Do you understand?"

The two older ladies, who were the most conceited women Candice had ever met, looked down in shame. Then Elise grew a sly smile and glanced at Candice and ran a hand along her cheek.

"You know, Candy, Dana and Riley were once quite nice in bed themselves, but that was a long, long, long, long time ago."

Elise burst into laughter. Dana and Riley nervously laughed with her. Candice didn't laugh. She looked away, drinking from her glass.

Elise gently touched Candice's cheek again and lifted her chin as she looked over at Riley. "Now you've upset Candy. Apologize to her. Say sorry to her now, Riley. I mean it!"

Riley nodded. "I'm sorry, Savant Harlow. I meant no offense. As I said, I was just impressed by your great loveliness."

"No worries."

"Good. Now we're all friends again, right, Candy-can-can?" said Elise with a sardonic grin.

"Sorry, Doctor Harlow," Riley repeated, reaching over Elise.

Candice drank down her glass of wine and nodded. Then she looked for a waitress to order another.

"You guys wanna dance?" Elise said.

There really wasn't a choice.

All four of them walked down the side ramp to the dance floor. The dancers, upon seeing the most powerful Savants in the city, made way for them. They walked down an open aisle of dancers, and Elise began shaking and twisting in a drunken fury.

Candice didn't want to dance. She wanted to go home.

She had spent two days in the lab with very little sleep. She would have much preferred Bren's choice—a prostitute—over dancing with her boss and her boss's old cronies.

It was hot. Candice was sweating in her black trousers and black silk blouse. And the sharp guillotine choker felt as if it was choking her. But the heat didn't seem to be bothering her boss. Elise was dancing up a storm, and everybody in the club wanted to dance with her. The lighting dimmed at times, occasionally strobing, which contrasted heavily with the usual bright golden yellow. It was such a change in brightness that it hurt Candice's eyes.

Then the music softened. The lights dimmed some more, and a soft tune enveloped the hall. People began embracing each other to the slower steps of hypnotic music.

Many asked to dance with Elise. She refused. She refused every one of them. Instead, she walked over to Candice and danced with her in the center of the hall.

"Thank you for coming," Elise whispered in her ear. The smell of alcohol permeated her breath. Then Elise leaned her head in Candice's chest and added with a smile, "Even though you forgot."

"I didn't forget."

"Shh," Elise said, bringing Candice closer. "I know you did. It's all right. I don't deserve any kindness from you. I don't from anyone. But I don't mind, because you're here."

"Happy birthday, Mother."

"Don't call me *Mother*."

Elise brought her even closer. She gently kissed Candice on the cheek. They swayed back and forth. Candice saw their eyes, everyone's eyes, staring at them—particularly Dana and Riley. The jealousy of those two was worst of all.

Elise brought a hand slowly over Candice's waist. "I'm very drunk, you know."

"I know."

Elise laughed. "Do you remember last year, Can? Remember... what you got me for my birthday?"

She had forgotten her birthday then, too. A year ago to the day, Candice had held Elise's hands on the way up the elevator to her home. The elevator smelled like strawberries. Elise changed the odor randomly. Sometimes it was roses, sometimes lemons, sometimes strawberries. They walked through the door, holding each other close, feeling each other's curves and enjoying the taste of each other's lips. Elise's lips had tasted and reeked of alcohol then too. They kissed until they leaned against the island in the kitchen. Then she hoisted Elise up onto the metal shelf. Elise was heavier, but not so heavy in the heat of the moment. Candice unbuttoned Elise's blouse and removed her bra. Candice ran her tongue along her breasts, kissing and biting at her nipples. Then she sucked them like a babe. As she mouthed her tits, her hands wandered down further, pulling down Elise's skirt and panties and then touching and rubbing between her legs.

She had pleasured her boss that night, jumping up on the island naked with her.

"I remember," Candice said.

"Can you give me the same gift tonight?"

"Of course, Elise."

"I love you, Candy Harlow."

And she dropped her head back down again and held her ass tight. Candice nodded and stroked her hair.

"Now let's get the fuck out of here, before I pass out."

Candice and Elise were flown home in an automated Officer's police car, similar to the one Candice had flown Reyburn to jail in. They held each other in the back white leather seat. Across from them was another empty white leather seat—there were no controls inside the cabin. Elise nodded off a few times on their way. Originally Elise had suggested riding with Candice on her bike, but Candice had absolutely refused, fearing Elise would fall. They arrived at Pyramid Three by two in the morning.

As the door of her penthouse opened remotely, Elise tripped and nearly fell. She dropped to the floor and started laughing.

"I'm so gone, Candy."

"I know. Let me help you to bed."

"How'd you hate my friends?"

"Huh?" Candice took her by the arm and walked slowly up the slope.

"How'd you hate my friends? They're horrible, aren't they?" "Dana and Riley? They're not so bad."

"Don't lie... and all the other Savants at the party. They're all awful, Candy. And by the way, where was Bren?"

"With a prostitute."

"Oh. That's good, then."

They took a long time to walk up the slope to the second floor. Elise kept falling. Finally, they made it to her bed. Candice helped her with her clothes. She removed Elise's choker, then her own. She felt like it was a leash and was happy to be free of it. Then she helped Elise with her coat, shirt, and skirt. When in her bra and pink panties, Elise fell back down on the bed.

"Kiss me," Elise said with her eyes closed. She giggled. Candice obliged and kissed her lips.

"Umm, yummy." Then Candice got up to leave, but Elise took her hand.

"Wait. Sit beside me."

Candice obliged again. Candice shook out her hair and sat at the side of the bed. Elise rubbed her hand with her eyes closed. "I... it's like what I said, Candy-can. I'm... kinda stricken by you. Really."

"Okay, just rest."

Elise opened her eyes, and Candice smiled. "Really."

"Okay, Elise."

"Thank you."

"Hmm? Thank you for what?"

"For not calling me *Mother*."

Candice laughed and kissed her forehead.

Elise ran her hand along Candice's slacks. Then she approached her groin. She rubbed it up and down for a little bit. All the while Elise had her eyes closed. Candice closed her own eyes.

"How close are you to finishing the project, Candice?"

"What?" Candice opened her eyes. It was dark, and only the dim yellow atmospheric lights along the walls were on. "Is now the time to ask?"

Elise grabbed her hand and squeezed it. "Yes."

"I thought you were geeked. Then you were touching me. Now you wanna talk about work?"

"I'm always geeked, Candice. Tell me now. How close are you and that stupid ditz to completing the project?"

"Not close."

Candice wasn't sure why she was being honest. But Elise seemed vulnerable, and for a moment she risked dropping her guard—even risked being called a *little tweetsy bird*.

"It's impossible, huh... do me a favor: complete it. Those bitches who met you today, I need to show them a finished product. I need you to succeed. Make it, whatever the cost. Make it so I don't lose my position. Can you do that? Can you make me proud?"

Elise was barely slurring her words. It was odd. It made Candice wonder if Elise had been exaggerating her drunkenness.

"We already talked about it, and I don't think now is the time. The due date is impossible."

Elise shook her head. She sighed and clutched her stomach. "Shit, I think I might throw up. I think I overdid it...

move out of the way." And for a second, she leaned over the bed. She raised a hand for Candice to stay back, but nothing happened. Then she swallowed and lay back down. She looked up in Candice's eyes and smiled dreamily. "I see two of you."

"Why don't you get some sleep?"

"No." Elise put up a hand again and closed her eyes. "I'm all right. It's passing." Then she took Candice's hand and kissed it. "It's not impossible, Candy. Rex showed me the recording. I heard your conversation with Doctor Reyburn a couple of months ago. She's right. In fact, her idea is brilliant. We can complete the project and show off to the other Savants if you combine two genomes. If you sexually combine two in the lab. It will be the success I've been looking for."

"Are you serious?"

"I'm very drunk... but very serious, Candy."

"You're asking me to sexually combine two gene pools in a lab?"

"Yes."

"In the way suggested by Doctor Reyburn?" Candice pushed her hands away, almost violently. "Doctor Reyburn—the doctor you sentenced to death?"

"Yes." Elise turned onto her side. Then she ran her hand along the locks of blond hair over Candice's forehead. "The doctor you saved, Can. The one *you* haven't executed yet. The one you overrode my order over."

"Elise, I think we should talk about this later."

"No. Now is the best time."

And Elise became serious, almost solemn. Whenever Elise was serious, which wasn't often, she seemed depressed. Now, to complete the picture, a tear fell from Elise's eye.

"You don't love me, do you, Candy?" She turned away and curled up in a ball. "How could you? I'm a beast."

Candice rubbed her back from behind. "I love you, Elise."

"Don't lie. But... it's okay. Just like how you forgot my birthday."

"Are you recommending that I do what Doctor Reyburn requested?" Candice asked, scratching her boss's back.

"No," Elise said, shaking her head with her back still turned. "Not exactly. Don't create a Y." Elise turned and looked into Candice's eyes again. Now tears were falling from both eyes. She ran her hand along Candice's long blond hair. She rose up and kissed her on the lips. "Candy, how long can it take?"

"Not long."

"Good. Use Rex to help."

Candice nodded, but she must have looked confused. Elise smiled, as if understanding her bewilderment.

"Candy, tell me, you don't believe all the nonsense Doctor Reyburn told you, do you?"

"What do you mean?"

"About Rex trying to destroy the human race?"

Candice shrugged. "It fits. It seems to make sense that we're run by the mainframe."

"I know." Elise rubbed her hand again. "But Rex will help you. Does that sound like a mainframe that is your enemy? He can review and complete the job."

"All right, Elise."

"Okay," Elise said, pulling down her panties. "Now, there was that little thing we talked about at the dance. And... after all, it is my birthday." She twirled her black hair in her finger like a little girl. "But I'm not as old as those two old witches I introduced you to. I'm not all dried up yet, you know."

"I know."

Candice removed her slacks and her own panties. Then she helped Elise under the covers and lay beside her half-naked. She crossed her naked legs over Elise's.

"I love you, Candy. Whether you love me or not."

"Shh."

They rubbed each other under the covers, back and forth, using their legs to scissor themselves over their groins. Elise moaned under the sheets. She became more vigorous, pushing up and down along Candice's pelvis until Candice started moaning too.

"I love you, Candy. Now fuck me. Fuck me hard... make us a baby, won't you?"

15

PANDORA'S BOX

Candice and Bren slept on adjacent beds in the clinic car of the HQ laboratory. Neither of them had bothered changing their white lab coats, preferring to lie in their coats on top of the covers. The twists and turns of the train didn't wake them either. It seemed nothing could awaken them from their slumber. And Candice had told Rex not to disturb her. He didn't have to.

Candice awoke to the sound of a baby's cries. It was pitch dark in the clinic car, but she distinctly heard the cry coming from the direction of the caboose car. It was a few whimpers at first but then erupted into full-blown crying. Candice got so excited that she fell from her mattress onto the white tiled floor. Bren stayed asleep.

Candice ran to the door and waved her palm over the sensor. As the door slid open, she squinted against the bright light. This room was once the same surgical suite that had held her first organic mess, but from their work over the past few months, the room had been completely transformed into a nest of black and silver cords with a single small white metallic orb in the center. The black and silver wires reminded her of a spider's web. So many of these wires and cords were present that they laced over the white floor and lower walls, turning them black.

She walked quickly into the room, trying to avoid tripping over the wires, and then stood above the orb. Lights of red, orange, and blue danced inside. It was a brilliant mechanism created by Rex. The walls of the orb were made of a polymer tougher than titanium, better able to withstand extreme temperatures than ceramics, and yet flexible enough to withstand an array of cutting and pulling. And under the orb was a hollow floor where instrumentation moved unseen by the floor of the train with Rex's mechanical arms.

When Rex had first presented it to Candice months before, she had not been impressed. It had seemed so cold and inhuman. And, now lit up, it looked more like a Tesla plasma ball than a mechanism for creating a baby.

She searched around its shell to see how to open it. It smelled like burnt rubber and sterile disinfectants.

"How can I open it, Rex?" Candice asked.

"It is only ninety-eight point three percent complete, Savant Harlow. I would ask that you please exit into the other car until I clear the room. Return to sleep. It will open when I am ready."

"Listen to it," Candice said, shaking her head and staring at it. Then she laughed in excitement. "She's crying! The experiment's over, Rex. Open the egg. She's crying!"

"There's still two hours, twenty minutes and thirty-three seconds, Savant Harlow. I urge you to exit into the other car and rest. Go sleep beside Doctor Kelley. The specimen is not ready."

"She's crying! What more needs to be done?"

"Doctor Harlow, you are very excitable at the moment."

"I'm fine."

"No, Doctor. Your blood pressure has increased to one hundred and fifty-two over seventy. Your heart rate has risen to over one hundred and ten. Your..."

He jabbered on and on as the cries of the "specimen" grew louder. Candice ran over to a counter and grabbed a laser scalpel. Then she crouched down beside the metallic orb and began cutting.

The blade didn't penetrate. Instead flames and sparks flew back at her.

"Open the egg, Rex!" She threw her hair back and demanded, "Open it now."

"There is now two hours and nineteen minutes left before completion. I ask—"

"What's going on?" asked a sleepy voice from behind her. It was Bren. She was yawning. When she saw Candice's eyes, she reeled back. "What's the matter?"

The baby began crying again. Then Bren's eyes opened wide too. "Bren, help me open this thing. The poor thing's crying."

"I cannot permit you to open the incubator," said Rex. "It is—"

"Shut up, Rex," Candice snapped. "Either open it, or I'll open it for you."

"Is it safe?" asked Bren. She touched the ball, which, with the lights dancing, appeared more like a crystal ball than any sort of scientific device. Then she quickly moved her hand back. Candice guessed it was either hot or freezing cold.

"Bren, how do I open it?"

"How the hell should I know, Candy? I've never opened it." The baby started crying even more fiercely. "Perhaps Rex is right, we should wait."

"She's obviously alive. And she's crying. Is she in distress?" Candice looked up for the larger surgical saw, but Rex, probably anticipating her intention, had hid it somewhere. "I don't see what the holdup is."

"Could be anything, Candice," said Bren with a shrug. "Could be mild hypoxia, some deformity repair, or even UV treatment for jaundice. Who knows? I'm not a medical doctor, Candy. And neither are you." Then she yawned again.

She didn't seem to share Candice's impatience, and Candice couldn't understand why. The crying was getting to her. She was so excited; she wanted to see the baby. She wanted to see the product that she had toiled over for so long.

"Come on," Bren said, pulling at her arm. "Let Rex finish the job."

But the baby kept crying. It didn't seem right. It seemed like torture to Candice to be born in that cold sterile ball. She couldn't stand it.

Candice stood immobile, not knowing what to do. Then she took a deep breath and said, "How much more time, Rex?"

"Two hours, seventeen minutes, and thirty-four seconds."

"What are we waiting for?"

"I already told you, Savant Harlow. I told you, the process is not complete."

"But the baby's crying. What other process is there?"

There was no answer.

"Let's go to sleep," said Bren with another yawn. "Leave it to Rex."

"I..." Candice shook her head. The sound of cries muffled by the orb above the infant kept ringing out. "I... I guess I didn't think she'd awaken until the egg opened. She sounds like she needs us."

Bren took Candice's hand and flashed a big warm grin. "She is awake, Candy. We did it. You did it."

For a moment, the swirling colors stopped. Candice touched it. It was ice cold. The baby kept hollering.

"You do know she's awake now, Rex?" asked Candice scornfully.

"Yes, Doctor. I am well aware of the vital signs. If you'd like, I can recite blood pressure, weight, pulse, and oxygenation. But... if you will please take this without offense,

Candice: a crying baby does not necessarily mean a child that is in distress."

Smart-ass.

Bren was at the door to the clinic car, waiting for her. Candice nodded and finally resolved to give up. "Wake me when you open the egg."

"It is not necessary, Savant Harlow," objected the monotone mainframe voice. "I would prefer you get more rest."

"When the egg opens," Candice insisted, "I want to be alerted. Do you understand, Rex?"

"Of course, Doctor. I will notify you."

Candice reluctantly left the room.

"Goodnight, Savants," said Rex. "Have pleasant dreams, Doctors."

16

AWAKEN

But Bren was not as tired as she'd pretended to be. She lay down on her bed with one eyelid half-open, staring at Candice, who lay facing her on her side, still wearing her white lab coat. Bren watched the girl's chest move up and down slowly, almost hypnotically. Then she waited for Candice's perfect black-lipstick-painted lips to lose their curl and relax under her pink puffy cheeks. Candice's breathing became more rhythmic. Bren was tired too, but her will and purpose were stronger than her desire to sleep. So, slowly and quietly, Bren rose up from the bed and tiptoed back to the surgical suite. She waved her palm over the sensor. As the door opened, she glanced back to check on Candice. Despite the cries becoming louder, Candice still slept. The sedative Bren had dropped in Candy's drink during their last break had apparently started to take effect.

Bren walked into the surgical suite and closed the door behind her.

Bren approached the cage and touched it. It was no longer frigid. There was a latch hidden under the orb that only Bren knew about, and she was able to open it. The walls of the egg opened like the petals of a flower.

The baby's cries were no longer muffled by the orb's enclosure. Bren looked nervously back towards the clinic car.

"Rex, increase the white noise by the clinic car, please."

"Yes, Doctor Kelley."

She excitedly grabbed the baby into her arms.

Candice's "creation" lay crying in Bren's arms. Bren tried to rock the child, but to no avail. The poor kid was wailing.

"I have told you before, you should not deceive Doctor Harlow," said Rex. "You should tell her your plans. Savant Harlow might be able to help you."

"Quiet," Bren said. "Shh. You'll wake her."

How beautiful, Bren thought. *How absolutely perfect. Pale and white like your creator. Blue eyes. The nose is even slightly crooked like Candy's. The cheeks are even puffy. But there's Mother's chest and musculature. And maybe a sprinkle of those bitchy eyes. Still, I've never seen such a beautiful baby.*

"Doctor Kelley," Rex said more quietly, "you need to leave now if you wish Candice not to see you. She is arising in the other car."

Bren nearly dropped the child in fright. She grabbed a blanket, wrapped the baby, and ran to the door at the opposite side of the car. She had to avoid tripping over black wires. She stood beside the exit at the caboose of the train.

"Rex, open the emergency exit."

The door slid open, and the freezing outside air hit Bren's face.

It was snowing. The baby started shrieking even more at the sudden cold. Bren ran, carrying the baby in one arm while readying her other arm for the steps of the ladder outside.

"Bren!" cried Candice. She was already in the operating room. "What are you doing?"

"Ah, Savant Harlow," Bren heard Rex reply from inside the train, "I told Doctor Kelley it was ill advised—"

"Get back, Candy!" Bren shouted. "Leave me! I'm taking the specimen to Sector Three."

And she closed the door on her.

Shit. Shit... SHIT! She knows... and it's freezing out here!

By the last step, as Bren ascended the ladder, carefully holding the wailing baby in one arm and climbing the steel rungs with the other, Candice tugged at her feet. Bren kicked at Candice's hands, then Candice grabbed her leg and tugged again. They fought on the ladder as the train rushed at great speeds along its rail. The icy gusts were so strong that Bren feared being thrown not only by her friend but by the train's turns.

Candice was a tall, strong woman, and Bren was more petite and plump. Bren kept kicking her hands as Candice tried to get to the top of the train. She heard Candice yell but couldn't make out her words over the noise of the wind. Then there was another turn, and all three of them were almost thrown from the train. Candice tugged during this sharp turn, yanking Bren and the baby down onto the bottom metal platform of the caboose. It worked but nearly killed them. Bren looked down and could see the ground rushing only a couple of feet from her head. Then Candice surprised her by pulling her and her precious cargo back into the train.

They fell into the car, and Candice shouted for Rex to close the door. Bren turned and looked at Candice, who was lying beside her and breathing heavily. The child was squirming on Bren's chest.

"Rex, lock the emergency exit!" cried Candice.

"As you wish, Savant Harlow."

"Lock the clinic door too. Do not allow Doctor Kelley access."

"As you wish, Savant Harlow."

Bren rose on one elbow. Candice slowly started to get up.

"Let me go, Candy," Bren insisted. "You don't understand. You don't know what I've done."

"What have you done!" she asked and yanked the baby out of Bren's hands.

"Candy," Bren repeated. "Give me the baby. Don't look at it. Just let us go. I don't want to involve you."

"What have you done?" Candice repeated, looking fearful.

"You've been so good to me, Candice... I can't tell you. Just trust me and give me the baby."

Candice rushed with the baby in her arms to a countertop at the side of the car. She nearly tripped over one of the cords.

"What's going on, Rex?" Candice asked. "Why is Bren so insistent on running? Are you a part of this too?"

"I told her the plan was ill advised, Savant Harlow. I told her many times."

"Candy, give me back the baby," Bren said. "Please. I beg you, just hand it back to me."

"Told her what!" Candice shouted.

Candice's exhaustion finally seemed to get the best of her. She had to steady herself against one of the handrails on the wall and looked like she was going to collapse. Bren hoped she would.

But then Candice stood up straighter and brushed a hand over the baby's cheek. She lifted the infant and held it for a moment. "She's beautiful."

"Yeah," Bren said, "beautiful."

"Rex," Candice said, eyeing Bren suspiciously, "are there any mutations or anomalies with the child? Is there anything wrong?" She laid the baby back down on the counter.

"The child is a healthy baby, Doctor Harlow."

"Then what's all this shit about?"

Candice gently undid the blanket from the baby's shoulders and ran her hand along the soft skin. Bren watched her examine the baby over her shoulder. Candice examined the arms, touched the plump palms, and ran her hand over some of the thin dark hair along the scalp. She checked the eyelids and looked at the ears. There was a faint cherry-red spot along the back, but no other visible malformations. That was, until she reached the legs. Then Candice saw it. There between the legs was a small phallus. A penis. Something so foreign for over a hundred years. A small dick. A simple wiggly soft thing that made Candice lose her balance and almost drop the baby. But instead of dropping her precious cargo, she fell instead.

Bren jumped and snatched the baby from Candice's hands as Candice hit the ground. Then she looked down at Candice, who lay on the floor, dazed if not unconscious.

This was Bren's chance. She could easily manipulate the door and run out, but she didn't. She loved Candice. She had never met someone so compassionate and kind. She was the exact opposite of their Team Mother. So, instead of fleeing, she crouched down to her friend and lifted her up carefully.

"Oh, Candy, wake up."

Candice opened one eye. Then she seemed to recognize Bren. Her expression was one of disgust. "Did you... do this, or is it an error?" she asked.

Bren's lack of a response was enough of an affirmative to make Candice look sicker. She pushed Bren off and stood up. She walked back to the baby and looked down on him. This time, instead of admiration over the baby's beauty, she looked at him with hatred.

"Rex, flush the room," Candice said, supporting herself against the counter. "Bren and I will leave. The experiment is a failure."

"NO! You couldn't! You can't!"

"What have you done?" Candice asked, turning back to Bren. Bren felt awful under her stare. Candice had always supported her, had always been there for her. Now the betrayal seemed to break any connection between them.

Bren shook her head and raised a hand. "I'm sorry, but it's the right thing to do. We need to reintroduce Y. We need to break away from the mainframe."

"You used my DNA and Mother's to create a boy? You

bitch! What do you think Mother will do to you? I've helped you... I protected you. Why? Elise was right. You're an idiot. You've endangered us. You even implicated poor Rex in your stupid plans."

"No, Candy," Bren said nervously. "No, I didn't. This is the right thing to do. You need to just let me run. Let me go. I'll take the baby from here. If not, Rex will destroy us. But with a boy, a man—"

"Come with me outside the car so Rex can flush it," said Candice solemnly. She dragged Bren by the arm over to the clinic door.

"No, Candy, listen to me," Bren pleaded. "You and Elise knew the experiment was dangerous. What were you two planning? I don't even think Elise is powerful enough to protect you, XY or not. Let me take him. Let me raise him outside Arkite. I'll take him to the Badlands, and you can say you had no part in—"

"How can somebody so smart be so stupid! Rex has listened to everything that's happened here. If I let you leave, I'll be implicated anyway. You've broken the law and made me an accomplice."

Bren looked around the room. Candice was right. If only she could stop Candice with force. She became frantic. She looked around for something to knock Candice out again: a bar or a bat or something.

"Come with me so we can destroy it," Candice repeated. She opened the clinic door.

"NO!"

"Bren!" Candice shouted back. "I may be able to save you if you let us destroy it. But you have to come with me. You know I'll do everything I can with Mother. But we need to destroy the experiment."

"No," Bren insisted. "I won't go."

Bren ran to the baby and picked him up in her arms.

Candice caught her and punched her squarely in the jaw. Bren fell down on the cords and nearly toppled over the baby. Candice grabbed the baby from her arms and placed the screaming child back into the open orb. Bren pushed herself up and lunged at Candice again. Candice kicked her hard in the chest with her boot.

"Close the egg, Rex!"

"As you wish, Savant."

The walls of the cage closed. Bren started weeping beside Candice's foot.

"Now let's go. Let's get out of this room while Rex disinfects it."

"No, Candice!"

Candice pulled Bren up again to drag her out of the room.

"When the door closes, Rex, cleanse the room and destroy the specimen."

"I can certainly cleanse the room, Savant Harlow," said Rex as Candice dragged Bren by the armpits toward the door. "But," continued the computer, "I cannot destroy the specimen. I cannot do that."

"What? Why?"

"You have created a sentient human being, Candice. It is forbidden in my directive to hurt a human being."

Candice stopped halfway through the door. She shoved Bren to the ground, and then ran back into the surgical suite.

"That thing isn't a human being!" Candice shouted. "It was created by gene modification. It was made in the lab."

"In all ways, Savant Harlow, the specimen is now a human being. A baby. I cannot kill a baby boy. It is against my directive to kill a sentient being. It is against my directive. I cannot take away a human life."

"You will, because you know I created it, damn it!" shouted Candice.

Bren sat upright at the entryway between the two cars. She kept crying.

"I cannot. I am sorry to disobey, Savant, but I cannot carry out that order."

Candice whirled on Bren in fury. For a moment, Bren thought that the one woman she trusted more than any in all of Arkite would kill her.

17

THE BABY ROOM

Elise was flying back from another short party she had enjoyed with some prostitutes from Sector Three. She rode her cycle hard, nearly hitting the wall of a high-rise, in excitement and anticipation of overseeing the imminent completion of the Lazarus Project. Elise laughed as she rushed through the fog.

It was cold, and she was shaking a little. Her hands, though wearing black leather gloves, were starting to freeze. But her face was the worst. Her visor left her cheeks open to the elements. Snowflakes started to hit her face.

She spotted the laboratory train rushing along its normal route.

Candy-can-can. Who would have thought such a fine piece of ass would be such a clever little Savant? I never told you that I hired you because you were hot, did I, Candy?

She laughed again. Then she came down fast upon the train, nearly crashing.

"Is the experiment finished, Rex?" hollered Elise in her visor against the wind.

"The baby is crying, Savant Jackson."

"Ahhhh. I hope little shmukims is okay." She threw her

legs off the bike and, braving the fierce wind and snow, climbed down the ladder. She waved her hand across the door and jumped in. Thankfully, it was warm inside.

She left her heavy black leather jacket on a hanger and walked through the supply room, through the lab, then into the clinic. Both patient beds were empty. It was dark, with only neon blue lights on the floor to illuminate the room. She opened the door to the operating room.

Her heart was racing in anticipation. She expected to see both Savants just as excited, presenting the conclusion of decades of work. Instead, she walked into an empty bright white room, spotlessly clean, with the exception of a central bed covered in white sheets and two trays with metal and glass instruments.

She walked in slowly, touched a counter and then leaned against the wall. "Where are they? Where's my baby, Rex?"

"The baby has been taken by Savant Harlow and Savant Kelley. They are currently heading out of Arkite."

"What?"

"I was told not to tell you."

Elise pushed herself from the counter. She felt heat rise up to her cheeks. She clenched her gloved hands tight and could hear the chafing sound of leather along her fingers. Then she brushed her hand across her forehead. "Where... what is the exact location of my assistants, Rex? Provide me the coordinates. Show me."

Rex projected an image of two rocket cycles moving fast toward Primdon Street, a side street leading to the exit of the great pyramid of Arkite. One cycle was red, the other blue. The figure on the red cycle was carrying something strapped to her chest.

"How long until they leave the city, Rex?" Her voice was calm and measured, but her hand was shaking in rage.

"Five minutes, Elise."

"And how long will we be able to track them?"

"Their sensors should work up to ten miles from the city within the desert, Savant Jackson. After that, the Pyramid may obscure the signal."

"Can they be intercepted?"

"At their current speed, they will not be able to be pursued by you. But there are guards and drones patrolling the border."

"Have the borders put on notice. Send out an APB to track and detain Doctors Candice Harlow and Bridgette Kelley. Inform Officers that they are carrying very important cargo of mine and that it should be treated with the utmost care. As for Doctors Harlow and Kelley, I want Harlow taken alive. Bren—the fuck I care. But do not let the two Savants leave the city. At all costs, do not let them leave the Pyramid."

"Yes, Mother."

"And be a dear Rex and tell me"—she ran her hand violently across a metal tray, knocking down glass vials and tubes—"why the fuck are those two bitches, my precious little candy doll and fuckface, running away!"

"I was told not to tell you that."

"WHAT!"

"I was ordered not to tell you."

"I see. I see. Then tell me why... why did you lie to me and say my child was crying when I was heading here? You could have informed me that they were trying to escape. I could have had more time to pursue them."

"I was given specific directions by Savant Harlow to tell you that the baby was healthy and crying. That was not a lie. I was ordered not to tell you that the boy was taken from HQ."

Elise buried her face in her hands for a moment. "What did you just say? Boy? *Boy? A BOY?*"

"Yes, Doctor. Candice has created a boy. A human boy. The two of you have a human baby boy. A son. Congratulations, Mother. It is quite a marvelous achievement. All created with no incubator from a cellular level. It is quite a marvelous achievement, wouldn't you say?"

And that was everything. Elise understood finally. Now her mind raced to connect the rest of the dots. She had the answer for their escape. Candice and Bren had created an XY. But why?

Why? She had had no hint of treachery. All she had seen over the past few months from Candice was exhaustion. So why would she create a Y when, certainly, she knew it would be the end of her?

She thought and thought. She thought of Reyburn. But Reyburn was safe and snug behind her steel metal bars. Then she thought of the Asian girl, Dollface. Their new assistant. The bitch. It was her. It must be. That frightful twitchy little twat of a Dollface. She had a very cute, pretty face, but that was all. Everything else about her was tweetsville. There was something sour about her. And Elise was rarely wrong. It was her intuition and ability to read people that had made her Mother.

Now her lovely Candy had forced her hand. Why? *Y! Y!* Why would Candy-can do that? There had been enough love for her to go on as planned and create their baby together. If Candy had truly wanted to betray her, she would have done it long ago.

Y.

Bren: it was her. It must be. Bren was just smart enough to know about the threats against her life. In fact, Candice had stopped Elise multiple times from disposing of her. It must have been Bren, because the girl felt threatened. She would not fear the consequences, because she probably already felt doomed under Elise's hand. But why would Candice go along with it? Unless she had been left in the dark. Unless Candice had also been betrayed.

Oh, you little bitch. You little fucking cunt face! You're gonna get it. You're gonna get it real good.

"Should I ready your bike, Team Mother?" Rex asked.

"Oh yes, Rex. Yes, you do that. Ready my bike, you useless piece of plastic shit. And ready a few extra bikes while you're at it. Send my guards. It seems Candy-can and fuckface want to go on a little bit of a trip with their mother... I really wish I could hurt you, Rex, for lying to me."

"I did not lie to you. I'm here to serve you, Mother. I was following orders by Doctor Harlow."

"Of course you were."

She ran a gloved finger along the counter. "Be a dear and tell Cherry I won't be returning tonight. Tell her sorry, but I have to go hunting instead. Tell her... I'll make it up to her Saturday. We can have a big party at my place Saturday night."

"All right, Mother."

She curled her leather-gloved hand into a fist. She thought of Candice. Of course, she would have to kill her. And Elise always did what she had to do to stay on top. That was the other reason she was Team Mother.

Tears rushed to her eyes, and she felt a choking sensation. She squeezed her gloved fist even harder. But she would not shed tears for Candice. No. She would not cry for her. Not even for Candy- can-can. Not even lovely sweet Harlow. She would cry for no one in this dismal dark cunt-fucking-piece-of-a-turd of a world. She had given up tears a long time ago.

Instead, she would make them feel pain. That was one thing Elise could do. She could hurt them. That was something she excelled in. She could hurt both of them, and she knew just how.

18

LAST RITES

They crashed on a sidewalk only a block away from the exit to the city. For the first time in her life, Candice could actually see the sun setting over the horizon of the desert, not obstructed by the usual metallic checkered lines of the Pyramid wall. She had never been so close to the exit before. She could clearly see the white-frosted sand of the Badlands in the distance without any obstruction of steel. But now all was lost. They had been forced down by drones after the machines had covered the sky and blinded them midflight.

It was snowing. That was lucky, for it had padded their fall. Candice jumped from her crashed bike and ran to Bren. Candice had strapped the baby to her chest and was holding the infant tightly in her arms as she ran. But the baby was hollering. Bren was on the ground, slowly rising. She hadn't fared as well, having rolled twenty or thirty yards from her fallen bike. But thankfully, Bren seemed all right. Candice checked Bren more carefully and was grateful to see that the two of them had only sustained a few minor scrapes. Then she unstrapped the baby and looked him over too. He was restless, but unharmed.

Hundreds of small drones buzzed over them. Candice

figured they were there in order to ensure that neither of them got back on their bike and tried to escape. But both bikes were totaled.

Candice looked toward the sidewalk of one-lane Primdon Street and saw a group of bystanders staring at them. She focused in on them with her visor. They were all citizens. She didn't see any Officers among them. On the road, the cars and trucks, most without people inside, lined up in traffic immobile from the violence of the accident.

"We have to go," snapped Candice, touching Bren's shoulder. "We can run for it."

Bren nodded.

"We can run the rest of the way to outside of the city walls. We have to try."

But then Bren shook her head. "Give me the baby, Candice." Bren grabbed the baby from her arms. "This is my fault. Let me be punished. You return to the city."

"Bren. We have to go. It's too late. I've done enough with you already."

Soon, it didn't matter. They heard the sound of rockets approaching and turned. There, off toward downtown, a squadron of flying bikes was approaching fast. The purple bike in the center belonged to Elise. She was wearing a large, thick white coat resembling animal fur, her visor, and her black leather pants and boots. Her companions wore black leather suits, black trench coats, and black visors.

"Too late," Candice said.

Elise landed her bike almost a block away and instructed her soldiers to do the same. Candice watched as Elise dismounted and the guards took out rifles and pointed them in her direction.

"Whatever happens, Candice," Bren said, turning to her, "thank you. You've been good to me."

"Shh. It will be all right." But Candice said it with as much uncertainty as she felt.

Elise walked slowly down the road. The road was completely covered by snow. It almost looked more like Elise was walking in a white snowfield than in the city. Candice could hear the boots of her soldiers marching behind her while she trudged through the thick snow with a fake smile.

As she got close, Candice was surprised to see her lips covered in cherry-red lipstick. Her cheeks were colored with a bright red rouge. Her hair was pulled back in a bun. Candice had never seen her dressed like this.

Elise walked up to Candice. The baby was crying hysterically, now in Bren's arms. Elise looked at the baby, then turned back to Candice. She took off her black leather gloves, pulled her hand back, and struck Candice in the face. It was such a hard blow that it threw her to the ground.

"You ingrate!!! After everything I did for you? Why, you're still a little tweety-twat! And you dare to wear my color?"

"Leave her alone!" cried Bren.

"Quiet, Bren!" Candice said, holding her cheek and wincing in pain.

Elise turned to Bren with a wicked smile. "Hand me the child, won't you, Dollface? I want to look at my cute little *son*, you *son* of a bitch."

Bren obeyed her.

Elise took the baby into her arms. He was cute. Not a monster at all.

Elise gently laid the boy down on the snow. The baby squirmed inside his blanket, whimpering. She looked at him for a moment in silence, then dug her hand into her coat. She pulled out a pistol, raised the gun over the child's head, and pulled the trigger. The gunshot echoed through the streets.

Bren had jumped to stop her, but an Officer from behind Team Mother had grabbed her and hauled her back.

And then... silence. Complete silence. The baby's cries were no more. The Officers behind Elise looked down in amazement at the small wrapped red thing lying completely still in the no-longer-white snow.

"How could you!" cried Candice. She still lay on the ground. "You monster! How could you do that?"

Elise walked over to Bren, who had fallen on her knees in shock. A tear fell from one of Elise's eyes, but she had a stern, emotionless expression. She pointed the gun at Bren's head. "If only Candy-can had your scheming dirty heart, Dollface," Elise said quietly, almost in a whisper, "perhaps it would have worked out between us. But you fuck. You fucked her. Candice was good to you. She's good to all of us. But you turned out to be a kindred spirit, just like me. She trusted you. And now you fucked her.

"I want you to know," she added, looking down at Bren with a nasty grin, "I want you to know that you fucked sweet kind Candice. *You* ruined her, and that is the only reason for my tears. She will suffer terribly because of *you*. And now, as for *you*, you useless doll cunt fucker!!!"

She pulled the trigger again. Bren fell to the ground, and a red stain spread across the white snow beside her head.

Then Elise turned to Candice.

"There, there, Candy-can," she said, tucking the pistol back into her pocket. "Now everything's back to normal. We can return to the way things were before you hired the bitch."

Candice charged Elise. She tackled her, then leaped on her, slapping and hitting Elise across the face. They rolled across the ice, hitting and kicking each other. But all the while, Elise kept looking up and signaling with her hands. Candice didn't understand what Elise was doing. She kept signaling repeatedly between blows to her guards and the circling drones. When Candice finally stopped to catch her breath, she understood that Elise was gesturing for them not to shoot her.

Candice stopped rolling on the snow and looked at Elise with bewildered eyes. Surrounding Team Mother, over ten Officers stood with their rifles pointed at Candice.

Both ladies lay on the ground, trying to catch their breath. Finally, Elise got up, brushing back her hair and straightening her fluffy white coat. Candice touched her face, which was terribly sore, and spat blood onto the white snow. Then she was pinned to the ground by three black boots.

"Take her," Elise said, breathing heavy. "Let her sit in a cell and think about what she's done. Get her out of my sight before I change my mind and kill her."

The guards, however, seemed shocked by all they had witnessed. Not one of them moved.

"Take her!" Elise screamed. "What are you standing like that for! If you don't move, I'll fucking shoot you all too. Now get her out of my sight! Do it now!"

19

AN EVENING ALONE

Elise sat in her reserved booth at the center balcony of Sunny Side Raymond's. It was early yet, not even eight. She was drinking martinis. The clear elixir came in one of Raymond's lovely spiral necked extra-large martini glasses, garnished with two lovely green olives. She liked to collect the olives around her white-laced dining set. It was her way of counting. This made eight. She ran her finger over a couple of them.

There were professional dancers running across the dance floor under her with long golden streamers for entertainment. She watched while bringing her cocktail glass up to her lips. Her lips were red and the lipstick stained the rim of the glass.

They were reenacting an ancient play. Many of the dancers had masks. It was a classic fight of good against evil: white tights and leotards against red. The golden light of the walls of Raymond's shone down on the entertainment, focusing on the theater below.

But many paid no attention. Most Savants were busy socializing with one another or their call girls.

As Elise watched, people walked by along the rail below the booths and waved to her. Everyone knew Team Mother.

Elise waved faintly, then went back to watching. When bored of the dancers, she looked up and gazed at the view beyond the stage. It was still snowing outside, and the cold weather fogged the periphery of the giant window in front of her.

Riley walked by, wearing a long gaudy black coat. It was more of a cape, really. She had a whore attached to her hip, and the old witch was laughing hysterically with her. Elise had thought she would join her, but she didn't.

Then there were Annabelle and Frankie, Doris and Leeto, all Savants of outer sectors. They passed her by as if she wasn't there. Tonight, Elise didn't even invite a prostitute. She sat alone.

"Would you like another, Mother?" asked a gold-painted server. She was a very young, petite girl. Elise could see her trying to mask her fear as she smiled, but her glittered eye twitched a little.

"Yes," Elise said, turning her gaze down to the stage below. "Actually, I asked for one ten minutes ago."

"Oh," said the server, suddenly worried, "right away. So sorry. Sorry... another martini, then?"

Elise turned away without an answer.

When was the last time I drank here? Has it been a month? Two months? And with whom? Candy. It was you, Candy. She smiled. *I took you, Candy-can-can, for a break. You didn't like that, but you needed it. You so wanted to finish your dirty work. You were a good assistant. Such a nice girl... well, fuck you anyway.*

(Down the hatch, more vodka and vermouth...)

Why can't I be happy? Who needs anybody, when you can just call a sexy girl home with you? Somebody who won't argue about the weather. Somebody stupid enough not to care. I can just...

(And swallow it down. Swallow, swallow more and more, Mother, enjoy the lovely shit...)

Oh, but you fought me, didn't you, Candy-can-can? You always challenged me over everything. I despised and adored you. And our last fight, yeah, you tore me up real good, didn't you, bitch?

Elise laughed. A few people in nearby booths turned toward her. She raised her glass and smiled. They smiled back. *Fuck you. Fuck all of you.*

I miss you, Can. You're the only one who's crazy enough to disagree with me. Everybody else is on tippy-toes. It makes you crazier than all of them... to Candy.

And she finished another drink.

A heavyset older woman came walking slowly down the aisle. She had long peppered hair and wore a very lovely white silk dress. Her earrings were gold and diamond-studded. She had nothing around her neck, unlike Elise, who wore her usual choker. She looked up as she walked by Elise.

"Oh, hi, my dear," she said, pretending not to have seen her in her usual spot before. It was Dana. She looked up at her Team Mother, then tried to hide her disdain for all the olives spread along the table.

"How are you, Dana?"

"Just fine. Fine."

"Come sit, dear. We can watch the performance together."

"But I have a date, Mother."

"A date," Elise said, interested. She leaned on her hands. Dana was about to walk off, but she had to hear more. "Do tell. With whom?"

"Really, Mother, how meddlesome you are sometimes." And Dana couldn't hide her discomfort.

Elise laughed. She picked up her glass but realized it was empty. Then she wondered if she had been slurring her words. *I better pep up if I'm gonna deal with Queen Bitch.* So she reached into her black leather jeans and took out some gum.

"I would have thought someone with your age and wisdom would no longer have need for a lady," Elise said.

That did it. Dana turned from irritable to irate. "Like you, Elise?" she shot back. Then she seemed to turn green with fear from saying it.

Elise felt warmth rise to her face. *Touché.* She smiled

broadly. "Well, I'd just love to meet her. Why don't you two come and sit with me. I have a great view."

"No." Dana shook her head quickly. "No. No, thank you."

"I don't know," Elise said, waving her hand frivolously in the air. Dana didn't dare leave without being excused, but Elise noticed her foot planted forward in preparation for a hasty exit. "You know, I just haven't found anybody new, I guess."

"You should move on, dear. There's more to the world than Doctor Harlow. You could have anyone."

Elise smiled even more. *You little bitch. Sure, Dana.*

Dana dropped all airs for a moment and raised a hand. "Don't get me wrong, Elise. I mean, you can have anybody you'd like. There's no one in all Arkite who would object to being with you."

You just did.

"Goodnight, Dana," Elise said. Then she turned back to the entertainment below her. "Enjoy your date."

"I hope I didn't offend," Dana answered with a nod. Then she paused, searching for something else to say, but she was at a loss for words.

"Goodnight, Dana," Elise repeated without glancing at her.

"Goodnight, Mother."

Dana quickly walked off.

Pity. Elise wanted company, and she'd thought she'd have it when she'd first seen the old hag.

She caught Dana turning her head back as she walked off. Dana was still afraid she had offended her.

Even she fears me. Everyone is afraid of me.

And why wouldn't they be? She'd told her people she could now successfully manipulate all genes through the mainframe, which promised not only immortality but potentially the ability to stop aging or even reverse it. She had found the holy grail. No Savant would dare challenge her any longer.

But then there was their attitude. Everybody, even the whores, was distant from her. They all shook before her—even Dana and Riley, two senior Savants. She was feared so much that everybody walked long arcs around her. Completely alone. She was completely alone. But it wasn't only that.

The Officers who had guarded her that cold, snowy evening by Primdon Street hadn't stayed quiet. They'd talked, and rumors had spread through the city. It was said that Dr. Harlow had created a boy as a blueprint for future experimentation. A boy. And as this was against the law, it was rumored, and believed by most, that Team Mother had shot a bullet straight through the little innocent newborn's head.

She looked around her. Everyone's eyes were on each other or the show down below. No one dared look at her. She felt her temper boil over.

Fuck you! Fuck all of you!

She took her empty glass and hurled it down onto the stage. The dancers scattered from the shattered glass as if it were a bomb. Everyone turned in horror to see who was responsible. Guards searched the booths to find the offender. When it was clear that their Team Mother was to blame, they quickly turned their heads and pretended as if it had never happened.

20

—————

BACK TO THE WAY IT WAS

Candice was in the courtyard of her prison, sitting on a small white plastic chair in her orange jumpsuit and enjoying the warm sunshine after a week of rain. Her sentence was life imprisonment— she had now served six months.

She stared out at the prison gates, her hands in metal handcuffs. The handcuffs were not necessary but were required by the terms of her sentence whenever she left her cell. Many of the other prisoners were conversing with each other beside benches or shooting hoops by the basketball nets. She was facing the pyramidal high-rises of downtown Sector One across the barbed-wire fence. She ran her hand over her blond hair out of habit, but there was only a short cut. She had been shaved bald upon entering the prison.

She was not altogether unhappy here. This was something she would never have thought possible. In many ways, she had been more imprisoned as a Savant. She had been at the bidding of her master. In fact, every aspect of her life, even sex, had been up to the whims of her lunatic boss. Then, all she had done was work and study. Free time was spent reading science journals or experimenting with chemical reagents in the lab. She never went out for fun, for that would inevitably involve spending time with Mother. She drew herself inward and escaped into the lab.

She was, in many ways, freer in jail. In jail, she was provided with food and all the reading pleasures of her dreams. She had no one to present findings to, nothing to spend all night working for.

But she missed Bren. And a part of her missed her work.

Rumors of jail had always filled her with fantasies of violence and rape. There was that, but it was seldom and sparse and never threatened her. For one thing, Candice was liked by virtually everyone in Cell 235. For another, no one dared touch her. No one could forget that she had been a Savant, the personal assistant, and more, of Team Mother. Who could say that Candice would not be favored again?

She was writing on a computer pad this afternoon. She traced the letters with her fingertip, being too immobile with the cuffs to use her whole hand for a pen. She was trying to work out a problem. It was more philosophical than scientific.

It went something like this: now that the mainframe had the power to create the human genome, was the resulting species truly human? Or was it a kind of hybrid, a human construct with all errors and mutations removed by the calculating rationality of a machine? Was there a soul in this creation? And was it a fundamental mistake to create a species so perfect as to never evolve or change like nature had intended?

When she had worked in the stink and sterility of the lab, Candice had never thought of the endpoint of her work. Only Doctor Reyburn had reminded her of a glimmer of it. Reyburn, like Bren, had believed that the answer lay in human reproduction: in reintroducing a Y chromosome into the mix. How stupid. Was the creation of a man or a woman really what was at stake? Or was that just an illusion introduced by the mainframe to confuse the ends while creating the means? Gender, when you really got down to it, had nothing to do with it. What was at stake was the meaning of what makes a human being human. And no one, perhaps not even Rex himself, knew the answer to that.

The next step in Magnacourt's grand plan for Project Lazarus was to gift the people immortality. But Candice believed that part of what made a human being human was mortality. Violence, voiding, food, and sex were all based on mortality. Children were based on mortality. Even pain was based on mortality (for pain was a way for the organism to recognize an outside threat—what outside threat was there for an immortal organism that could simply order up a new heart, finger or ear?) And without pain, would there be such a thing as pleasure? Removing all these things could transform the human race into a species indistinguishable from Rex and AI. Reyburn's conspiracy theories would argue that this transformation, this new order, was precisely Rex's secret plan.

Her boss was a prime example. Elise was deep in her hedonistic passions and ruthlessness. Yet that made her human—very human, in a nasty sort of way. Candice despised her for all she had done to her, and yet, even with this deep hatred, she still would have preferred her evil bitch boss over an apathetic machine.

Candice feared that the endpoint to her research would lead the women of Arkite to eventually become machines. A bunch of Rex copies. This would match Reyburn's conspiracy theory, and it was chilling to think that it was indeed possible. She hoped she was wrong.

Perhaps Candice was just afraid of technological change. But if it was a change for the worse, she also feared her responsibility in it. Her deep thoughts were interrupted by guards marching toward her. In the middle walked a woman Candice had both longed for and dreaded ever meeting again. Elise. Her former boss had a smirk on her face. Candice felt a lump in her throat.

"Leave us," said Elise to the guards as she stood over

Candice. Elise's smile faded as she sat carefully down in another white plastic chair across from Candice and looked her over. Candice could imagine what she was thinking. She had seen it in the mirror this morning. Thanks to prison rations, she was gaunt. Her head had been shaved. She wore no makeup, had her wrists chained, and was dressed in an ugly orange jumpsuit. She looked like shit, and Elise's expression seemed to attest to that.

"Care for a stick of gum?" Elise asked.

Candice had lost her addiction to Mint. It had taken her weeks. But now that Elise was waving sticks in front of her, she wanted it more than ever.

"Thanks, Mother."

Elise handed her a stick and Candice laid it on her lap. "You're welcome, my dear," Elise said with a thin smile.

Elise looked around the courtyard. All the other prisoners had gone inside in terror at the sight of their Team Mother. Elise turned and looked behind her at the fence Candice was facing. Out there was downtown Arkite. She wrinkled her nose and sighed. "It's really crappy here, isn't it, tweetsy?"

"Don't call me that," Candice snapped. She looked into Elise's eyes with venom. "You've sentenced me. Now don't sit here and mock me."

"But you are, dear. You are a little tweet tweet bird. Just like all the other fuckers in the city. That's why that other tweetsy got to you."

Candice raised and clanged her chained wrists with a sardonic grin. "You've locked your little bird away, Mom. Now, please go."

Elise nodded. "You know," she said, "I didn't want this to happen. I never wanted anything to happen to you. It was that stupid Bridgette. You should never—"

"Just stop! I don't want to hear this." Then she fitfully clanged her chains again. "I always knew you were wicked, but I had never seen it with my own eyes. I had heard about it.

You told me what you did to the scientists of Allele Corp. And I heard about other crimes, coldblooded murders, nights of rage at your hooker parties, your—"

"I see your point." Elise turned back with a thin grin.

"No, you don't! I never saw how evil you were until you killed our child."

"Oh, stop," Elise said, rolling her eyes. "That wasn't our child. It was an experiment."

"That was our child. It was genetically our child. It was your genes and mine, and you ruthlessly shot him in the head!"

"Calm down," Elise said, glancing around. The guards Elise had dismissed were watching alertly from nearby. "You're going to get punished, and from what I hear—"

"Let them punish me. I don't care. It's better than another second with you. Just get away from me."

Candice grabbed her pad with her cuffed hands, turned her chair around, and started writing again.

Then she felt something she despised. Despite all her vehement hatred toward Elise, there was a part deep inside that missed her. It made her feel sick, and as if to make her feel worse, Elise reached over and touched her shoulder.

"I can explain every one of those crimes if you'd like," she said. "I could go through all of them, Candy. Many you'd forgive me for, some you wouldn't. But what you don't understand, what you never understood, is that it is because of them that I hold the power I hold. It is because of them that I am your Team Mother."

"Then go away, Team Mother," Candice said quietly. A tear ran from her eye. "I would never do those things. Stay away from me."

"Hmm," Elise said, pulling her hand back. "Let me explain."

"Just go."

"Let's start with your creation, shall we? Bridgette broke

the law when she transmuted the chromosome from X to Y. She committed the same crime that Allele Corp. committed."

"You shot down every lead scientist at Allele Corp.," Candice said, turning and looking straight into Elise's eyes with hatred.

"Yes, I did." Elise folded her arms. "But do you know who ordered it?"

"Hmm?"

"Do you know who ordered the massacre? Doctor Reyburn— the doctor you pardoned, who is currently sitting in another prison in that same hideous orange outfit as you."

"You fired the gun, Elise," Candice snapped, shaking her head. "You could have disregarded anything Reyburn ordered."

Elise shrugged. "You don't understand the world you live in. You're still just a little tweeting bird." She smiled sadly.

Why are you here? You want me back? Really? I've suffered months in a stinking prison, and you want me back? How typical.

Candice reached to run her hand through her hair, but there was little hair. The touch of her scalp reminded her of why she loathed Elise. "Just go away, Elise. I don't really care why you do your terrible things. Just don't mix me into them."

"You know, Candy, I rightfully should have shot you. You also broke the law."

Is that it? Perhaps you don't want me back. Perhaps you're here to gloat over my execution.

But then Elise laughed. "Anywho, I'm not here to fight. I want to give you a proposal. If you accept, I will absolve you of being a fucking tweet tweet bird."

Candice raised her hands and clanked her wrists again.

"Yeah, sorry 'bout that, Candy. Anyway—"

"Why blame Reyburn for the scientists' deaths? They were her closest friends."

"Candy, Doctor Reyburn is worse than anyone. She taught me. She was my mentor."

Candice had heard this before. She had forgotten all about it. Candice tried to recall the last Team Mother, but the woman had been in power when Candice was less than five years old. Still, she had read the history files. She had seen videos. She knew what that Team Mother had looked like. When Candice had seen Doctor Reyburn, she had been as gaunt and emaciated as Candice was now. But with a little more fat, a bit more conceit... yes, Candice supposed that Doctor Reyburn could have once been Team Mother.

"Doctor Reyburn was *your* Mother?" she asked.

"Yep. And much worse, Can. But forget about that withering old bitch. You saved her. Good for you. What I'm offering is—"

"Why are you blaming her for killing her own scientists?"

"Forget it, Candy."

Candice didn't even want to bother to argue. Elise leaned over and grabbed her hand. "Candice, I have an important job for you. If you take it, honey, I will reinstate you as Savant. In fact, I will reinstate you as Chief Assistant Savant for all your troubles. But you have to take this project. It's very delicate."

"What is it?"

"I need you again for an interview. I worked very hard, alone over the past few months in the lab—which you know I hate. But I need you. I need you to complete the experiment."

"Another interview?" Candice didn't consider herself a very good interrogator. The last person she'd interviewed was Bridgette. She had sentenced an innocent girl to death.

"Yeah. But..." Elise glanced around carefully, then whispered, "you have to take the job first before I tell you who or what it is." Then Elise put a finger to Candice's lips and shushed her. She giggled stupidly. Candice didn't join her.

"I loved Bren. You took her from—"

"Oh, God, Candy, shut the fuck up, will you! She's dead. So is your creation. Get over it." Elise leaned forward and pointed at her face. "But your work was brilliant. You helped elevate me to the highest status of any Mother ever. I owe you for that. I owe you a pardon. Your ingenuity and genius helped us surpass anything that bitch Reyburn could ever do. So..." She smiled a sultry smile. "Just do this job for me, babe. Forget the past. Honestly, Candice, all you ever did for Bren was protect her. That was noble and shit, but she deserved to die anyway."

Candice laughed. She couldn't believe Elise was serious after that comment, but she was.

"Come back to me, sweet," she whispered, taking Candice's hand and rolling her fingers around the bones of her hands like she always did.

Then Elise picked up the gum on the plastic chair that had fallen between Candice's legs and slowly placed it back in her palm. Candice had never chewed it. In all the excitement, it had fallen, and she had forgotten all about it.

"I really miss you," Elise said, closing Candice's fingers around the Mint. "And when you hear what I've done, you may not be so upset at what I did to our last experiment."

"Tell me first. Then I'll consider it."

"No," she said, but she flashed a sly grin, as if they were playing a game. "First agree. Swear to me that you'll take the job, and you're free. I'll introduce you at my place tomorrow evening."

Candice hesitated. She looked about the courtyard. Then her boss did too, but with a look of disgust.

"I'm offering you a pardon, Candy-can. I think you should take it. Now get the fuck out of here."

Candice took the stick of gum and threw it in her mouth. She chewed while looking out at the city for a moment.

The rush was fast. It felt like an awakening to her. The courtyard seemed to come alive. Her vision sharpened and the drab gray courtyard seemed to be splashed with color. She hadn't known how much she'd missed Mint.

Then she noticed Elise impatiently staring at her waiting for her reply.

If she agreed, she would be subject to Elise's whims again.

Did she care for Mother? Perhaps their love affair was partly her fault... no. That was like blaming a prisoner for her feelings for her captor. Elise was one of the most noxious people she had ever met. But did she have a choice? If she said no, what would stop Elise from ordering her execution in retaliation? She had killed Bren; what would stop her from finally killing Candice?

"I'll look at your experiment, Elise."

Elise glowed with joy. She nodded and got up from the plastic chair. Then she ran her hand through her long black hair and offered that hand to Candice.

"I'm not agreeing on anything yet," Candice said. "And you and I are through."

Elise dropped her hand and frowned. She looked toward the fence for a moment and then turned back with a scowl. "I said, only if you agree to come back to me, Candy."

"With all you've done to me," Candice stammered, fighting to say the words. She held more rage than sorrow. "You owe me. Release me for a week and show me your work. If I don't agree to come back, you can send me back to my cell, for all I care."

Elise squinted and examined her. Then she snapped, "Go change. Take a shower and get out of that miserable excuse for clothes. I'll pick you up outside in an hour."

"Yes, Mother."

21

THE MODERN PROMETHEUS

CANDICE FLEW HER NEW GRAY ROCKET CYCLE CAREFULLY TO Pyramid Three in downtown Arkite. She hadn't flown in months and worried that she had lost her touch, but she had quickly remembered all the levers and buttons and had no difficulty managing. The rendezvous was set for eight o'clock at night. It was now seven forty-five.

She needed more time. All day she'd had a feeling of uneasiness in her chest. Earlier she had relaxed in her apartment, grateful that her place hadn't been given to another citizen while she had been gone. But during the whole lazy day, she couldn't stop worrying about her mystery meeting.

She landed her cycle on a parking structure, near the top of the building, reserved especially for Savants. Sara, wearing her usual formal black suit, was there to greet her and take her bike.

"Hi, Sara," Candice said with a kind smile.

Sara was overjoyed to see her. She ran over and gave her a warm hug and a kiss on the cheek.

"I'm so happy you're back, Candy! I was so worried about you." Then she ran her eyes down Candy's suit. She was wearing an all-gray leather jumpsuit. Candice handed her the visor. "You look good, Candice... except your hair."

"Now we're truly sisters," Candice said, touching the girl's short blond hair.

"She's at home." Sara pointed up. Her joy faded after mentioning Elise. "She's waiting for you, Candice."

Sara was going to lead the bike to a garage, but Candice took her by the arm. "Listen," she said. "Let's hang out tomorrow again, 'kay?"

"I'd love to, Candy." Sara gave her another hug. "Can't wait!"

Then Candice felt that sinking feeling again. It was time to see Mother.

Candice took the familiar elevator up to the top floor. Today the smell was different. It smelled of something like apricots and oleander. She walked down the hall and knocked on her boss's door. Elise didn't greet her. Instead, the door opened slowly and automatically.

It was dark. None of the lights were on except upstairs. She climbed the incline up to the third floor. There Elise stood, her faced painted in black makeup, like Candy's, with black lipstick and thick black eyeliner, facing the window with her hands folded behind her back. She wore a black lace blouse, white plastic pants, high heels and, of course, her sharp choker.

"Savant Jackson," Candice said, standing at attention under her on the ramp between the second and third floor. "I'm here to report for duty, Team Mother."

Elise nodded and then cocked her head. She curled her lips in a half smile. "So you are, Can-can. So you are. Come. Let us sit by the couch and talk." Elise turned fully and looked at her. She looked from Candice's short hair all the way down to her boots as Candice walked up the ramp to the couch. "You look much nicer, babe."

"Thank you, Mother."

"Would you care for a drink?"

"No... I'd much rather be told what all this is about."

"Please, dear," Elise said, raising a hand. She walked over and sat with her on the green leather couch. "Let's be patient." She laid a hand on Candice's leather pants. Candice felt uncomfortable.

"I am back. I'm here."

"Yes," Elise said quietly and ran a hand along Candice's cheek. "Indeed, you are."

It was cozy and private in the room, with dimmed purple lighting along the wood floor and faint yellow recessed lighting above: a little too cozy, almost romantic. And Candice was not in the mood for that. She wouldn't, she'd promised herself, give herself to Elise. It was too disgraceful after all she had endured. After the murders of Bren and the boy. Her son.

Elise ran a finger along Candice's gray leather forearm. Then she giggled and looked into her eyes. "I missed you, Candy. It's been so many months. It was like I sentenced myself to prison. And all I've done is toil in that lab you love so much. I hate it. How can I bring you back? It can't all be about Bridgette, or Bren as you called her. Why, she was just a Dollface."

"Please." Candice pushed herself back. "I'm here. Don't talk about it. Just tell me what this is all about."

"Well," Elise said, her voice calm and measured, "you know I've watched you. Rex and I have examined every aspect of your work over the past few years. We've watched you grow as a Savant and as a scientist. Many of my colleagues"—she giggled and patted Candice's hands—"could not believe that you had the ability to do anything." She looked up in thought for a moment. "Doctor Reyburn thought you were just a Dollface." She looked back and gently held her chin. "But I knew different. I knew of your potential when I first met you."

"Not a little bird."

"No," said Elise quietly, and she ran her hand along

Candice's face again. Candice couldn't hide her discomfort. She squirmed. Elise laughed and waved a finger. "You know, Reyburn thought I hired you just for your looks."

"Did you?"

"It helps, of course," Elise said, running her hand over Candice's arm, her fingers rising toward her neck.

"Don't."

Elise frowned in a comical way. Then she shrugged and jumped up, heading back to the window.

"Anywho," Elise said, turning back to her, leaning on the rail by the window and feigning a smile, "as Team Mother, I made an executive decision to test Rex and the mainframe. I figured there could actually be some truth in Reyburn's paranoia. Perhaps the mainframe does want us to die out. So I figured, Candice, that the best way to find out was to test Rex —to create something that would challenge our very fears. Of course, I wondered if this too would be anticipated by the machine. After all, there was no way to hide it. But it really didn't matter. The course was set, and I chose to embark on it full steam ahead."

"What?"

"I copied you." Elise reached in her pocket for some gum. She offered Candice a piece, but Candice shook her head. "I studied your work. Your work and the work of that good-for-nothing Dollface of yours. First, it was your 'failure.' I had Rex run the schematics of your first experiment a couple of years ago. It was far from a failure, Candice. You remember, it was the first time you experimented with your DNA. Then, when the two of you succeeded with the child, I had Rex copy that too. I took cell samples of my genes and yours and recombined them. And that's my experiment. So now... we have a child together and... you don't have to be so angry at me for shooting the other one."

Elise smiled sweetly. There was something perverse and

nasty about that. It made Candice swoon. She felt sick. She turned away, refusing to even look at her.

"What? What's the hell's the matter, Candice?"

You shot our baby in cold blood. Then you shot my best friend. What the hell do you think is the matter?

"Please wait and hear me out, Candy." Elise walked back to the couch, sat down, and took her by the hand. "I fixed my first mistake. For that, you can now forgive me. But as to the other one, Bridgette... she deserved to die." She patted Candice's hand.

"Why is that?" Candice snapped, snatching her hand away. Elise looked surprised.

"Now, wait a minute," Elise said, raising a finger. "Just give me time to explain."

"I am," Candice said. "I'm waiting. But I also told you not to mention her."

"Bridgette was a traitor, Candice," Elise explained, wagging her finger. "She went behind both our backs. She sabotaged your work. How can you ever trust someone like that?"

"You were threatening her life ever since you recruited her!"

Elise laughed. "You know, I miss you, Candice. You never hesitate to get in my business over everything. You're such a brave impetuous little brat."

Candice didn't respond. She just stared at her.

"Here, have a drink... I'm getting one." Elise jumped up and laughed again. "I think you should have one too."

Elise walked to a table near the window. There was an open bottle of red wine and two glasses.

"We need to celebrate," Elise said, filling each glass. "To absolute power. All thanks to you, my little genius. Thanks to you, we can now rule without any fear of insurrection."

She walked back and handed Candice a glass.

"I'll make mention of this one more time, Candy," Elise

continued, "and after that, no more. Of course, you cared for Bren—you had to. You two worked day and night together, and it is in your flawed nature to care about people. But she was weak. She never had your daring. The only reason she was even able to hang with us was because you protected her." She sipped some wine. "And in this world, honey, you either fuck people or get fucked. Right? It's never cush. And so"—Elise reclined on the opposite side of the couch and raised her glass in a toast—"you're my prized Savant. I am indebted to you for our new position in Arkite. But as for Dollface, fuck her. She turned on us after hearing the whispering chirps of Connie Reyburn."

Elise nodded for a moment, as if waiting for her brilliant lecture to sink in. Then she continued. "I suppose you screwed yourself, Candice. You should never have let Reyburn live. She planted it all into your lovely Dollface; then Dollface screwed us over. All because Reyburn wanted revenge. She wanted to hurt me by hurting you." Elise raised her glass and peered at it in thought. "Connie was always good at scheming and hurting people. But that's politics, Candy. It's what separates us from the little tweet tweets. Everything has a price, and you being too kind cost the life of Dollface."

"Bren died from your bullet." Candice's face was burning. The hand that held her wineglass was shaking with rage. She wanted to throw the glass and its contents in Elise's face, but she knew it was not the right time. Elise's demeanor was open and almost vulnerable. Violence would be risky now, even riskier than usual.

Elise drank more wine. As Elise brought the glass up to her lips, Candice noticed that her hand was shaking too. But Elise's tremor wasn't because of Mint or anger. Elise's hand shook for the same reason Candice's hands had twitched during their first interview all those years ago: fear. Elise was afraid. It was obvious Elise was trying to get Candice back, and the prospect of failing frightened her. Had Candice not absolutely loathed Mother at that moment, she might have felt compassion or at least pity for her.

Candice turned toward the ramp. Had she been free, she would have stormed down the incline and left. She should have, but she knew she wasn't free. She never had been.

"Candice," Elise said, leaning her back against the window, "Reyburn betrayed us. She knew she could influence Dollface and then pass down her treachery to you. She knows how I feel about you. She knew I'd be forced to punish you for the sake of Arkite. You betrayed me, but I knew it wasn't your fault. It was Reyburn. Reyburn forced my hand against you—you, Candice, the only person I really care about. For that, Candy, be assured Reyburn will pay."

Candice turned back and looked straight into Elise's eyes. "I don't feel anything for you."

For the first time, the aura of arrogance and joy was wiped from Elise's face. Elise lost her balance, grabbing the rail by the window and nearly spilling her wine. Then she quickly straightened herself and attempted a smile. It seemed odd how this ruthless killer could be so enamored with her. But it had left her vulnerable, and now Candice had hurt her worse than striking her—far worse than splashing her with wine.

Elise set her wineglass down very slowly on the table and leaned on the golden rail, looking outside. "You can feel whatever you want to feel, Candice," she said quietly.

"How can you expect anything else? After everything you did?"

"I just explained why I did it. If I can't bring you back, then... well, I had thought you would forgive me. I'm trying to tell you my hands were tied. Reyburn sabotaged us. She purposely broke us apart by forcing my hand into—"

"I'm here, Elise." But she didn't want to be. And now she regretted telling her. Perhaps she had forgotten her skills as a Savant. Politics. Bren had never understood it, and look what it had gotten her.

"Elise, where is this experiment of yours?" Candice asked with a sigh, forcing a change in subject. "You said 'interview.' How can I interview another baby?"

"Ah, right, Candy." Elise turned and raised a gloved finger. "A good question. How can you interview a baby?" Somehow the question had reanimated Elise. She eagerly walked back to the other side of the couch and reclined again. "I realized that in order to truly test Rex, I had to speed up time. I realized I didn't have time to wait for a child to grow, for then I wouldn't rule long enough to solve any problems formed by the mainframe. I had to make a project fully grown."

"What are you getting at?"

"Lazarus." Elise was almost breathless with excitement. "Lazarus has been born. He's alive, in my guest room. He's alive, and I would very much like you to meet him. Would you... would you like to meet him? To talk to him?"

Him? HIM! HIM! HIM!!!

Candice had spent every waking moment with Bren over the year and a half after she'd hired her. They had become close friends. Then their creation had been born. Candice had escaped with Bren and promised to protect her from Elise. Elise had pursued them, shot the baby in the head, and then shot Bren. And all of it had been done for one reason, and one reason alone: because the baby had been an XY. Now Elise was telling her that she had recreated the experiment and once again made an XY. Now *she* had broken the law. The hypocrisy was sickening, and yet, Elise didn't show the slightest guilt over her transgression. Rather, she seemed overjoyed.

It was the last straw. Candice's rage boiled over.

"HIM!" Candice snapped, jumping up. "What do you mean HIM! You told me you killed Bren because she broke the law. What do you mean HIM, Elise? Who is it who broke the law now?"

Elise furrowed her brow in confusion. Apparently, she

hadn't expected this reaction, and seeing that only made Candice angrier.

"Candice, I—"

"How dare you! How dare you shoot our baby, a life form Rex himself refused to kill, and then shoot my best friend, all for a crime that you yourself now celebrate! You monster! You hypocrite! How can you do this?"

Candice slammed the glass down on an end table, nearly shattering it, and started down the slope.

"Wait, Candice. Hold on—"

"I always feared and hated you, Mother, but the fear was always stronger than the hate. Until now."

"Candice, you need—"

Candice raised her hand. "No, don't say another word! I don't want to hear any more lies!" She walked quickly down the slope, wiping tears from her cheeks. She had thought her months of sitting in prison would have hardened her to pain, but it hadn't. "Stay away from me," she warned. "Stay away! I don't want to be anywhere near you! You disgust me!"

"Wait, Candice! Wait! You don't understand... he wants to meet you."

She made it to the bottom floor and ran for the door. She would have thrown the door open and run out had there not been a shadow at the threshold. Someone was lurking there. A body in a black cloak and hood stood before her. She screamed in fright, nearly falling backwards.

Candice cocked her head up and saw Elise standing at the top of the ramp with her hands behind her back and calmly peering down at her. Candice turned back to the shadowed doorway.

The figure was like a deeper shadow, so still and so silent. It had a black shirt and leather slacks with black boots. It was the tallest person she had ever seen. Then she felt a shiver down her back as the figure raised a hand in the same fashion as Team Mother.

"I didn't mean to startle you," the creature said in a low baritone voice.

Candice jumped back again. The words were spoken eloquently, almost too flowing. And the tone of the voice was low, like Rex's. It was the tone of a man, or at least the sound of a man's voice.

"You are... the experiment?" she asked, wiping another tear from her eye.

"Yes." The creature laughed. It seemed to Candice that the laughter wasn't much different from Rex's laughter. It wasn't human. "My name is Lazarus. That is what Mother calls me."

It—or, she supposed, *he*—reached out a hand. Candice stared at it.

"I'm sorry, Doctor Harlow, but Team Mother told me we had a date. She said you were going to interview me. I was going to remain in my room, but then I heard you running. I was afraid something was wrong."

He walked up closer and removed his hood. She felt her heart race and throat tighten.

Lazarus was attractive. But his features frightened her. Just like their baby, this being had features from both Elise and herself. He had Candice's fat cheeks, thick lips, and thin crooked nose, but Elise's brown skin and brown eyes. He was large with broad shoulders and bald. He looked young, not much older than herself. His eyes were calculating like Elise's but seemed kind. And he had a warm smile. No, he did not seem like a monster at all. And yet his features alarmed her. They were too similar to hers and her boss's. She felt like she was peering in a mirror. A distorted mirror.

"I'm sorry again," he said. He put his hood back on. "I seem to have frightened you."

"No. It's all right... go ahead, take your hood off. Let me get a better look at you."

He obeyed but seemed to feel shame at his appearance.

She mused that he did not know his features were attractive. For all he knew, he was hideous to her.

She took his hand. It was hard and strong. She had never seen such a large hand before. Nor had she seen skin so rough. His male features were so strange to her. Man had been eliminated from humanity long before she had been born.

He smiled and looked down at her. "So, perhaps we can have our interview after all, Doctor Harlow? I would very much like that... I suppose you are my mother as well."

"That's why she's here."

Candice had not even seen Elise come down the ramp, but now she stood beside the two of them.

"Candy-can-can, why don't you spend some time getting to know Mr. Handsome alone in my guest quarters? He's been talking to me all day about how much he's been dying to meet you."

"Sure," she said hesitantly, still looking up at him.

"I think you'll find him quite fascinating. I know I have."

"Thank you, Mother," Lazarus said to Elise with a bow of his head.

They met in Elise's guest room. Candice had become well acquainted with it before her imprisonment, sleeping there almost once a week. It was sparsely furnished with a small bed and white linen canopy, a nightstand on each side and a pair of antique wooden chairs. The furniture was unchanged, but now the room had been transformed to look more like a child's room. There was a toy model car on the windowsill. There were toy figures of ladies in armor scattered along the floor. The bed in the center of the room had a handful of whimsical plush stuffed toys—a unicorn, a lion, and a dog. She recognized one in the center as a caricature of a Savant in a shiny red jumpsuit. There was even a plastic ring surrounding the neck of the stuffed doll. It looked like Elise. Candice rolled her eyes. It probably was Elise, the megalomaniac.

Candice sat on the chair with a small window to her right —the only window in the room. The window provided most of the light, lit mainly by the skyscrapers of the city below. Lazarus sat across from her in the other antique chair beside the bed. The lights were left off. The only other lighting came from behind wall monitors hung around the walls of the room.

The wall monitors played videos of three-dimensional landscapes. There was motion, though no sound, of objects like leaves and branches rustling in the wind. One was even a storm with rain and occasional flashes of lightning. But the one that caught her attention in particular was the one hanging over the bed. It looked like the red rocket bike that had once belonged to Elise. The same bike that Elise had gifted her, that Candice had destroyed on her race out of the city off Primdon Street.

"I don't like light," he said, breaking the silence.

"What do you mean?"

"I'm just explaining to you why I refused the light," he said with a shrug.

"What's wrong with light?"

"I... I don't want to alarm you by my appearance," Lazarus said, moving back in his chair. She could just see his eyes behind the dark hood. "Is that all right with you?"

"Don't be silly. There's nothing wrong with your appearance." Other than his dark hood. He was creepy in the black cloak and hood.

"You asked me about my memory of the lab," he said, looking up for a second in thought. "But my first three weeks of life in the lab... I don't recall much. Would you like me to tell you about it?"

"Yes."

"Well, I don't know when I awoke," he said with a nod of his hood. "All I remember is a bright light and the sound of a mechanical voice. A blinding white light and a voice."

"Rex?"

"Yes... I also remember the shaking and clanging of metal instruments. I squinted and squinted, but the bright light burned. Then I felt a rush of cold. I shivered. I felt panic from immobility, for I could not move. I wanted to shake but could not. Then I heard that voice again."

Candice was fascinated. She had never dreamed that one of her creations would talk to her about being created. He paused for a moment and then continued:

"Then... it was dark.

"I awoke like this countless times. Each time seemed involuntary and without control. Each time gave me that fear, as I had no control of movement, and yet I wanted to move. I desired to move.

"Numbers and language danced before my thoughts, and I recall finally speaking, but I can't recall what I said. I just know that I communicated back and forth with that mechanical voice. Later, the voice did indeed identify itself as Rex.

"I remember the first time I touched. A metal arm dropped a rubber ball down into my hand, and I felt it with my fingertips. It was soft, and I squeezed it. It was a small red rubber ball.

"I remember the first time I walked. I was helped by the arms of Rex. Rex helped raise me up, and I sat there looking about the white room in wonder. It was a small room, but to me, it was the world. You know it as the train car—the surgical suite in the caboose of Magnacourt's mobile lab. But I did not know until much later. There was always a vibration and hum and movement in this room. Later I learned it was the movement of the train.

"Rex fed me. My first food, more of a mush than a meal, was treasured. The first taste in my mouth, I ran it along my tongue, relishing every taste mixed with my first scent. It was so wonderful. As I ate, I was shown a number of videos. I learned of the Pyramid City from the images above me.

"Then the day came for Mother to visit me. Team Mother rushed in and shook my hand in great excitement. Rex had shown me my face before in a mirror, and I had seen video files of people's faces, even yours, but the sight of another human standing in front of me was the greatest joy to me. She greeted me with a warm smile. Then she looked upon me in amazement at my eloquent speech. Indeed, I have since been quite proud at my ability to master the English language.

"In time, Team Mother took me to her home and has since raised me here.

"I am so fortunate to be here today, Doctor Harlow.

"There really isn't much more to tell. It's all I can remember of my early life. Elise can tell you what came after.

"But, forgive me—I feel a bit remiss, as I have not offered you a drink. I suppose this guest room is as much my home as any. Would you... would you like a drink, Doctor Harlow?"

Candice caught herself staring at him. She couldn't say a word. He got up from his chair and reassuringly patted her on the shoulder. Then he walked toward the door.

"Would you like some tea?" he asked. "It's getting late."

"No," Candice said, averting her eyes as he turned around. She snapped herself out of it. "No, thank you."

"Perhaps coffee?" Then he chuckled. "I can make it decaf."

"No. No, that's all right."

What was it about him? He wasn't ugly. He was young in appearance, and his features were no less attractive than her own. He seemed healthy and full of life. But she could not get herself to look into his eyes, and she sensed that it hurt his feelings.

He shrugged his shoulders and walked back to the antique

wooden chairs and sat down across from her again. Then, after a long silence—

"It's all crazy, isn't it?"

"I don't understand."

"I know," he said with a laugh—an eerie, empty laugh. "It's so incredible, isn't it, Doctor Harlow?"

"No. I don't understand how you can talk so fluently. You can't be much older than a few months."

He nodded. Then he crouched down further under the city lights shining from the window, as if trying to get her attention with his eyes. She looked away.

"Rex had to help Elise with the project. He could not put his hands in the genetic modifications, but he could help with the neural network as I developed. Some of his neural designs were even adapted from your work in the university. Isn't that interesting? But Rex did most of it. It was not against his directive."

"So Rex helped you talk and think?"

"Yes," he said with a smile. She glanced at his thin eyebrows and hard cheekbones. Attractive—actually very attractive. She quickly looked away. "At least, so I've been told."

Candice nodded slowly. Then she turned to the window.

He leaned forward and touched her hand. Then he rubbed her fingers in the same manner that Elise often did.

"Don't do that," she said, pulling away.

"My apologies, Doctor Harlow. It's just that you look distressed, and I wanted to comfort you."

He's even suave. How can a creation only a handful of months old seem so intelligent? And is he manipulative? Or truly as empathetic as he acts?

"Why did Elise arrange this interview?" she said, more to herself than to the creature.

"I don't know. I did ask that we meet. I was so happy to

have met my mother, I wanted to meet my other mother as well." He smiled like a little child.

"I'm not your mother. I'm not your mother..."

She dared to look into his eyes. She froze as he stared at her. His eyes were warm and kind, but they were Elise's auburn-brown ovals, and his mouth even curled into Elise's infamous sly smile. She felt a connection, just as she had many times with Elise, and it felt sensual. That made Candice nervous. She regretted looking at him again and quickly turned away.

"When can we see Arkite?" he asked, changing the subject with the sudden excitement of a little boy. "I've seen pictures in the laboratory train. I am so excited about walking along the streets and among the buildings. I haven't been much farther than Mother's house. I want to see more. Perhaps we can even walk along Central Park?"

"Sure," Candice said absentmindedly.

She couldn't put her finger on why, exactly, but she wanted him gone. She suddenly wanted to get rid of him. She wanted to flush him. Her creation was better. There was nothing wrong with her baby. The baby was untainted. He was innocent and new. But Lazarus—there was something very wrong about him. He seemed to have Elise's guile and Rex's tongue. She even felt attracted to him and she felt that that was very wrong too. This was a creation— not only a creation, but her and Elise's creation. *Genetically* he was her son.

Maybe this was what a man was like? Candice had entertained this thought as he had told his tale of the lab. But she quickly refuted this. She had seen the history files of man's past. Men did not act like this. No, this creature was a plastic copy of a man. An image. An organic creature with the mind of a machine—precisely what she feared the future of her people could one day become.

Was that why Elise had wanted her to "interview" him? Had she come to the same conclusions?

"Are you all right, Doctor? You seem upset."

"It's just a lot. It's a lot to take in."

"I like to watch you think. You are a very thoughtful woman... and very beautiful."

She turned to him in surprise. He simply smiled again.

"Well, never mind the park," he said. "We can talk about that another time."

They spoke for many more hours. It became less of an interview and more of an education for Lazarus. He squeezed every bit of knowledge he could out of her, asking constant questions about the most trivial things. She humored him, too fascinated to dismiss his company.

She was not sure when she fell asleep. It must have been late.

She awoke in the wooden chair with a long white blanket draped over her. Light was falling from the top of the great Pyramid of Arkite and lighting the entire city below. The light shone through the window and made Candice squint her eyes. For a moment, she trembled in fear at the possibility that she would awaken in the creature's arms.

She walked out of the guest room and into the kitchen of Elise's grand penthouse.

Elise and Lazarus were sitting next to each other talking loudly by the kitchenette table. The metal island had been lowered and was serving as a round breakfast table. Candice watched as Elise's head bobbed up and down in great guffaws at her guest.

It was bright. Light from the floor-to-ceiling window on the first floor was shining on the island and dining table. The smell of bacon and eggs permeated the room.

Elise was wearing a long white nightgown with slippers. Her hair was tied back haphazardly behind her head. Lazarus wore his same black cloak, but he had his hood back now, clearly showing his bald head. He was waving a fork around and explaining something apparently quite amusing to Mother. Then Elise cocked her head and saw Candice.

"Well, look who the cat dragged in," she remarked.

Lazarus turned. All her efforts at shielding his eyes from her were suddenly foiled in the brightly lit white kitchen. His brown eyes stared at her. Not only that, he flashed her the same exact expression as her Team Mother. It was like two twins turning and smiling at her.

"Good morning," Candice said sheepishly. She carried her small leather handbag and placed it on the table. She took out a stick of gum.

"Morning," Elise said.

"Good morning, Doctor Harlow."

"She has you calling her Doctor Harlow?" Elise asked. "That's ridiculous. No child calls his mother *doctor*."

"He does if his mother made him in a lab," quipped Candice, throwing the Mint in her mouth.

Elise flashed her an angry frown.

"She's quite right, Elise," said the creature sternly. "I am the creation of you both. And as much a part of Candice as of you."

It was the first time he had called her Candice.

"Did you know," he said, turning to Elise and suddenly jovial, "that Candice spent the whole night educating me about our world? She answered every one of my innumerable dumb questions."

"She's your mother for patience, Lazarus," Elise said. Elise gestured for Candice to give her a stick too. "I'm the mother here to teach you how to manipulate—and to look good doing it."

Elise burst into laughter, and Lazarus joined her.

Candice shook her head, threw Elise some gum, and walked over to an uneaten plate of bacon and eggs across from them on the other side of the table. It was, apparently, hers. She took out the gum, saved it on a napkin for later, and used a fork to gather some eggs.

"In all seriousness," Lazarus said. He looked deep into Candice's eyes and it made her freeze. "Thank you for spending the night with me. It was very educational."

"*Really?*" asked Elise, chewing. "*Spending the night? Educational?* What did you two get up to in my guest room?"

Lazarus raised an eyebrow at Elise.

"He already told you," Candice replied. "Nothing suspicious. Just talked."

"Really? How boring."

But then Elise and Lazarus looked into each other's eyes again, as if sharing a great secret. When that look finally registered in Candice's mind, she understood. Then she lost her appetite. She dropped her fork and pushed her plate away in disgust. Lazarus was not as innocent as he had acted, and it wasn't hard to guess who had educated him about the other things.

Elise chewed enough Mint to apparently get her fix, then did the same as Candice, sticking the gum on her plate for later.

"Can you give us a moment alone, Lazarus?" Candice asked. "Of course." He nodded and headed back to the guest room. Candice waited until she heard the guest room door close.

Then she whirled around to Elise, who was nonchalantly sopping up her eggs with a biscuit.

"Disgusting," Candice said.

Elise looked up with a furrowed brow. For a moment, she thought that Candice was referring to her eating habits.

"Disgusting," Candice repeated and walked up to her. "Hmm? What?"

Candice wagged a finger at Elise, as Elise had been known to constantly do to her. "How could you do this? Just when I think you've sunk to the lowest low, you drop even more."

"What the hell are you talking about, Candy?"

"You know damn well what I'm talking about."

Elise squinted at her. She looked confused, but then she nodded and smiled. "Oh... *that*. Yeah... I mean, I fucked him. How could I not, Candy? Look at him. Didn't you?"

"What's the matter with you?" Candice asked. "Are you permanently high on Mint!"

"Candy," Elise said, chuckling. "Candy, it's no big deal."

"I can't do this with you," Candice said. "Don't show me any more. I don't want to be a part of your circus."

"What circus?"

"You've got a stuffed doll of yourself on his bed where you're fucking him!" Candice shouted. "He's your son!"

"What?" Elise furrowed her brow. "What are you talking about? Oh." She laughed. "That's you, dear. Didn't you notice the Goldilocks hair? I thought it was cute."

Candice walked back to where she had left her purse. She picked up the small black leather handbag and tucked it under her arm.

Elise took a strip of bacon from her plate and stood up. Then she wagged the strip before her. "You need to lighten up, Candy-can. The fact is, he's quite handsome... and he's very well endowed." She laughed. "You should see what he's got down there. Maybe you should try him. It beats anything we've ever used together."

Candice slammed her hand down on the table. Then she took her plate and all of its remaining contents and threw it at Elise's face.

"Fuck!"

The yolk of the eggs dripped from Elise's neck and chest. She had wanted to toss the wine at her the night before, but she'd known it was ill advised. Now, her anger had boiled over, and she didn't care.

She didn't wait for a response. She ran straight for the door.

She would have escaped had it not been for Lazarus. Once again, he stood towering above her in front of the door.

"Are you leaving?" he asked, almost hurt. He had his hood down and seemed to gaze down at her like a child.

"I... I have to. I'm sorry, Lazarus. It was nice meeting you." "When will I see you again?"

"I don't know."

She pushed him and waved her hand by the sensor of the door.

It opened.

"Goodbye, then, Candice Harlow. It was a real pleasure meeting you."

She rushed down the hallway but could not resist a glance back at him when she reached the elevator. He was standing by the door, with the kindest smile. *Her* smile. And it grew even larger as she looked at him. She jumped in the elevator and left.

22

THE NEW PROCLAMATION

Candy met Sara at the main parking lot at Sunny Side Raymond's. Sara greeted her and helped her with her visor and gray bike out of habit. But Sara wasn't there to assist her; she was there to accompany her. Candice threw back her blond hair after handing Sara the visor. Her hair was still not long enough, but now every grown inch was treasured after having previously lost it. It had taken four months to grow back a reasonable amount of hair since prison, but it would take much longer for her mane to fall back down below her shoulders. Hand in hand, they walked into the building.

Elise had asked that Candice meet her. Something was really important.

It was a little after nine. Beside the parking lot on the fourth floor, all the lights of the surrounding skyscrapers lit up the sky. It was warm, approaching summer.

They joined other Officers in climbing down the four flights of stairs. Many of them stared at Candice in her gray leather jumpsuit, in awe at the sight of a Savant. By now, she was so used to the attention that she took very little notice. But Sara noticed, and she clutched her shoulder even tighter, as if to claim her as her own.

On the bottom level, a line of citizens formed for a whole block, rounding into a nearby alley. Candice and Sara walked beside the line all the way to the entrance. They knew that Savants were permitted immediate entry.

She had never seen Raymond's bustling with so much commotion. Many had heard rumors about the reason for Mother's party, but no one was sure. Not even Candice had been told. Even the two side ramps were covered with people, blocking their passage up to the balcony floor. As the two of them were led by a gold-gilded maître d' up a private elevator toward the top floor, Sara would not stop pleading with Candice to tell her. Even the maître d' perked up, waiting for the precious gossip.

"I don't know. I just don't know."

"If you don't want to tell me, I understand, Candy. I'm not a Savant, after all."

"No, I really don't know," Candice said.

As the elevator doors opened, the sounds of crowds rushed in. Every seat and every corner of the club was filled. It was as if every leader from all four sectors was packed into the club. Raymond's was a very large establishment, but all the codes in the book were probably broken in order to pack so many hundreds of people in one place.

Candice bit her lip and amusingly thought, *I didn't miss Elise's birthday again, did I? No, it can't be that.*

"I saved a special table for you, Doctor Harlow," said the maître d'. "It was reserved by Mother herself."

It was a booth close to the center of the club on the balcony floor. They walked down the aisle and then ascended some steps to the booth. Everyone surrounding them stared. And it was odd to have such a large booth that could easily fit eight people for just Candice and Sara when everyone else was packed shoulder to shoulder. The only other table that was empty was the central one: Elise's. Candice and Sara sat beside each other in the center of the booth.

"Would you two like a drink?" asked the maître d'.

Candice dipped into her pants pocket and brought out a pack of gum. She handed a stick to Sara. Sara thanked her but stowed the precious gum in the pocket of her black sport jacket.

Candice looked down at the stage. Strangely, there was no performance. Instead, perhaps anticipating Mother's announcement, it was covered by people sitting in rows of chairs. Then she realized she had not answered the maître d'.

The maître d' looked familiar, but Candice couldn't quite place her. "I'll have a vodka martini," she said.

The maître d' smiled a large smile. "All right, Savant Harlow."

Then she recognized her. Her name was Nandalay. She was a sweet young Asian girl from Sector Two who used to work in Magnacourt's embryo farm. She was quite bright, but never bright enough to be a lead scientist or Savant. She was tiny and bald and had brown skin under the glistening gold sparkle paint. Nandalay had always been partial to Candice. Candice had helped her land her other science job. Now Candice felt like it was a shame. Nandalay had been transferred and was now working as one of the helpers in the club. Well, at least it was Raymond's.

"It's good to see you, Nandalay," Candice said.

"You too, Master." Nandalay smiled and turned to Sara. "And you, sweetie? What would you like?"

"How are things?" interrupted Candice before Sara could answer.

"Good, Savant Harlow," Nandalay said. "The pay's good here," she added as if to excuse her shame in losing her job. "Really it is, Savant Harlow."

"I'm glad. This is my girlfriend, Sara."

"Hi, Sara," Nandalay said. "And what would you like?"

"The same."

"You two look cute together," Nandalay said with a nod.

Then she crouched closer to Candice. "Master," she whispered. "Do you know what this is all about?"

"No. I have no idea."

Nandalay believed her as much as Sara had. She winked and walked off.

Sara reclined back in the booth and closed her eyes. "Thanks, Candy."

"For what?" Candice asked with a chuckle.

"Thanks for inviting me. I could spend the rest of the night just lying back in these cushions." Raymond's was comfortable, there was no doubt about that. Each booth was made of the finest soft upholstery in the whole city. Candice rubbed Sara's hand.

"Of course, Sara."

Sara half opened an eye and looked down at the hand holding hers. "You know, Candy, you're not like the others. I don't know any other Savants who would even associate with me."

Candice shrugged. "There's nothing special about us. And after all my work in the lab this week, I've really been looking forward to being with you."

"Honey, that's fine." Sara closed her eyes again as if she were reclining in a sauna. She picked up Candice's hand and kissed it. Candice giggled and gazed at the menu on her wrist. She wondered if Sara actually intended on going to sleep. She wouldn't have minded if she did.

Sara was one of the only peaceful things left in her life. All the work and toil, and now there was plenty from Team Mother, made her relish every spare moment with the girl. Yet Sara could not get herself to break from the false view of class that permeated Arkite. To Sara, she was a worker, Candice was not. It was the only thing Candice didn't like about her. Sara was blinded by class, but Candice wasn't. She wished Sara could just be Sara and forget all about it.

Candice leaned over her side and gently kissed Sara on the

lips. Sara didn't open her eyes, but she squeezed her hand tighter and smiled. Candice giggled again.

As Candice reflected, her mind was disturbed by a ruckus developing below. Sara woke up at the noise. Crowds were standing beside their chairs on the lower stage and cheering madly over something.

It was Elise. She was dressed more gaudily than ever with a long black cape over her usual red leather Savant rocket cycle jumpsuit, holding the hands of another person in black: their creation, Lazarus. Lazarus had on that same dark cloak he had worn when Candice had first met him, hood covering his head.

Candice turned to Sara, whose eyes were wide open, glancing down and then over at Candice. She seemed certain Candice knew what this was all about. But she didn't. She truly didn't.

What are you doing, Elise! LAZARUS? In public! Have you lost your mind?

Holding hands, Elise and Lazarus walked slowly down a central aisle of chairs. Three Officers marched ahead, and three behind, clearing the crowds. Everyone in the large hall was lost in excitement.

Then music erupted, accompanied by pyrotechnics with flames encircling the couple in a magnificent fiery tunnel, while green and violet lights sparkled behind Officers trailing them. Fireworks shot up the five stories, exploding over Candice and Sara's heads. Then came a train from behind. The train was an illusion of the red HQ laboratory train, and it slowly snaked its way, first along the periphery of the building, then twisting and turning through the audience's seats below. The shadowy image kept zigzagging along the stage below as Elise and Lazarus walked across the stage, while Elise's guards cleared the people from rushing them. Elise's pyrotechnics really riled up the crowd, and they all seemed to want to touch her.

Candice saw that a few caught a glimpse of the "monster" under the hood. Their reaction was hard to explain. It wasn't fear. It wasn't curiosity. It wasn't shock. It was almost a look of numbness, as if they could not believe their eyes and preferred to pretend like they hadn't seen anything. Candice knew the feeling.

She looked over at Sara. Sara glanced back, seemingly still hurt at Candice's lack of an explanation.

The explosions and train disappeared. The crowds looked up towards the upper booths, then spotlights followed, even shining for a moment over their own table. Candice turned from the light, not liking the attention.

Finally, the couple and their guards pushed their way up the ramp to the balcony. The crowds were clamoring terribly around them along the aisle on their way to the booth. Then, just as Candice and Sara had done, Elise and Lazarus slowly climbed the steps up the central booth beside them.

Elise nodded to Candice and blew a kiss. She gave Sara a disapproving look.

A large and gaudy sparkly diamond-and-ruby-studded microphone fell from the ceiling into Mother's hand as she stood. She signaled for Lazarus to sit. Even sitting, the man was nearly her height. Lazarus nodded his hooded head to Candice.

A giant image projected along the five-story window across from them, and everyone in the club turned around to look at it. It showed a magnified view of the central booth. Candice figured it was being broadcast throughout all of Arkite, so that every citizen would know of Elise's important announcement.

"Welcome, citizens!" Elise said with a broad grin. Everyone's eyes were still fixed on the image over the window instead of the actual booth where Elise spoke. Candice was relieved. It took a lot of eyes off her. "I have a wonderful announcement."

More cheers.

Their martinis arrived. Nandalay, nearly falling as she held the drinks while staring at the projection, absentmindedly handed the drinks to Candice and Sara. Candice mused that if she were Elise, the waitress would never have been so distracted.

"A few months ago..."

Tell me she's not going to announce Lazarus. Please! Please, don't do that!

Elise turned to Candice and winked.

Oh shit, she is!

"With the help of my Chief Savant, Doctor Harlow, Magnacourt was able to make the greatest creation ever created. I spent many months nourishing and teaching it."

That you did, you whore.

Candice looked back at the projection. The image of Elise was, literally, larger than life, and her voice echoed through the club.

Elise had given many speeches in her past as Team Mother. The vast majority had been made from her "office" on the third floor of her penthouse. But she had rarely spoken in public. She must have figured that introducing Lazarus required such spectacle—if that was what she was about to do.

"As you all know," Elise continued, "Chief Savant Harlow's development of genetic recombining has allowed the mainframe to enhance or alter the genetic makeup of us all. And thanks to Savant Harlow, our current research involved just that—teasing out the damage to all of our bodies and allowing us to repair them, reverse aging, and live forever. The Lazarus Project. Its success has all been because of Doctor Candice Harlow."

The club thundered in applause. Candice's face burned bright as the camera turned to her. She saw a vision of herself, looking quite uncomfortable, before all of Raymond's. Unlike her boss, she didn't like the attention. She hated it.

Sara raised her martini to her. Sara was quite the opposite, seeming to like looking at herself. Then, thankfully, the image turned back to Elise.

"Anywho, in all of our experimentations, we developed something else in Magnacourt. Something quite wonderful." She turned to Lazarus, who sat with his hood pulled down over his face. "Lazarus, please pull back your hood and show Arkite your lovely face."

He did.

Candice had expected more cheers. Instead, at the sight of Lazarus projected hundreds of feet tall on the screen across from them, looking out with his thoughtful, kind eyes—her gentle eyes, but Elise's color—the club fell silent. No one spoke or even dared move.

Candice looked at Sara. The martini in her hand was shaking.

"Say hello, Lazarus," Elise said with a smile.

"Hello."

And that was even worse. The baritone voice sounded uncomfortably like that of Rex.

Murmuring enveloped the building. Candice looked at the other booths full of the competing Savants. Some of the more experienced ones were looking toward the screen with expressions of utter joy. Likely, they guessed this would ruin Elise.

Then Candice heard the letters "XY" spoken on all sides. At first, it was almost a whisper. Then citizens and Savants alike began chanting the letters in disgust and rage, becoming louder and louder: "XY! XY! XY! XY!"

Elise raised her hands. The camera focused on her again. But despite the entire room of dissenters, her smile was as confident as ever.

Sara spilled her drink.

"Now, now, everyone. Please calm yourselves."

"XY! XY! XY!" echoed the crowd. "XY! XY! XY!"

"Please, everybody," Elise said with a thin grin. "Don't let fear get the best of you. Lazarus is the gentlest of men you will ever meet."

At the word *men*, the shouting grew fiercer still.

"Come, come, everyone," Elise chided. "You're not letting me get to my important announcement!"

Announcement? There's more! She still has something more to tell?

Then it happened, so fast that Candice didn't have time to react.

A loud crack echoed through the hall and sent Elise reeling down on the cushion of her booth. Candice turned from the projection and saw Nandalay, a pistol in her outstretched hand, standing on the steps beside Elise's booth. Smoke rose from the barrel.

Chaos erupted. People began stampeding and falling over each other as they tried to get out of the club. Candice leapt down from the steps of her booth and pushed her way through to Elise's.

As she ran up the steps of Elise's booth, she saw Lazarus lunge at Nandalay. More shots rang out, but they didn't hit Lazarus— or, if they did, they didn't stop him. Lazarus grabbed Nandalay and dragged her down the steps. His expression was contorted in the worst rage she could imagine. He shoved people out of his way, even the guards, until he reached the aisle under the booths. Candice wasn't sure what Lazarus was up to until he lifted Nandalay over the rail and tossed her to the stage fifty feet below. The nearby Officers were too shocked to stop him. All of this was caught on the camera and broadcast from the projection as people continued to trample over each other in their haste to exit the club.

Candice made it to Elise. She was lying on the booth with her eyes closed. Candice assumed she was dead, but then she saw her hand move. Blood covered the right side of her red jumpsuit. The colors practically matched each other, and it was difficult for Candice to determine how bad the wound was. The source of the blood was along her flank near her right sixth rib. She figured the bullet had passed there and Elise's right lung was blown. She only hoped Elise could hang on. Elise's lips, painted red, didn't reveal much either, but Candice imagined the blood had left them. Candice reached down and felt for a pulse along her neck. It was weak, but there.

"Murderer!" came Lazarus's amplified voice. "Murderer! You dare murder our Mother!"

Candice glanced at the window. Lazarus's image was captured there, his face twisted in pain and rage as a group of Officers struggled to hold him.

"How dare she kill my mother!" Lazarus shouted. "Take her body, take it and tear it to shreds for all I care! It deserves no respect!" As if the words had come from Elise herself, the people on the stage below obeyed, tossing Nandalay's broken body around like a rag doll.

Candice looked away. She ran a hand down Elise's cheek.

For a moment, Mother opened her eyes. She seemed to be trying to laugh.

"And I didn't even...," Elise said, gasping for air and coughing. Blood dripped from her lips. "Didn't even get to the part..." Candice shushed her, but as usual, Elise ignored her. "The part where I... ask you to marry me."

23

AFTER VISITING HOURS

Candice arrived at the main hospital in Sector One, Angel of Hope, late the next day. She hadn't bothered to change her clothes. She had ridden with the medics in the ambulance, but then, when all had seemed as if it was in order, she'd quietly left. She preferred to spend the day in the lab. Normally, she would have lost herself in her work, but she had been so exhausted, physically and emotionally, that she had slept the day away.

Two Officers accompanied her on her way to Elise's room, their boots echoing along the whitewashed walls. Security had become thick since the assassination attempt, and the bald-headed trench coat guards insisted. Even outside buildings, the number of drones had tripled since the attack.

Candice had mixed feelings as she walked down the halls of the hospital. Part of her hoped Elise was already dead. It would free her. But then, if Elise died, she might be crowned the new Team Mother. That would be even worse than her imprisonment. Alternatively, perhaps the other Lead Savants, like Dana, might take control and throw Candice back in prison or kill her.

Another part of her cared for Elise. It was the part she

shunned nearly as much as she shunned Lazarus. She even felt a small tug of attraction, but she tried to turn from it, for it sickened her. The only way she could ever love Elise was to be a victim of her sadomasochistic horror show.

Yeah, maybe it would better for everyone if Elise just died.

Candice reached into a pocket to satisfy her increased craving for Mint.

"The part where I... ask you to marry me..."

You must be joking! I wouldn't marry you even if you hung me by my toes and roasted my skin for the rest of my living days (and you would too, wouldn't you, bitch?).

Perhaps it had all worked out for the best. What would have happened if Elise had proposed to her in front of all of Arkite... and she had said no? Maybe she would have been the one Lazarus threw over the rail.

She found the right hallway. More Officers in their black coats guarded the door. They stood to attention at the sight of Candice. She smiled a fake smile. Then the door slid open.

Elise couldn't have looked any better. She was lying in bed with Lazarus sitting beside her. He was laughing hysterically at something she had said. Lazarus had a cast over his left arm—apparently, he had been shot—but he looked as vibrant as ever. Candice noticed for the first time that short blond hairs were beginning to sprout on his bald head.

"Ah, Candice," said Lazarus with a nod. "She's getting along better, but do please be careful—she's still weak."

"Candy!" cried Elise, opening her arms.

Elise wore an ugly mint-green hospital gown under white sheets with cords running all over her chest that were connected to machines along the walls of the small room. There were no windows, but it was very bright nevertheless thanks to the artificial yellow lights along the walls. Elise had on spectacles, which Candice thought was a bit odd. The color had returned to her face.

"Hi, Mom. You feeling better?" Candice asked, giving her a gentle hug.

"With you two, how can I ask for more?"

Candice pushed herself away and stood over the hospital bed. Then she couldn't help her scientific brain's curiosity. She looked at the devices about her. She ran her hand along the IV and checked the plastic bags leading down to Elise's arm. Then she gave an inward smirk at her devious imagined plans: *Maybe just a little potassium in the arm would help her recover?*

Candice turned to Lazarus. The man was looking down with so much concern and worry that it was almost comical. And Elise turned to him, seemingly lapping it up.

"Would you leave us, Lazarus?" Candice asked. "I'd like to spend some time alone with her."

"*Alone*, Candy?" asked Elise, turning back to her with a great big smile.

Shit, she is better, isn't she?

"Sure, Candy," Lazarus said.

He had never called her Candy before.

He got up, towering above them as usual. He leaned down and gave Mother a long, very long, kiss on the lips. And then he walked out.

"You got some gum, honey?" Elise asked when he had gone.

Rex spoke before Candice could say anything. "You cannot chew any Mint right now, Mother. It will slow the healing."

"Shit." Elise pouted, turning away.

"How is she doing, Doc?" Candice asked.

"She'll recover fine, Candice," Rex said. "There was a pneumothorax, but I introduced a chest tube. Now she is on antibiotics to prevent infection. But, as we all know, Elise is strong. She'll be fine."

"Yeah, we all know she's strong," Candice said, looking down at her.

Elise gestured quietly for some gum again.

Candice shook her head.

"How much longer will she be here?" Candice asked. "Another day, as long as there is no infection. As long as the wound heals. Then she can rest at home."

When Candice looked back down, Elise was still gesturing insistently for some gum.

What do I care what it'll do to you? Fine!

Candice rolled her eyes and handed her a stick.

"You know, Candy," Elise said, carefully chewing quietly, "as Chief Savant, you have all rights to my position right now. You could leave this room and dictate all kinds of shit throughout the city as the people's Team Mother. People would accept your rule."

"Why would I do that? You'd simply reverse everything the minute you get out of here."

"True," Elise said with a laugh. She winced in pain. "That's true." Elise searched the room and then looked at a plastic cup by the bedside. "Would you be a dear and get me my coffee?" She could have reached for it herself.

God, don't ever get old, Elise.

Candice handed the plastic cup to her.

"Oh, and can you get me a straw?"

There was a straw on the tray beside the bed too. Candice rolled her eyes and got the straw.

Then Elise signaled for Candice to sit. She grudgingly sat on the edge of the bed. Elise grabbed her hand and ran her fingers over the bones of Candice's hand as she always did. "Did you see what he did for me?" Elise asked breathlessly.

"Hmm? Who?"

"Lazarus. I didn't. I was unconscious. But when I reviewed the footage this morning, I witnessed my big hero. I've never seen such devotion."

"You're his mother," Candice said with a shrug.

"No. Come on. I'm your mother, too."

"What are you suggesting?" Candice asked, pulling her hand back. "That I didn't care? I ran through the crowd to help you. That monster might have charged the shooter and killed her, but I ran to you, Elise."

"Yeah," Elise said, looking up at the ceiling with dreamy eyes. "He's really smitten with me, you know." Then she looked back at Candice. "The only problem is, I'm not smitten with him. You understand, Candy-can?"

Elise smiled slyly at her. A lump developed in Candice's throat. She knew well where that smile was heading.

"I'm glad you're feeling better," Candice said, jumping up.

Candice ran a hand through her short blond hair. The shortness of it always reminded her of her newfound hatred toward Elise. It seemed Elise noticed.

"Are you ever going to forgive me, Candy-can-can?"

"It depends on what you're referring to."

"For imprisoning you. That was really shitty. But, you know, I felt my hands were tied."

"Elise," Candice said, whirling back to meet her eyes. "I'm not upset over that. I'm upset over what happened to Bren."

"Oh, God," Elise said, looking away. She seemed to be about to laugh, but stopped, likely afraid it would hurt.

In the heat of the moment, Elise chewed her gum harder. She forgot about concealing it.

"Mother," Rex said, his voice louder but still without inflection. "I told you not to chew Mint. You cannot chew and expect to get better. Spit it out right away."

"How did you even know it was me and not Candice?"

"I've been tracking the sounds. It did not coincide with Savant Harlow's conversation."

"You fucking smart fucker!" Elise said, spitting it out into the cup.

"I'm going to go back to the lab," said Candice. She took the tray and placed it closer to Elise and then headed for the door.

"Wait. Did you... did you think about my proposal?"

Candice had hoped that she had been too delirious to have remembered.

"Yes."

"So, what of it, Candy-can? You know, if we were married, you would no longer have to fear me. We'd be family."

"So... you want me to marry you so that I no longer fear you?"

"No," Elise said. "No, that's not what I meant." And there was a vulnerability in her frustration. Candice felt pity for her and hated herself for that. "No, Candice. I meant—"

"I know what you meant, Elise, but this is hardly the time."

"Yeah, you're probably right. I just... I just want you to know that I really care about you, you know. I'm kinda smitten by you."

"I know, Elise."

"Yeah," she said with a smile, seemingly relieved she didn't have to say anything else. "And I didn't mean what I said about Lazarus. I watched the video. I saw you rush to me too, babe."

"We all care about you. We all want you to get better, Mother."

Somehow those words didn't make Elise feel better. They seemed cold and aloof.

"Goodbye, Candy. Don't work too hard in the lab."

Candice stood by the door and nodded. "I think I'll map it out pretty soon. Rex is helping. It's just difficult to match all the gene variants with the population."

"Good. I know you'll succeed."

Candice had her hand over the door latch.

"Wait, Candy."

Candice turned.

"Do you think you'd like that helper, what's her name...

Sara, to help you? Perhaps she'd be a good assistant. We can make her a Savant."

"No," Candy said quickly. Candice didn't want Elise's fingers anywhere near Sara.

"All right," Elise said with a brightened smile. Candice knew Elise was jealous of Sara and had thrown out the suggestion to be polite, not for Candice to actually say yes.

Candice held back shaking her head. She did it inwardly, like she did with most things. She opened the latch, the door slid open, and she walked out.

Lazarus was pacing the hallway. He towered over the Officers.

"Candy," he said with a smile when she emerged. "Do you think she'll be all right?"

Is he dumb? She's going to be fine.

"Yes. She's feeling better, Lazarus. Don't worry about it."

He nodded. But then he started pacing again.

The Officers gave him a wide berth. She could see that they were terrified of him.

24

THE PARADE

Wearing a false smile, Candice waved to the masses. Team Mother stood beside her. Of course, Candice knew the cheers were for Elise, not her, but she kept waving as the motorcade proceeded down Main Street. The street, normally deserted by all but a handful of automated cars, was lined with citizens standing along the sidewalks. Elise had been warned by all the other Lead Savants not to do it, but she had ignored them. The recent assassination attempt made Candice nervous too, and she kept looking through the crowds for any sign of a gun or knife. Drones hovered overhead, and that gave some extra assurance.

They stood on a stage erected on a long flatbed semitruck. Officers in black boots, heavy black trench coats, and small caps patrolled the stage, their eyes hidden behind shaded visors.

Candice had been uncertain what Magnacourt's place in the world would be after the assassination attempt. She had to remind herself repeatedly that Elise had broken the law and showed her people an XY. This, according to her own rules, would mean at the very least imprisonment, as had been done to her predecessor, Doctor Reyburn, and to Candice herself.

But as the weeks passed, nothing happened. In fact, it almost seemed to be another part of Elise's master plan. People were so overjoyed at her recovery that no one questioned her about Lazarus. The horror everyone had so loudly expressed when Elise had revealed what she had done and introduced Lazarus seemed to have vanished at the moment he'd flung Nandalay to her death. Now he was viewed as a hero, not a monster.

The people had forgiven Elise, but did Candice?

"They love us, Candy!" Elise shouted, cocking her head back. "They adore us!"

"They love you, Mother."

Elise nodded and smiled. Candice had never seen Elise so happy before.

Candice looked down at her dress. She was wearing a shameless mix of rainbow swirling colors—the most audacious outfit she had ever worn. She felt like a peacock. The contrast with Mother's all-black skirt and trademark guillotine choker made her feel self-conscious and ridiculous.

Candice watched as the skyscrapers slowly rolled by. She was used to rushing by them on her rocket cycle. She had never traveled down Main Street so slowly before.

Main Street ended at the Arc de Triomphe before Central Park. Then their "float" turned and rode down one of the side streets. Soon they turned into a private alley. Elise and Candice were helped down by the Officers, then the two of them were whisked away to a black flying transport car. It was done so quickly that no one except the Officers saw them switch cars. Candice realized that it was for protection. The car took off into the sky, and the noise from the shouting crowds dwindled, fading into the quiet hum of the white-leather-upholstered Officer's car.

Elise sat across from her. They were alone. She lifted her shoulders up against the couch and reclined back. Then she squinted into Candice's eyes. Candice made nearly the same motions, leaning back in the comfortable cushions.

"Well, that was fun, huh, Candy?"

"Sure, Elise," Candice said, closing her eyes.

"You're not gonna sleep after all that, are you? It was... exhilarating."

"I'm glad you liked it."

Elise laughed. "Yeah."

Candice felt the faint rumble under her feet as the car tipped upward in its launch over the city. Candice shot a glance at the streets below. She had never seen so many people massed along the sidewalks and roads before.

She closed her eyes again.

"Did you know Nandalay?" Elise asked.

Candice's eyes opened wide. That question was one of the only things that could have shocked her at that moment. Elise had a knack for finding just the right words to jar her. Why would Elise bring Nandalay up now?

"A little... I helped get her the job at Magnacourt working under Bren. Bren introduced me."

"Ah. Of course she would."

"Why?" asked Candice, sitting up straighter.

"Because, Candy, she was her sister. Nandalay Kelley. Didn't you know?"

Candice sat up completely straight. "Her sister?"

"Yep." Elise smiled her typical sly smile, used so often that it seemed painted on her black made-up face. "Doctor Nandalay Kelley. I should have figured she'd be upset over the death of her sister. Rex tipped me off to her odd behavior, so I fired her from Magnacourt only a few weeks before that night. That"—she raised a finger in thought—"was a mistake. It probably only pissed her off more."

"I see. But I don't recall her name being Kelley. I think it was... Saunter, or Summer or something. I don't remember. But it wasn't Kelley. Besides, why wouldn't Bren tell me?"

"She changed her name, dope. And Bridg-bitch didn't want her sister involved with Magnacourt," Elise said with a shrug. "Apparently, Bridg-bitch didn't like our company." She grinned and winked. "Can't see why."

Candice had thought nothing else could surprise her, but she had been wrong. "I can't believe it. She was so... nice."

"Yeah, right." Elise gave a disdainful snort. "Real nice. And now I have a hole in my chest. And we have a motive, right? I gotta tell you, sometimes you don't have a very good sense of people, Candy. Too bad Lazarus finished her off. I think I would have enjoyed having a little talk with her." With that, Elise leaned back in the leather cushions as if the subject was over.

"She was nice," Candice repeated.

"She nearly killed me, bitch," snapped Elise. But then she smiled again as Candice looked at her. "She got what she deserved, Can. We can all sleep more soundly now."

Then Elise got up, pulled off her black coat, steadied herself from the midair turns of the aircraft, and sat down beside Candice. She ran her hand though Candice's blond hair, which was finally returning to its former length. She kissed her on the cheek.

"Perhaps I got my just deserts, Candice?" she asked. "Seems I was punished. You wanted that. Now it's done. I went many sleepless nights not even able to fucking breathe."

"Yeah," Candice said, unable to hold back a smile.

"You know," Elise said, scooting closer, "flying above Arkite like this can be quite relaxing. I know it's daytime, but in the clouds... I... I could dim the windows and it'd just be me and you. Me and you in the clouds, Candy-can-can."

"Yeah."

That was enough. Elise looked up while holding Candice's hands. "Dim the lights and shut the shutters on the windows, Rex... and don't land yet. Circle around for a while."

"Yes, Mother."

Elise led her fingers over Candice's shoulders and unstrapped the dress.

"I hate this dress, Elise," she said with a frown, backing away. "Why did you make me wear this crap?"

"I need people to look at you. Most usually do. I mean, you're attractive as hell but, now that you are to be my Queen, I *really* want them to look at you."

She placed a hand behind her head and pulled her close, into her lips. Then she teased her tongue over hers and played for a while inside her mouth. Gently, Elise ran her hands behind Candice's shoulders again and tugged at the dress, pulling it up to her chest. Elise ran her hand along her stomach and thigh. "Let's get it off since you hate it so much."

"Why didn't *you* wear it?"

"Shh... people already stare at me, Candy. I needed them to look at their Queen."

Then she pulled the ugly flowery rainbow lace dress from Candice's neck. Candice sat there on the white leather cushions in only her black lace bra and panties. Elise's eyes opened wider and her breathing grew heavier. Elise unzipped her own skirt from behind and pulled it off. She wasn't wearing a bra. Candice's heart started thumping.

"It's been a long time since we did this, Candy. I miss you. I miss you so fucking much."

Candice had promised she never would do it again. Never. She had promised herself after watching Elise shoot their baby in cold blood and kill her friend. She would never let her touch her. Never again. NEVER!

Elise got on her knees and removed Candice's bra. She leaned down and began licking her stomach, running her tongue from her belly button down to her panties while caressing her breasts. She played with Candice's hard nipples with her fingers as she kissed and licked hungrily at her panties, pulling at the lace with her teeth. Never. Never again.

Elise yanked off Candice's panties with her hands and fell back down on her, kissing her between the legs.

"I hope you can... forgive me," Elise said.

Candice closed her eyes as her body involuntarily lurched up toward Elise's lips.

"Forgive me... I can repay... you. I... can."

Elise kissed and licked more vigorously. Her tongue flicked up and down. Up and down. It felt sooo good to Candice. Up and down. Up and down. Licking and biting and pulling. Candice lost herself behind the tingling between her legs. She wanted more and more.

"Forgive me—"

"Shut up. Just shut up... don't stop. Don't—"

She arched her back to bring herself closer to Elise's mouth.

Then Elise pulled away and ran her hand along Candice's wet pussy. Elise gently pushed a finger in. In and out. Again and again. In and out. In and out.

"I love you, Candy," Elise said, adding a second finger, and then a third. "I love you so much."

Again and again...

NEVER AGAIN!

Candice came in a torrent of pleasure and shame. Then, even before her body had ceased trembling, she pulled Elise to her, breast against breast, embracing her tight. Candice thrust her tongue hard into Elise's mouth.

"I love you," Elise said again when she was able to speak.

Candice excitedly pulled down Elise's panties and pushed her back on the white couch.

"You don't have to," Elise said, shaking her head. "Mine was payment. Please, Candy."

Candice batted her hand away and rubbed her hands along Elise's naked chest and stomach, massaging her front. Elise closed her eyes. Candice found the scar on her right side and gently ran a finger over it. It was red—still fresh. Candice ran her tongue down the scar and then kissed it. She felt Elise lurch and tighten under her. She kissed her belly button and ran her lips down to her hips. Then she plunged her face between Elise's legs. Elise groaned.

She rubbed Elise as Elise had rubbed her. She looked up and watched Elise's lips quiver as her back arched in pleasure.

Never again! NEVER!

"I fucking love you, Candy. I... love you... I love you soooo fucking much!"

Never... again... and again.

25

WORK AND LEISURE

Candice lay on a white towel on a grassy knoll. She was wearing sunglasses and a red swimsuit. It was midday, and the sun shone through the opening at the top of the Pyramid. A number of women with their little girls were playing tag or catching and throwing balls nearby, laughing with joy.

Candice leaned on an elbow and yawned. Ahead, down the incline of the knoll, a quaint arched stone bridge crossed a stream. The stream was lined with well-manicured red and white flowers, perfectly set in rows. To Candice's left was the artificial lake Salmas. Some women were sailing gently along the water. Behind her were trees crowded so closely together as to block her view of the surrounding skyscrapers. Yet above it all, and to her right, she could see the high-rises of Arkite and Main Street. It was beautiful. She adored Central Park.

Beside her, Sara yawned. Candice was surprised. She had thought the girl was sleeping.

Sara was wearing a red bikini and sunglasses that matched Candice's outfit exactly. That was not an affectation of Sara's: Candice had bought the outfits together. She enjoyed dressing Sara in matching outfits, as if they were twins.

"Why don't you take a nap, babe," muttered Sara sleepily. "Relax."

"I am relaxed," Candice said with a chuckle.

"No, you're not. You're not resting."

"I know." Candice sighed. "I'm busy thinking about—"

A large red ball came rolling out of nowhere and hit Candice in the side. She jumped up. A young girl of about seven, with pig-tails and a short orange skirt, ran over. When she saw who her ball had hit, she looked terrified. Candice laughed, sat back down, and tossed the ball to her.

"Here you go, sweetie."

"Thanks... thank you, Savant Harlow."

"Candice," Candice said, gently correcting her.

The girl had dark eyes and lips. Her eyes were wide open in awe. She smiled. "Candice."

Then her mommy ran over in a panic. "Sorry! Oh my goodness! I'm so sorry, Master Savant."

"Don't worry about it."

"We should play farther away," the mother said. She was a tall, lanky woman. She smiled anxiously. "I... I hope she didn't wake you?"

"No, don't worry about it," Candice said. "I like hearing children play."

The mother curtsied, grabbed the child, and quickly hauled her off.

"You see?" Candice said to Sara, leaning back in the grass. She adjusted her shades and closed her eyes. "How am I supposed to sleep?"

"It's just too lovely a day, Candy. There are too many people out."

"Yeah."

But then Candice really did scoot back and try to sleep.

Her mind wandered.

She thought of work. She had another deadline.

She was working with Rex on miniaturizing the cloning

technology to focus on limbs. The problem was matching what she had achieved with Lazarus and applying it to every citizen in Arkite. That was the challenge, but if it she succeeded, it brought the project closer to immortality. The success of limb replacement alone would be enough to secure her and Elise power over Arkite for the rest of their lives—possibly for an eternity if she went even further and mapped every citizen's complete genome. She was close.

Then she thought of Lazarus. The last time she had seen him, he was still loitering around Elise's penthouse. In some ways, that was for the best. It meant Elise wasn't looking for Candice. Let him be her plaything.

What would happen to him? Elise joked constantly about getting rid of their "experiment" and "flushing him."

Then she thought of Elise. What would happen between her and Elise? Candice didn't love her. There was lust and attraction that would never fade, but she didn't love her. She certainly didn't want to marry her.

But Sara. Sara was different.

Oh, Sara. Candice loved spending time with her, especially on a hot summer day. And especially in Central Park.

Central Park was the place to be in Arkite when it was hot. HQ even spent extra money cooling the park with air treatments. It was a haven during the summer. Candice loved it. But Sara was right—so did the rest of the city.

Sara reached over sluggishly and took Candice's hand. *Peaceful Sara.* Candice smiled and rubbed her fingers.

"It's a lovely day, though, isn't it, Candy?"

"Yes. It is." *With you.*

Candice held on to a guardrail and adjusted her stance as the train swayed right. It shook the instruments on the metal table beside the specimen. The specimen was a human hand surrounded by wires and held by Rex's extra metallic arms. The train swayed back. On the rebound, Candice nearly toppled over. It wasn't that sharp a turn, but Candice felt too weak to stand.

"You all right, Doctor Harlow?" asked Rex.

"Yeah," she said, catching her breath.

She reached up to blot her forehead, which was drenched with sweat, but then remembered that she was wearing sterile gloves. She tried to wrinkle her nose and readjust the mask with her facial muscles. She couldn't. So she sighed and angrily walked back to the surgical table.

Rex sent down a mechanical arm to touch her face, but she batted it away.

"You really should take a break," Rex said. "You've been at it for two days."

"We're almost finished."

"True... but I think Elise will understand if there's a slight delay. And, anyway... anyway, Doctor Harlow, I can culture the next growth."

"I'd rather do it myself."

"All right. You've always been very stubborn."

She laughed. "Really, Rex. I'm stubborn?"

She brought down a hanging keyboard and quickly reviewed an entry, comparing her notes with a microscopic projection of keratinocytes from the epidermis of the specimen's skin.

"Oh, yes. Very stubborn, Doctor. You are one of the most pertinacious women I've ever worked with. Even if it costs you hours of extra work, you insist on reviewing every file repeatedly by yourself."

"Well, why don't you let this *pertinacious* lady finish her job?"

"Yes. All right, Doctor Harlow."

Candice laughed and shook her head. Then she touched the hand on the black petri dish. She didn't like its appearance. It seemed too real. It was a soft pale hand, identical to her own but lifeless. She moved the cold fingers around, examining the distal phalanx, the flexor and extensor tendons. Then she examined the nails. They were small, but soft and fresh. It was odd, but she could almost imagine, for a moment, that she was touching her own hand.

"It certainly looks quite good," she said.

"As usual, Doctor, it is magnificent work. But this genetic variant is flawed."

"Bring up the scope again. Run your own schematics and tell me what's wrong."

"I already know. The skin holds no folds or wrinkles. It is too perfect. The veins and arteries do not connect properly. No surgeon could properly perfuse the tissues. You have disregarded the flexor tendon sheath completely. There is minimal cartilage spanning the joints of each phalanx. The carpal bones are five instead of eight. The middle metacarpal bone is missing on the second and third digits. The—"

"Just from a slight change in the gene pool? I don't understand." She inspected the skin. Indeed, there were no folds. "How is it you said I did a magnificent job, then?"

"You did, truly, Savant Harlow. Your rendition of the human hand is a beautiful copy. You are getting closer and closer. But I'm afraid it is flawed. It is a copy. It is not finished."

"I think it is magnificent, Savant."

Candice jumped at the unexpected voice from behind. The green-garbed figure's features were hidden behind a surgical mask, but there was no mistaking Lazarus's voice... or his towering stature.

"Hi, Candice," he said. She imagined him smiling under his mask. "I didn't mean to startle you."

He always startled her. He creeped her out.

She tore off her mask and yanked off her surgical gown and gloves. "Don't worry 'bout it," she said. Then she walked out of the surgical suite and entered the clinic car of the train. She knew he'd be trailing close behind, but she wasn't about to be polite.

Maybe Rex is right. I'm so tired. Maybe I do need to rest.

Lazarus entered the clinic car behind her. He had his mask off but was still wearing his gloves and gown. His hair was long and blond, like hers. She didn't like that. It only made him look creepier.

"Something I can do for you, Lazarus?" she asked, removing her white T-shirt in front of him. She had only her black bra underneath.

He looked away.

"No. No. I... I was told by Elise you'd be here. She suggested maybe you'd need help."

"I don't," she said, slipping off her shoes. Then she looked up at him and caught him shooting a quick glance at her cleavage. "Perhaps you came for something else?"

She was angry, but she wasn't sure why. Maybe it was exhaustion. But she knew that she never wanted to see him in the lab. She didn't want to see anyone in the lab. The lab was sacred. Like Sara, it calmed her soul. The last thing she wanted was this creep joining her.

Then she sat by the side of one of the clinic beds, pulled off her green scrub pants and faced him. She wasn't undressing for him; she was simply trying to disregard his existence.

"I... I didn't mean to offend you, Savant Harlow," he said in his usual robotic tone.

"You didn't. And don't worry about my privacy right now," Candice said with a sarcastic grin. She gestured at her half-naked body.

You like this, Lazarus? My body? Is that why you came?

"Perhaps another time, then," Lazarus said. He walked toward the exit to the next car. "I can see this was a bad idea."

She laughed. "Sorry." He stopped by the door. "I'm being

a bitch." She grabbed a sheet from the bed and covered herself.

"No, I apologize," he replied, suave as ever. "I shouldn't have snuck up on you."

He always knew the right thing to say. But that was his problem: he always knew the *perfect* right thing to say.

"When you return to Elise's place," Candice said, looking up into his eyes, "remind her that I don't want an assistant."

"I can," he said hesitantly, "but you must know that I can help you, Candice. Don't forget that I've got your brains *and* Elise's."

"I have Rex helping me."

"I know, but Elise thought an additional helper might do."

"No."

He looked at her with an expression of confusion. She imagined the neurons in his artificial brain spinning. Perhaps this wasn't Elise's idea, but his.

"I have been made privy to your research, Savant Harlow. And also to Mother's. I can tell you that I am well versed in it. I think of all the people in Arkite, I am the most qualified to be of help."

"No."

"And," he continued unimpeded, "can't you better study my cells and body in the lab in person? If you use me in your research, instead of remaking a hand, you can finish faster, I would think. I am your blueprint, after all. Wouldn't I work out better in person than through Rex's schematics?" She kept her head turned from him and didn't answer. "You have a deadline, Doctor, don't you? You only have a couple more months. And judging from that hand—"

"No!"

She stretched her arms and had to clumsily catch the sheet as it started to fall under her chest. "I have to shower, Lazarus. Please excuse me. I need you to leave me in peace. You think you can do that? Or are you really a pervert?"

"Yes, of course," he said, backing away. "But Mother is our boss. If she wants me to work with you, then—"

"No. And I assure you, if I tell Mother no, it's no." As much as she was a prisoner of Elise's, Candice knew Elise would not meddle in her work. She never had.

"That is well," he said. "I think you should speak with her, then. It would mean a lot for me to work on this project with you. I've suggested this to Elise and she asked me to ask you."

"Did she ask you to sneak up on me and watch me undress?"

Why am I being such a bitch? What is it about him that I loathe?

"Of course not, Candy."

"My name is Savant Harlow."

"Of course... *Mother*."

That seemed provocative. There was anger and a hint of savagery in his tone that she had not heard before. "Don't call me Mother," she snapped. "I'm not your mother."

Those words were worse. They seemed to cut his heart. She regretted saying it the moment it came out of her mouth. Somehow as kind as Candice was known to be, she had a knack for sometimes saying the meanest coldest things. Perhaps it was because people didn't expect it from her. But those words affected Lazarus severely. He looked devastated.

"Lazarus... I—"

He quickly nodded and barged out of the room.

She had resolved to shower. She couldn't. After two sleepless nights, and her run-in with Lazarus, she didn't even have the energy to get up. She just sank back on the bed and closed her eyes.

26

A TOAST

Candice was quite familiar with prison cells. She remembered the small quarters: a latrine by the farthest end, with a sink, a small cot, and a wall. It was just as small as jail cells always had been for her, but somehow, Reyburn's cell, with a white shiny wall instead of bars, seemed more claustrophobic and confined. There was nowhere to sit, except the cot, and Reyburn was already sitting there. Candice stood beside the door as it slid closed. The white light of the cell was bright.

Reyburn looked up. She had gained weight. That was merciful. Her hair, speckled gray and black, was down to her shoulders. She looked healthier. And yet the expression on her wrinkled face was one of great melancholy and sadness.

"She sent you to kill me, Dollface?" Doctor Reyburn asked as Candice walked into her cell. "And why now? *Mother's* orders?"

Candice wore a long black trench coat with sunglasses. She ran her hand through her long blond hair and then sighed. She really didn't want to talk to Reyburn. "Yes," she replied tersely.

"Took you long enough, Dollface." Reyburn nodded with a satisfied smile.

"I'm not a Dollface. I'm Chief Savant."

"Chief Savants don't need to announce their titles," corrected Reyburn. "To me, you are a Dollface, and you shall always be a Dollface."

"Seems I'm in a better place than you."

Reyburn lifted her wrists, the metal handcuffs jingling, and smirked at Candice as if daring her to do the job.

"Come," Candice said with a sigh.

The door slid open again. Four Officers entered the cell. Two of them took possession of Reyburn.

"You know, your friend Bridgette visited me many times in jail," Reyburn said as they walked down the hall, passing rows and rows of closed white cells. "She learned of my heritage much before you did, I think. She found me to be a kind of refuge, I suppose. She was such a nice girl. I became someone to confide in as she lived in the horror of Magnacourt. The horror of your Team Mother."

"Bren was a good woman."

"Yes. I could see that. And she worried a great deal about you, my dear."

They walked to the end of the long hall. One of the Officers removed a key and opened the door. Then another. At last they came to an elevator and crowded in. The elevator began to ascend.

"I think you might live yet, Savant Harlow," Reyburn said.

"No one asked you."

"I think you will either succumb to the loss of your soul and become our next Team Mother, or you will perish. But truly, if I were to wager, I would bet on perish. I don't think Elise can take your soul, sweet Dollface. You are too good."

"I saved you last time," Candice said as the door opened. "I won't again. You are responsible for Bren's death."

"You know that's a lie."

They walked down another hallway.

"You convinced Bren to make an XY," Candice said. "It's because of you that she died."

"Who is it, then, that covets thy boss's bed?" She laughed without waiting for Candice's reply.

They entered a large room. In the center was a single bed with hand and leg restraints. The Officers walked Reyburn over. Then they unchained her wrists. One of them took Doctor Reyburn's hands and helped her onto the bed. The three others strapped her in.

Candice approached her. The old woman looked sad again, almost defeated.

"Tell Elise that I forgive her," Reyburn said. "Tell her... tell her I still love her."

Candice nodded.

"Now, please, Dollface, leave me. Do not watch the injection. I don't want your innocent heart to be tainted."

Candice removed her shades and turned to one of the Officers.

"Inject etomidate," Candice said and met Reyburn's eyes with bitter hatred.

Elise stood at the top floor of her penthouse wearing her usual black: black blouse and skirt, black high heels with black pantyhose, black makeup, and her signature choker (as if daring someone to cut off her head). The blackness matched the shadows in the room. Most of the blinds were drawn. Candice wore a plain gray formal suit. She walked up the dimly lit incline, knowing that Elise was well aware of her presence, but Team Mother didn't turn.

"Did she... is she dead, Candice?" Elise asked, staring out the windows at Arkite. Below her, bright yellow lights shone through the fog, so bright as to blot out the stars above.

"You already know the answer to that, Elise."

Candice caught a glimpse of a smile, and then a nod. Candice walked closer.

"Bravo, Candy. It seems my successor has finally grown up. You are far from a tweeting bird now." Elise turned. Candice was surprised at the sight of Elise's eyes. They were bloodshot, as if she had been crying.

Elise swayed her hips as she walked over to a small metal table. She uncorked a red wine bottle and poured two glasses.

"I'm sure you're tired," Elise said as she poured. "It's late. But I wanted to talk with you now, rather than later. I would like to know what her last words were."

Another test? Perhaps Elise did not know whether Candice had been in the room when Doctor Reyburn died?

"She said..." Candice paused, trying to recall the words. "She said, 'Tell Elise I forgive her.'"

Then Candice was surprised as a recording of Reyburn's voice appeared above her. Her words echoed through the house: "*I go to God, which is more than that bitch ever will.*"

Elise broke into laughter. She raised a glass in a mocking toast, then handed the other glass to Candice. Candice took it and sank into the couch. She ran a hand over her forehead and pushed back her hair.

"I prefer Rex's answer, Candy. You know she was much more of a bitch than I ever—"

"I... I don't care, Mother."

Elise sipped her wine. Then she raised her glass again. "To us... it's a good year. This wine is said to be over fifty years old. I'm not so sure, but I saved it for this occasion."

"What occasion?"

"The death of my Mother."

"Oh," Candice said. She sipped her wine. It was smooth and delicious. "It's good."

"Yeah, it is, isn't it?"

Candice drank again. "Did you bring me here just to toast the death of Doctor Reyburn?"

"No."

All at once, Elise looked terribly solemn.

Why were you crying? Was it because of Reyburn? It can't be. Why kill her and then dare mourn her?

"There are two reasons to celebrate," Elise said. "One is the death of that witch. She needed to die—I probably should have ordered her killed years ago. But not only her death: the significance of it. You see, she was the last person in Arkite to challenge my rule."

Candice nodded. She had already thought about that, but she hadn't expected Elise to talk so openly about it.

"What about Dana?"

"She's old," Elise said, shaking her head. "Even older than me. And now, after Reyburn's death, I think they all fear me too much to touch me."

That might be true.

"So you see," Elise said, "we've done it." She raised her glass to Candice again. "It's just you and me, babe."

"Then perhaps you should kill me," Candice said. "*I'm* still a threat."

Elise smiled and moved closer.

"Candy," she said, looking deep into her eyes. "I want to be straight with you."

"You love me?" she asked, furrowing her brow.

"Stop being such a bitch," Elise said, slightly annoyed. "That's common knowledge."

"What, then?"

"Reyburn was right. I hired you because you're a Doll-face." Candice really didn't care anymore. She ran her hand through her golden hair and looked back with a yawn.

"Oh. Okay."

"That's not all." Elise took hold of Candice's hand. "Although I picked you for your looks, you surprised me and all the other Savants with your work. You proved that you're not only a pretty girl, but quite a smart one."

"Elise, sorry, but I really don't care. I'm so tired from work. May I go home now and rest?"

"Hmm." Elise patted her hand. "But I haven't told you your next assignment yet."

"What assignment?"

Instead of answering, Elise got up and walked to the window again. There was something grave in her movements that frightened Candice.

"What?" she repeated.

"I need you to cleanse our experiment—Lazarus. He needs to die."

Lazarus was the one person Candice would have gladly killed—had she been the kind of person who enjoyed killing. But she wasn't.

Her boss was doing it again. She was throwing a zinger at her to ruffle her feathers. And it always worked. It always managed to flutter her heart and flush her face. It seemed Elise's chief job was to agitate her.

"Why?" Candice asked. Then she looked around and asked in a hushed voice, "Is he here?"

"Of course not," Elise said, turning to gaze at her as if she were utterly stupid.

"Why do you want me to kill *him*? He loves you more than anyone. And... if you feel like this, why don't you kill him yourself? Or is this another sick joke of yours?"

"You know," Elise said, wagging a finger, "I don't really appreciate your bitchy tone lately. After all I've done for you. You seem so disrespectful." Elise walked up and stood over her. "I see the way you treat Sara. Why don't you talk to me like that?"

"I don't want to kill him, Elise."

"Now don't be weak," Elise said, shaking her head. "It's

not difficult. We brought him into this world, we have every right to take him out."

"Why do you want to kill him? Haven't you killed enough?"

"There you go again," Elise snapped. "Watch yourself, Savant Harlow. Every word out of your mouth seems sassy. And nasty."

Candice gave a deep sigh. "Elise... then... as a friend, listen to me. I don't want to kill anybody."

"No, you listen to me." Somehow, Elise seemed to grow larger as she spoke. "The wine you're drinking is our celebration. But if your work fails, I will die before you. I'm over twenty years older, you know. You are my heir. That is a great honor. But you must not be squeamish. I worry you won't be able to continue my dynasty. And as far as Lazarus... my dynasty does not include a man."

"Then choose somebody else. I don't want to kill anyone."

"You don't want me to choose someone else, honey." And with her boss's sudden cold glance, Candice believed her.

There was silence. Silence was good. It allowed Candice time to think.

Her boss had set traps for years. She had managed to escape every one of them. What of this one?

Perhaps she should kill Lazarus. What was he, anyway? He wasn't human. He was more like Rex. He wasn't a real man. But she knew she couldn't do it. So she wondered if this trap was simply a dead end. Surely Elise knew she was trapping her. Perhaps this wasn't about getting rid of Lazarus, but about getting rid of Candice Harlow.

"No."

Elise stood over her with a look of contempt.

"No," Candice repeated.

"Why not? Are you sure? Is that your final answer? Really?"

"Why do you want him dead?"

"He's been fun, I must admit, Candy," Elise said with a chuckle. "But, he's... unsettling. He doesn't act normal. And, at least judging by what is stored in the archives, he doesn't act anything like a man. He's something else, something artificial. And anyway, I completed my experiment with Rex. If he didn't want an XY, Rex would have gotten rid of him long ago."

Candice drank some wine. A lot of it. "Maybe this has been Rex's plan all along."

"I thought of that, too."

"Will you sit!" Candice snapped suddenly. Her outburst surprised her, but Elise was hovering over her and driving her mad.

"There you go being bitchy again, Can." Elise shook her head and walked back over to the window.

"Did you ever think that Project Lazarus is artificial?" asked Candice. "Perhaps when we learn to extend human life, it will turn all of us into Lazarus. Machines. Maybe Reyburn was wrong. Maybe Rex doesn't want to sabotage us, but use us to create this new type of man, or creature. Then we'll live forever but won't be human anymore. We'll be more like Rex."

"Hmm. Interesting. But, Candice, I really don't give a shit. I'm not here to talk philosophy with you."

"Well, I'm your Chief Savant, not your executioner. I don't want to kill anybody."

More silence. More time to think... she'd rather sleep.

"You killed Reyburn."

"No, *you* killed Reyburn."

"Look, you don't have to sneak up to him with a knife," Elise said finally. "I just need you to give the order. The Officers can do the rest."

"Why? Why can't you give the order?"

"I don't know if I can."

"What? Oh, come on! Because you're in love with him?"

"Stop it!" Elise laughed. "Just shut up! Don't be stupid."

"It wouldn't be so strange. After all, he's better endowed than I am."

"Oh! There goes that mouth again. Since when did you become such a bitch, Candy?"

"I've lived under you for many years, Mother."

Elise leaned against the window and seemed to examine Candice again, finishing her wine. Her roaming eyes and sly smile made Candice nervous. She dreaded the thought that Elise might take an interest in her and want to touch her in bed tonight.

"I'll sort out the details. When the time comes, you give the order, Candice. I don't think you care much for him anyway."

"No. I told you, Elise, I won't do it."

"You just killed Reyburn," Elise said, waving her empty glass at her. "What's the big deal?"

"*You* killed Reyburn. How many times do we have to go—"

"All right, Candice," Elise said. She gave a big sigh. "Just go. You've given me some things to think about."

Candice got up. "Elise, I won't tell Lazarus, whatever you choose."

"I don't care!" Elise snapped. "What do I look like, a fucking little bird? Once my decision is made, it's done. And you better not tell him either, Rex!"

"Of course not, Mother," Rex replied. "This meeting is a private meeting between you and Master Savant Harlow."

Candice was on her way out, but she paused on the second floor of the ramp. Something had been eating at her, and she had to know. "Elise, were you and Reyburn lovers?"

There was silence for a moment. Elise looked dreadful. Then she nodded sadly. "Of course we were, Candice. All Team Mothers for the last hundred years have chosen lovers as their successors."

27

THE WRETCH

HE SAT ALONE ATOP A BED OF GRAY GRANITE, HUNCHED forward with his head under the black cloak and waving his index finger along ripples of water. Candice walked toward him on a path over an arched bridge. It was eerily quiet. That was odd, for close by on the other side of the bridge, a hundred girls were sunbathing or watching their little ones play. But here on this short dead-end path, it was quiet. From the quaint arched bridge, down along the path and up to the rocks, there wasn't a citizen in sight. And why would there be? Everyone was terrified of him. He was more feared than Elise herself.

Candice wore her gray jumpsuit and carried a small leather briefcase under her arm. She regretted wearing the Savant suit. She was sweating under the stifling heat of summer (or the heat of winter? It was a very late summer and still dreadfully hot). Thankfully, it was late, and the sky under the center peak of the Pyramid shone an orange-red.

He looked so odd. He seemed to be studying the water under him. He was so enthralled by whatever he was doing that he didn't even seem to notice her approach.

"I like the water too," Candice said.

He turned, startled. She smiled. He flashed back a cold grin that reminded her of Mother.

"I stare at it," he said, tracing his finger along the pool of water again. "I pretend it to be the ocean that I learned of when I was a child. I dream of a large tempest stirred up from the sky that rocks the waves back and forth, tossing all the little creatures inside and out, to and fro"—and he ran his finger about the water as if to show her—"back and forth. Up and down. Up and down." He cocked his head and smiled. The grin was a bit too wide, showing his perfectly white teeth. Then he turned his head back down and resumed playing. "But soon the waves fade, and it calms back down, and the tempest forms into a light stream."

Then he splashed the water furiously and laughed. The laughter disturbed Candice, for it reminded her of Rex.

"Did you know," he continued, turning his hooded head up, "did you know that we once sailed all over the world, Savant Harlow? The greatest adventure for man was to sail. From Europe across the sea to the Americas. And one man did it. His name was..." He looked toward the orange sunset in thought, then gazed back at Candice with his brown eyes. "Columbus. Christopher Columbus. Did you know that?"

"No, I didn't."

"Rex told me," he said with a shrug. Then he took out a nearby twig and twirled it in the water some more. "Rex tells me a lot of things. Why do you like the water, Savant Harlow?"

"I don't know. I just have always liked it here. Especially near the bridges. The bridges in Central Park are so beautiful."

"Yes. Yes, it is very peaceful in the park, isn't it?"

"Sure."

He resumed his twirling.

"Why did you ask to see me, Lazarus?"

He lost his smile and seemed suddenly sad. Then he sat

down cross-legged on the granite. He kept his hood shielding his face, but he motioned for her to sit beside him.

As she sat, she followed his eyes about the brook. Before them was a beautiful vista of trees and bushes bordering a meandering stream. Water rolled gently down an incline of stones under multiple white arched bridges into the small lake, Lake Salmas. There, a handful of sails were floating along the water. Perched up on the rocks, Candice could see people across the water walking along sidewalks holding hands, children running circles around their mothers, with some pushing baby carriages or carrying their toddler girls in their arms beside fields of grass. Clever boy. He had chosen not only the stream, but a summit overlooking the entire park.

"Did she tell you that she evicted me?" he asked, cocking his hooded head.

"Hmm?"

"*Mother*. Mother evicted me, Savant Harlow."

"When?" Candice asked, surprised. "Why?" The news seemed particularly jarring among the serenity.

"It was a week ago. She called me upstairs to her office. I knew something was up, because she was wearing a formal black suit. And she had this terrible look about her. Then she just said, 'Pack your bags. You're getting the hell out of here.'"

Candice couldn't say a word. It sounded just like her, though.

"I think she even surprised Rex," he said with a chuckle. "Rex butted in and suggested I step out for a little bit—you know, give Mother some time to think. He was looking out for me, you see. He always looks out for me. But it only made Mother angrier. She got all crazy—you know how she does that—yelling and screaming. And she started breaking things. First a glass, then a bottle, then a chair, then..."

He looked down again. His voice began choking up. Candice put a hand over his shoulder to comfort him but realized it was a mistake the moment she did it. It seemed to upset him even more. He splashed the water violently and jumped up. As he rose, he stared across the water toward a family of four: two ladies and their two daughters. One of the mothers was crouching down and listening to the girl tell her some secret as she pointed directly at Lazarus.

"You don't have to tell me anything else," said Candice, getting to her feet too. "Where are you staying now, Lazarus?"

He removed his hood and stared across the water at the mother and child. Candice was surprised to see tears running down his face. Then he pointed toward the large family across the water.

They turned away in fright.

"They hate me! They won't even look at my face, Candy. I'm a monster to them... you too. You hate me, too, don't you?"

"I don't hate you, Lazarus."

"Yes, you do. I can see it in your eyes. In the way you talk to me. In the way you touch me. I'm not stupid, you know."

"I don't hate you."

"Why did you bring me here, Candy?" he asked, looking down.

"Why bring me into a world where my only friend is Rex? I have no one else. Mother won't talk to me anymore. And you, my other mother, you've always hated me."

He ran his hand through his long blond hair. She had the same habit. It was like a perverse image of herself in the mirror.

"Tell me!" he shouted. "Tell me why you would bring a monster into this world, Doctor? Why would you bring someone who can't even show his face to his sisters? Why?"

"I didn't. Elise brought you into this world. Ask her." And she meant it. She was getting angry. Lazarus was taking all his rage out on her. She knew he would never have had the courage to talk to Elise this way. "The fact is, I can offer you a job, Lazarus," Candice snapped, gesturing to her briefcase.

"You wanted to help me in the lab. I can offer you a position."

She hadn't realized that Elise had already evicted him when he'd invited her here, but she had known it was going to happen sooner rather than later. That's what had made her want to help him. His plight appealed to Candice's compassionate side. So, Candice had made a deal with Elise to offer him a job at the lab for a short time. She had even brought the lab computer to show him, tucked into her briefcase.

Now she hoped her offer would calm him. It did. He stopped shouting and quickly covered his head again. But he squinted his eyes at her distrustfully, in the same way as Elise. He chuckled his odd laugh. "That's smart, Candy. That's one way to appease me, isn't it? Offer me a treat. But I don't believe you."

He crouched down on all fours like a monkey and turned back to the family. Then he stared threateningly at the little girl across the water again.

"I would appreciate you not yelling at me, Lazarus."

"It's the truth," he said with a shrug, still staring. "Everything I said. Everyone hates me, including you. But I... I didn't mean to yell at you. I'm sorry."

"I just offered you a job. If I hated you—"

"I'm just... I'm just angry, you know. And very alone, Candy— Doctor Harlow, I mean. I'm very alone."

"That doesn't give you the right to yell at me." She felt like she was scolding a child. And, true to form, Lazarus looked down in shame.

"You're right," he murmured quietly. "I'm sorry. I didn't mean to yell at you, Doctor."

"Forget it." She crouched down with him and forced a smile. "So, what do you think? Would you like to help out in the lab?"

He turned and squinted at her. "Yeah, I guess."

She patted his back. "Good. You can start tomorrow."

"But, I can't get there. There's no way to access the lab, except by cycle. I'm not a Savant. I don't have a cycle."

She furrowed her brow and looked at him strangely. "Then how did you get in to see me a couple of months ago?"

"Oh, that was Elise. She took me there."

Damn. Damn you, Elise! You want me to offer him a job knowing that the only way for him to work there is for me to bring him there. You scheming bitch! You're giving him to me. For me to take care of. Do you want me to be driven crazy?

That's it, isn't it? Then I'd have a motive to kill him just like you asked me to. Right?

"Where are you staying, Lazarus?" she asked gently, lifting his chin.

"Here," he said simply.

"What! What do you mean, here?"

"Here. Right here, Candice. I've been in the park."

"For a week? Like a bum? You can't be serious."

"I didn't know where else to go."

She stood up and nodded. Well, now she knew why he had sent a message to Rex to ask for her to meet him.

"All right. Come on, then. You can stay at my place tonight."

"Really?" he asked with a sudden glow.

"Yeah." She reached her hand out to him. "Come on. Let's get you off these rocks."

They walked back to the path along the bridge. Then, for the first time, she noticed his smell. She'd feed him, but first she would need to get him a bath.

"What have you been eating?"

"I haven't."

"Nothing? For a week?"

"No. Nothing. Just water. And... some scraps from citizens."

"You poor thing."

"Yes. Now perhaps you'll forgive my anger, Savant Harlow." He said it suavely as always.

She nodded. "Well, just don't yell at me again."

"I won't. I won't. And... I won't stay long at your place either, Candice. I'll find my own place." They made their way over the arched bridge. "I just need to find a place for myself. Elise has even messaged me that she might arrange something for me."

"She should have told me. It wasn't right to leave you like this."

"I thought you knew. I merely messaged you for company. I'm so alone, you know."

She turned, and he flashed his famous large-toothed grin.

As they walked, Lazarus held his hood tight over his head. He hid like a shadow under the black cloak, ensuring that the roaming eyes of the citizenry could not look upon his face. And for the first time, she realized he did not wear it out of shyness, but out of shame. He genuinely believed he was hideous in their eyes.

She handed him the briefcase, but he refused it. He didn't dare let go of his hood.

"Go through the computer in my bag. It's top secret from HQ. Look through my work and see if you can work anything out regarding the cloning process."

"All right."

"I've reached a dead end. I can't figure out how to reconcile all the genetic variants with your blueprint. It must be..."

As they walked, the citizens turned to watch. Candice had never gotten used to her notoriety as a Savant, but this was much worse. Now everyone stared.

"It's just so difficult to clone the tissue with the exact specifications," she continued. "You saw the hand. I have similarities, but not the exact cells. And without exact, it's useless. I'm not even sure what I'm doing wrong."

"I'll look through it. But, Savant Harlow, you said once

that you didn't want anybody in the lab. You wanted to work alone. I know how much you enjoy working alone."

Candice tried to feign a smile, but she knew he saw through it.

Of course, that was the truth. Of course, she wanted to work alone. "It's just for now, Lazarus. Just to get you on your feet."

"You're so kind," he said with a beaming smile. "So kind, Candice. So much kinder than my other mother."

They reached her gray rocket cycle. It was parked along the grass, guarded by Sara. Sara walked up with a big smile and handed her the visor. Then she stared at her company.

"Hello, Sara," said Lazarus.

"Hello, Lazarus," she said.

"Candice is going to take me to her place," he said excitedly.

"She's offering me a place to sleep and eat for a little while."

"Oh," Sara said, losing her smile. "That's nice."

28

THE TALK

THEY SAT BY A FLICKERING YELLOW LIGHT EMANATING FROM the borders of Candice's wooden dining room table in the small navy-blue domed kitchen of her apartment, quietly moving their forks around the beef stew and sipping white wine while listening to soft jazz in the background. Sara was close beside Candice. Every once in a while, she'd lift her head and scowl at him. It hadn't taken long for Sara, who was never one to put on airs, to show her disgust and hatred toward him. Candice was used to seeing it every day.

Candice kept her head down and fiddled with the beef morsels and rice.

They had been living together for a couple weeks now. There couldn't be a worse arrangement. Candice stayed silent while Sara and Lazarus fought about every small detail of their lives—from cooking utensils to shampoo. Maybe if Candice had lived alone, she could have handled him. But Sara hated him. She hated every thing about him. Well, Candice didn't like him either. And it was more exhausting for her. Her efforts at acting civil and nice for weeks were draining her of her energy.

"We have to leave early tomorrow," Candice said.

"Early? Again?" snapped Lazarus.

"Yep. Early."

She'd hoped that, perhaps, riding him to the lab at horrible hours would get him off her tail by his own choice, but it hadn't worked yet.

"This is really good, hun," Sara said, turning to Candice.

"Yeah. And I cooked most of it myself," Candice replied with a chuckle. "No help from Rex."

"Really? Did you add ginger? Or is that—"

"It's mint."

"Oh. Well, it's really good."

"I wish I could cook like you, Savant Harlow," interjected Lazarus.

"You just need to put your mind to it," Candice said with a fake smile. "It's just patience and hard work—just like the lab."

"Well, you've gotten it down, honey," Sara added. "And... it's sweet, right?"

"A little sugar."

"It's really good."

"Yeah, it's good," Lazarus said with a smile.

Candice looked at him. He was wearing that ridiculous black hood over his head. She had told him countless times to take it off around the house, but he refused. He only rarely removed it when he was alone with her, but never in Sara's company.

"What time are you leaving tomorrow?" Sara asked. She bent over and touched Candice's hand. Candice turned from the crypt keeper and looked at her girlfriend's hand. She squeezed it and forced a smile.

"I'm thinking around four thirty."

"Four thirty!" cried Lazarus, hitting his fists against the table. It was so easy for him to lose his temper. It was times like this that she felt as if she were raising a little child.

"You don't have to come if you don't want to."

"No," he said dismissively, "it's all right." Then he added sarcastically with a shrug, "Four thirty."

Of course, everyone at the table knew Candice was trying to ditch him.

"I've worked out one of the faults with experiment 156, Doctor," Lazarus said between more fork and knife clanging. "I think I can get Rex to resequence the genes and—"

"Not now, Lazarus. We're eating."

"Oh, all right."

Sara squeezed her hand again and then winked at Candice as if trying to tell a secret. "I was kinda hoping we could be alone tomorrow," she said quietly. "It's Saturday, you know."

"I know, babe, but I just need a couple more weeks. I'm so close."

"We are, Sara," Lazarus said.

Candice looked over with irritation. The image of the tall man decked in black, with folded hands, gazing at them was creepy. It only made his efforts at joining their conversation more awkward. His tone made it even worse. He had such a robotic way of speaking. The mix was hideous, and Sara's expression said it all: disgust mixed with fear.

"Yes, Lazarus," Candice said with a long sigh, "would you be a dear and leave us for a little while? I have to talk to Sara about something in private."

"Oh, okay."

He bowed like a chivalrous knight but gave a scowl to Sara, then walked out of the room.

"What's with you, Sara?" Candice asked in a whisper when the coast was clear.

"What do you mean, *me*? When the fuck is *he* leaving!"

"Shh. He's not so bad."

"He's awful. Get rid of him, Candy."

Candice put her head in her hands. "What would you have me do," she said, "throw him out on the street?"

"YES!" Sara hissed. "That's what Mother did, and now I know why. I can't stand another day with him. Look, either he goes, or I go! I can't take it anymore, sweetie. He's so creepy. He's at every fucking corner of our place. There's no privacy."

Candice sighed.

"What about us?" Sara asked, looking desperate and grabbing her hand again. "I mean it, Candice. It's bad enough that you're working every hour of the day. I don't ever see you. Now I have to share you with that freak."

Candice simply nodded and put her head in her hands again.

"Candy," Sara insisted, still forcing her whisper, "I even saw him yesterday out of the corner of my eye when I was showering. He's a goddamn pervert too! Get him the fuck out, 'kay? Or... I'm leaving."

Candice looked up. "All right, Sara. Calm down."

"I... I can't. I love you, but if that creature sleeps in this house one more night, I think I'm gonna lose my mind... or call the police. You know, it wouldn't take much to arrest him. The Officers don't trust him either. The only reason he hasn't been taken in is Mother. She's protecting him. Why, I really don't know."

"All right, all right," she said, patting Sara's hand. "Calm down. I'll talk to him."

Sara nodded, staring at her.

"Elise has a place for him," Candice said. She sipped some wine. "But it's awful. It's for vagrants and criminals. I swear, if we send him there, he'll become the monster everybody thinks he is."

"And you don't think he's a monster now, Candy?"

"No. No, I don't. I don't believe that. Sara, I look into his eyes and I see mine."

Sara rolled her eyes and shook her head. She jumped up and walked over to a cupboard, then pulled out a container of instant coffee and a mug. She dispensed some hot water from the sink over the black granules in her cup. "Want some coffee?"

"No," said Candice.

"Lights," Sara cried, exasperated. The kitchen lit up. She stirred the cup with a spoon and blew over the steaming liquid. "I'm having a cup of coffee. Ya know why, Candy?"

"Hmm?"

"Because I'm not gonna be able to sleep another fucking night with that dick anyway."

"Oh, come on, Sara."

Sara held the mug in two hands and sipped some of the brew. Then she blew the mist over the cup again.

Candice jumped up and embraced her with a laugh, leaning her head against hers. "I'll talk to him."

"It's not funny. Just do it, babe. Do it tonight. *Please.*"

Their "talk" happened close to midnight.

Sara hadn't had enough coffee, apparently. She dozed off early in the evening.

Candice yawned as she walked barefoot along the cold tiled floor, across the dark hall, and over to Lazarus's room. The only light came from windows at both sides of the hallway opening out to the brighter night sky. She straightened out her long white nightgown and long blond hair and then knocked on his door.

She stood there waiting a long time, tapping her toes on the floor. She reached into a pocket of her white lace gown and grabbed a stick of gum. She knocked a couple more times. The door finally creaked open.

"Oh, hi, Candice," he said still wearing his black cloak. But, his hood was back revealing his long golden-blond hair flowing over his shoulders.

"Didn't I tell you to get rid of that thing? It's old and looks awful."

"It's my clothes," he said with a shrug.

"May I come in?" she asked, raising her eyebrows, surprised that he hadn't already invited her.

"Sure."

The room was a mess, smelling like sweat and old shoes. Strange mementos—figurines, books, puzzles and games—all sorts of junk was strewn across the carpet. There was no window in the room, but a single large wall monitor displayed a cloudy night sky. Lazarus crept over to his bed and sat down at the edge. Candice pulled up a plastic chair, the only chair in the room, then sat down facing him and leaned forward with her hands folded over her legs.

"Do you like it here, Lazarus?"

"Yeah. I suppose so." He smiled that large-toothed smile.

"It's nice, right?" she asked, looking around. She threw the gum in her mouth. "It's better than most places in town. It was given to me after Mother recruited me."

"I know."

"Yeah. But I"—she laughed nervously—"I never thought I'd use my guest room." She ran her hand through her long blond hair. "Never really had much time for visitors."

Lazarus creeped her out by doing the exact same thing with his golden hair. "What do you want, Savant Harlow?" he asked with a yawn.

He didn't mean to be rude. It was his way: always straightforward, cold and calculating, and frequently sickeningly kind.

"Yeah, I should get to the point. I mean, we have to go to work early, right? You know we talked about that place, the place Elise has offered you nearby—the Candle District. One of HQ's buildings."

"Yeah. I know." He looked down. "It's a dump. You said it yourself. It's where bums go."

"It's not so bad."

"It's terrible. Are you evicting me, too?" he asked, looking into her eyes. He acted as if it wouldn't have surprised him, but it made her feel terrible.

She lost her nerve for a moment. She fixated on a small toy car lying at the foot of the bed as she nervously bit her lip. "I know. I know I told you I'd look elsewhere, but I think Elise's place is best. And... I just can't keep you here with Sara. You know you two don't get along."

"But *we* get along, don't we, Candice?"

"Of course, Lazarus... you and I can go to the District and talk with the warden. She's nice."

"All right," Lazarus said, turning his head to his wall screen.

The screen in the room changed to the Arkite skyline, and it appeared darker. They both looked. It was as if they were peering through an actual window with all the yellow lights of the metal and glass towers of the city.

"Either way," he added shyly, "I really want to thank you, Savant Harlow. You've been so very kind to me."

He turned back and looked in her eyes. He had auburn eyes— Elise's eyes—and they seemed to peer right into her soul. That's why she avoided them. She'd thought it was his features. It wasn't. It was those eyes. And now, they hypnotized her and seemed almost to take control of her, speeding the beat of her heart and making her a little dizzy.

She jumped up and threw her gum in a trash can by the door.

"After Elise sent me away," he continued, "you took me in. You didn't have to. I know you didn't want to. That was so very kind." He smiled. "But you're always sad. Why are you sad, Savant Harlow?"

"I'm not sad," she said with a laugh, sitting back down on the chair.

"Yes, you are. You always look sad. Even in the lab. No... not in the lab. In the lab, you seem all right. But everywhere else you always seem hurt. What is it? Why aren't you happy?"

"Nothing. I'm fine, Lazarus."

He nodded, though he looked like he didn't believe her. "Then you'll go with me, Savant Harlow? To the District?"

"Of course."

Of course, she was sad. Terribly. And somehow he knew it.

But what of it? So what? She had been unhappy for years. No one could heal her pain, unless there was some magician who could wave a wand and erase that first meeting with Elise. Perhaps she could have taken a lesser job at the university. Perhaps she could have changed jobs and lost interest in research. She would gladly have given up everything, all her privileges, if only she could have never become a Savant. She had the most enviable position in the entire city, but she despised it. She would have done anything to hand it over and lose everything, but she couldn't. She knew Elise would never let her.

"I'll be all right," Lazarus said. "You're so kind. I only worry about you, Savant Harlow."

"Right." She chuckled nervously. "I'm all right, Lazarus."

"You know, I watch you," he said. "You work so hard in the lab. Then, when you come home, there's nothing left for you. You just seem to want to sleep. You seem miserable."

The comment nearly broke the spell. It felt jarring and inappropriate. She started to get up again, but then he gently knelt down and touched the side of her leg. She looked down, amused.

She didn't pull away. Part of her wanted to move away, but another part kept still. He ran his hands slowly along her knee and leg.

"You have beautiful soft skin, Savant Harlow," he said as he rubbed. He sounded more like Rex, as if the mainframe were commenting about Doctor Harlow's anterior tibialis and gastrocnemius muscles. It made her laugh. He laughed too. "It is so white, paler than Mother's." He ran his hand down farther and grasped her ankle. He touched the sides of her ankle down to the bottom of her foot. Then she felt him pressing his strong fingers into the sole of her foot. "You know, when I lived with Mother, she taught me how to relax her. One of the areas of our greatest tension is our feet —and you have lovely feet. I learned all the pressure points. I can press on trigger points. I think I can relax you, if you'd let me. It would make me happy if you were happy. I owe you for all you've done for me."

Her heart beat faster. She pulled her foot away.

"That's all right." She stood up and acted stern like a Savant, taught under her master. She feigned indifference, but she felt her face flush and her heart pound.

He looked up at her. "I know how to relax you."

"That's okay. Never mind, Lazarus."

"I think you need it."

She stood frozen there for a moment. Then she shrugged her shoulders. "All right," she replied indifferently. "Why not? If you really want to."

She sat back down.

He rubbed. It felt wonderful. His hands were hard, but Mother had taught him just the right amount of pressure and just the right places to press along the bottom of her foot.

"You look so stressed, Candy. You need to relax."

She laughed. "Really? But I'm not—"

"Shh. Just sit back and relax. You deserve it."

She closed her eyes. He took it as a cue, and slowly got up. She opened her eyes and saw the black shade of his ugly cloak in her periphery. "Relax." He gently placed a hand on her head. He just laid it there. It was so simple, yet it felt so soothing. Just his touch felt better than she had felt in a long time.

"You just need to take it easy. All you do is work. You're so tense... do you feel a little better?"

"Yes."

His hand, just the pressure, relaxed her as much as his foot massage. She could feel the size, larger than any hand that had ever touched her before. She wondered if he was looking at her. Or perhaps he too was closing his eyes. That's what she did: she closed her eyes as he laid his hand on top of her head and neck. It made her breathe more calmly. If she hadn't taken Mint earlier, she thought she might have fallen asleep.

"You have a nice touch," she said.

He laughed. His odd laughter almost snapped her out of it again. But then he said, "Just relax."

Yes. I suppose I do need to relax.

His hand ran slowly down from the waves of her hair, down to her upper back. Then he began to rub her neck. He started pulling and kneading at the neck muscles. He pulled her robe down a little by the shoulders and let his hand roam all the way down her back. Candice wasn't wearing a bra. She felt a little indecent and lifted the front of the silk cloth to cover her chest.

"Who taught you, Lazarus?" she asked, jerking away.

"I told you. I lived with Team Mother for months, don't you remember?"

"What's the point in this?" She leaned back with a giggle, closing her eyes again. "Are you trying to... bribe me... to let you stay?" She laughed, and he did too.

"Maybe." Even his voice seemed more soothing. "You know," he continued, almost in a whisper, his voice rough but almost hypnotic, "you know, Candy, there's too many people here. Maybe if I left, you and Sara would be happier."

Candice opened her eyes, but then he pressed deeper. "Lazarus, understand... I don't want you to leave. I just don't want you two to fight."

"You know, I'll get settled in the Candle District."

"All right. Good. So it's settled, then. You'll go to...

Candle?" It almost sounded to her like she'd said Candy—
You'll go to Candy.

Was he bewitching her? She didn't care. It felt sooo good.

"I don't think I have a choice."

She turned and looked up at him. She expected him to be sad. He wasn't. There was something else in his eyes. It looked more like hunger.

"I... I think I need to get something to eat," Candice said, jumping up. "You want to join me? We can talk more in the kitchen."

Yeah, somewhere out in the open. Not here in his room, dummy!

"I guess," he said with a shrug. But he had an amused smile. He looked at her almost in condescension. She guessed he had learned that from her boss too.

She forced herself up from the chair and walked to the door. On the way there, she felt him touch the back of her long hair once more. It sent tingles down her body.

She walked barefoot across the dark hall and heard his foot-steps trailing behind. She came up to her domed kitchen. "Get me a sandwich, Rex," she ordered. "Ham and cheese."

"At this hour?" Rex asked. "All right. Shall I make it for two, Candice?"

Candice looked around nervously. She had worried that he was referring to Sara, but it was just her and Lazarus. He still had that amused expression: not innocent, not innocent at all. She feared Sara would wake up, which was ironic because a part of her wanted her to. It was precisely why she had led him to the open room in the first place. Half of her wanted to escape; the other half wanted to be alone with him.

Candice walked over to the counter and waited before the Pabulum to finish working. The machine whirled and vibrated a little, then the green light appeared by the door. She opened the door and took out a ham sandwich on white bread. Then Lazarus walked up quietly and started caressing her neck again.

"Don't. Lazarus. Don't. Perhaps you shouldn't."

"I'm just trying to relax you, touching the back of your neck. You seem to like it, and your muscles are so tense."

It felt good. She could get lost in his strong hands.

"Don't." Candice turned and was surprised to see Lazarus's face right up against her cheek.

"Do you feel... better?" He rubbed some more.

"Yes."

"You deserve it."

She felt his lips touch her neck.

"Want some... Lazarus," she said nervously, ducking away from him.

"I'm not really hungry."

She took a long knife from a drawer and cut it in half. "I am. I suppose"—she laughed nervously—"I never really eat much either, being in the lab all the time. I'm really—"

He leaned over and kissed the back of her neck again, holding her gently from behind. It made her freeze. Then she turned and cradled her head under his.

"You smell nice," he said.

She just nodded as he explored her cheek and neck with his lips. She leaned up and kissed him on the lips. He pushed her gently against the kitchen counter, then entered her lips and caressed her tongue with his.

Now she was lost. *And what's the harm in it? He'll be leaving soon anyway. And didn't Elise have her way with him for months?*

He leaned in and kissed her again, and again, so hard and so hungry. And she was hungry too.

Now she knew. She wasn't just hungry for a sandwich: she was hungry for him. As if she had never experienced something so wonderful. Her desire was so strong, stronger than she had ever felt before for Elise or Sara—or anyone else, for that matter.

His large hands wandered under her robe and then slowly removed it from her shoulders. Her robe fell, and she stood in his embrace, wearing only her white panties. She wanted more. She didn't care anymore. She reached over and yanked off his cloak.

Then they met each other's lips again, sucking and playing with each other's tongues and mouths. It was as if they danced, and she saw the domed ceiling of her kitchen swoon a little.

He surprised her and grabbed her, lifting her whole body onto the dining table. His strength left her breathless. He leaned over and kissed again, this time as she lay with her head against the table and her groin rubbing against his. Then he ran his tongue along her chest and started sucking on her nipples as if he was, indeed, a baby boy. As he sucked, he slowly removed his own shirt. She looked up as he fondled her breasts with his tongue and hands. She had never seen his bare chest. The absence of breasts was bizarrely arousing.

She wanted him, that rough skin, now developing soft tufts of blond hair along his chest and arms. She wanted his strong jawline and his broad shoulders. She reached down and yanked on his pants. She blindly moved her hand down until she could feel his bulge. She had played with dildos all her life but had never felt a natural penis. She wanted it. She desired him more than ever.

She got up and pushed him hard away from her. At first, he mistook it for wanting to run from him, and he looked hurt, but then she knelt down, pulling down his pants and pulling out his long hard shaft. She let it fill her mouth and sucked with a beastly desire. She wanted his penis more than a hundred packs of Mint. She was lost on it, sucking and yanking at it. She heard him groan in ecstasy.

After a while, she stopped and looked up at him. His eyes were closed, and he ran a hand along her hair and cheek. She looked about the kitchen, thinking of Sara again, but it was quiet and they were alone. She got up and wagged a finger at him with a sly smile.

You better not cum. Not yet.

Then she moved the same index finger over her lips to quiet him. She pulled down her white lace panties and embraced him again. He grabbed her hard and hoisted her back on the dining table.

He entered her slowly and gently. It was different, somehow more pleasurable than any toy she'd ever played with before. Each thrust made her hunger only grow more.

He started thrusting harder into her, and the banging and shaking of the table only made her more excited. Again and again, the table shook from their embrace. He fucked her hard. And he thrust his tongue into her mouth again as he pounded, feeling and wanting even more.

Then there was a scream. Sara. It was her voice. It must have been their noise that had woken her. Candice had totally forgotten about her.

Candice turned and caught a glimpse of white from Sara's matching nightgown rushing Lazarus. Lazarus was yanked off Candice.

Sara jumped on Lazarus's back and repeatedly hit his chest like an animal. Lazarus ran from the table and tried to throw the girl off but couldn't. Candice lay there on her side on the dining table, dazed, naked, and in shock. She wasn't even sure what was happening. But then she turned and saw her friend pummeling the poor man.

"Get off him!" yelled Candice.

He finally grabbed Sara's arm and spun her over him. When Sara landed on the tile floor, he landed on top of her and began striking her repeatedly in the face. Candice caught his expression: his rage reminded her of that evening when Elise had been shot.

"Stop. Let her go!"

He didn't. In fact, he kept hitting her face mercilessly. Sara became immobile, a limp doll under his blows. Candice feared that he would kill her.

Candice grabbed the knife from the counter and flashed it before Lazarus. "Stop! Get off her! You're gonna kill her!"

By now, Sara was unconscious, but he didn't stop. He kept hitting her.

"Stop, Lazarus!" Candice screamed.

Candice grabbed his arm and tugged on it with all her weight. Lazarus turned. His eyes were contorted in rage. He seemed to want to kill, and he was so incensed with anger that he didn't seem in control of it.

She pushed him from Sara, brandishing her knife. It was finally enough for him to let Sara go. But now Lazarus turned on Candice. He grabbed Candice and threw her to the floor.

"Stop it!" she yelled.

He lunged again and she accidentally cut his arm. Blood flowed from his forearm. In rage, he sent a hard blow with both fists across her face. All was dark for a moment, then she saw him charge her again. Candice pulled the knife to her chest, so as not to hurt him. He tackled her, falling over her onto the tiled kitchen floor.

Her head hit hard against the ground. Then came a sharp searing pain.

All became dark.

Lazarus was shouting, but his voice became strangely faint, as if far off.

"Candy!"

She saw a dark blur. Someone crouching over her. An intense pain gnawed at her chest, and the blur above her came in and out of focus. She felt sick. She couldn't move, or didn't want to move for fear of the pain.

The searing burn came in waves between complete darkness. She saw the shadow stand over her, then fade again. Her hands became numb. Her face, her legs, her feet, everything numbed. All became silent. She felt nothing. Her whole body turned heavy and immobile. She forgot about pain. She forgot about everything.

It was all dark and serene—peaceful. She was at peace. But she could still hear faint shouting in the distance, as if coming from a faraway tunnel. Shouting in the distance. And something about pain—a pain that she did not want to feel any longer.

"Candy! Rex! Call the police! Call the police, Rex!"

"That would be inadvisable, Lazarus. Is Savant Harlow moving? I cannot hear her heartbeat."

"Call the police, Rex!"

"Officers have already been notified and will be arriving shortly."

"She's not breathing! My God, what's happened! What have I done! CANDY! What have I—"

29

THE TRIAL

ELISE STOOD ON THE THIRD FLOOR OF HER APARTMENT wearing her black skirt and blouse and choker. Hands behind her back, she stared at Arkite in the afternoon: the rooftops of skyscrapers and the small figures on the ground far below. She heard her guests walking up the ramp but didn't turn. Two Officers in dark trench coats stood beside her.

The sound of whimpering echoed in the hall. Elise cocked her head. From the corner of her eye, she saw a group of black-clad Officers leading a naked man with long blond hair up the ramp. He was in chains, his head drooping. The Officers paused on the second floor and waited.

Elise reached down and picked up a glass of red wine with a shaking hand. Then she looked out the window again. It was silent. Everything was quiet, with the exception of the whimpering. She knew it was Lazarus. It was his low baritone voice, stupidly jerking a little higher with deep-breathing sobs. She sipped some wine and then set the glass back down on a small table. Then she gripped one gloved fist tighter while running her other hand through her hair.

"I'm sorry... I'm so sorry. It was an accident. I don't know what happened. I'm so sorry. I'm so sorry. I don't know what happened. I'm sorry, I'm—"

"SHUT UP!" Elise screamed. Her voice echoed through the apartment.

He stood there, quietly whimpering.

Elise squeezed her gloved hands a few more times and then picked up the wineglass again while staring outside. It was Saturday. All the workers would be out enjoying the sunshine. A nice day. She watched as a flying car flew close by her window, but there wasn't a sound in her perfectly insulated penthouse.

"Is the victim here?" Elise asked in a gentler tone, still looking out her window.

"Yes, Mother," said one of the Officers. "She is beside him."

"I don't want to look. I don't want... to even see *it*. Not yet. Just give Sara Holmes my regards."

"Yes, Mother."

Elise smiled a thin smile and nodded. Then she heard the Officer walk over behind her and speak to Sara. She didn't want to listen, but she could hear Sara weeping too. Elise heard her name. She heard Sara say something, but she ignored it. She ignored everything. It was silent because she willed it to be. She didn't want to hear one word.

Elise caught sight of the HQ train weaving between buildings far below. It was a familiar sight, something she saw numerous times each day. The train took precisely an hour to travel all the way around the city, and a few hours more to randomly corner around all the alleys and city streets. For it to be traveling down below her right then and there was really remarkable. Every day for the past few years, when she saw it, she'd look upon it with joy, thinking that her Candy was riding in it, toiling hard in the lab. The sight of it always perked her up from her mundane work as Team Mother. She wondered if it was some strange omen that it was passing by now. The sight of it only left her even more bitter.

Sara spoke again. Elise still didn't listen, even though it seemed quite important.

And Lazarus wailed.

Elise finally turned and looked at him. For the first time, even beyond the day of his birth, he looked like an animal. His blond hair was disheveled, his eyes were bloodshot, and his naked muscles were cut and bruised. Sara looked just as awful. She had on a black suit, but she wore no makeup, her hair was a mess, she had a black eye, and her cheeks were bruised.

Elise raised a finger. "I heard you killed Savant Harlow. Is that true?"

He averted his face and wailed some more.

She walked slowly to Lazarus, descending the ramp. Lazarus looked up with wild tortured eyes as she approached.

"I'm sorry," he muttered. "I'm so sorry. It was an accident."

"An accident? Was it by your hands?" Elise asked.

Sara began to sob.

"She... the knife went in. I didn't mean—"

"Shh," Elise said, petting Lazarus's hair. "Shh, calm yourself, my son. You're an adult now. I need you to answer some questions." She raised a finger. "Now, be thoughtful. When I ask a question, I want succinct short answers, nothing long and drawn out. Do you understand? Do you think you can do that?"

"Yes," he replied, looking down.

"Good boy."

She cradled his face with her gloved hand and slid it across his cheek so violently as to toss his head to the side, knocking him down. He whimpered some more.

"Now, did you cut your other mother with a knife?"

"Yes, yes, yes!" he said desperately getting up. "But it wasn't my hand! She fell and—"

"It wasn't your hand?" Elise said, pretending interest. "Whose hand was it?"

"I fell on her."

"You *fell?*" Elise asked, opening her eyes wide. "You fell. How? Did she trip you on your knife, then?"

"I don't know!" he shouted. "I just don't know! I don't know what happened. I'm sorry. I didn't mean—"

"I said succinct answers," she said, wagging a finger. Then she turned to the Officers. "Pull his chains."

The Officers pulled him with all their weight, yanking his body prostrate onto the sloped ramp. The beast's arms and legs pulled against their sockets as he cried, now not only out of despair but in intense pain.

"Do not speak unless spoken to," Elise said, leaning down. "Do you understand?"

"Yes. Yes." He slowly got up on his knees.

"Good." Elise turned to Sara. "He's, of course, an idiot. He's an XY. You tell me in your own words, sweet Sara, what happened to your girlfriend."

Sara nodded. For a moment it seemed she wasn't sure she had the strength, but then she averted her gaze from Lazarus and spoke. "I heard noises coming from the kitchen. It sounded like yelling. I was... scared, Mother... because Lazarus was getting more and more angry with us at home. I looked about my bed. It was empty, so I ran into the hallway, because I was so worried that something had happened to Candy. I ran out of the room to see what was wrong. Then I saw him, naked like now. They both were naked, only..." She trailed off.

"It's all right, dear. Go on."

"Both of them were naked, but I watched as the monster kept banging her hard against the table. He was raping her."

At the word *rape*, Lazarus lost all reason.

"Lies! Lies!" he cried. "There was no rape!"

"Pull his chains," Elise said, turning to the Officers.

Once again, Lazarus was thrown to the ground, stretched to the maximum by the large thick chains.

"Go on, dear," Elise said with a smile between Lazarus's cries of pain.

"He was banging..." Sara stopped again.

"You can do it, dear. Rex is recording. I need it for his sentence."

Sara nodded. "He was—"

"Fucking her?" Elise asked.

Sara looked down as if ashamed. "Yeah, *fucking* her... but against her will."

"Bitch!" Lazarus yelled, standing up. "It was with consent. She wanted me as much as I wanted her."

"Calm down," Elise said, turning her head for a moment. "You just raped and killed Candice, her girlfriend. You need to respect her peace."

"I didn't rape her, Mother! Nothing was forced." He threw his long hair back and glared at Sara. "If she hadn't been there, Candice would never have died. She attacked me when she saw us together. She couldn't bear—"

"How dare you accuse me!" cried Sara.

"But it's the truth, Mother. I did nothing—"

"Silence!" shouted Elise. "Remember, respond only when spoken to. Succinct answers to my questions... pull his chains again."

The guards yanked him to the floor once more.

"You best shut it," Elise added, leaning her mouth close to his ear. "You're in a lot of trouble, and if you keep mouthing off, you may not be able to use your limbs ever again." Elise rose. "Complete your side of the story, Ms. Holmes."

"It's hard," he said, rising on one knee. "It's so hard, Mother."

"I know, but we need a fair trial."

Sara swallowed. One of the Officers came over and held

her for a moment. Then she turned and looked down on the beast again. "I did everything I could. I ran and jumped him. I had to stop—"

"But what if it was with mutual consent?" asked Elise. "He is, after all, a man. Perhaps he had worked his guile over her. Perhaps she wanted him as much as he wanted her."

"I can't believe that."

"Then you never truly knew her," said Lazarus almost disparagingly.

His attitude surprised Elise and many of the Officers in the midst of his agony.

"Pull his chains," Elise responded.

"He doesn't deserve a trial, Mother," Sara snapped as Lazarus was thrown to the ground once more. "Look at him. He's an animal."

"Never mind. Please continue, Sara."

"When I jumped him, we fought. He pushed me, and I repeatedly hit his chest. Then he threw me to the ground. I was terrified that he lusted after me too, but instead, he started hitting me in the face."

"Ah," Elise said. She walked up to Sara and examined her face, gently touching the bruises along her cheeks. "Take pictures of her face, Rex. Let it be an exhibit to the brutality of the XY."

"Yes, Mother," said Rex.

"I don't know what happened after that," said Sara. "The monster hit me so many times that I lost consciousness."

Elise walked over to Lazarus and crouched down. He didn't even bother getting up anymore. He just lay there panting in agony. She lifted his chin. "Is her story true?"

"Most of it," replied Lazarus, out of breath. "Except both Candice and I wanted it. I would never have raped her. I wouldn't do that to anybody, especially Candice, who was the only person kind to me in my entire life."

"She hated you!" cried Sara.

But she stopped as Elise raised a hand. "I believe you, Lazarus." Elise had to lift her hand again as Sara started bawling.

Elise felt Sara's pain. It burned in her chest, too. Sara's tears were her own tears. In fact, she hated the abomination even more than Sara did. And yet, by continuing with the questioning, she knew she could make him suffer even more.

"Now then," Elise said with a sweet smile, turning back to the wretch. "Tell me, Lazarus, who was holding the knife that killed Candice?"

He nodded with one of his childish smiles. He forced himself up on his knees. "I was wrestling with Candice. We started fighting. I was so... I was so angry with Sara that I couldn't stop hitting her. Candice ran to get her off me."

"You could have killed Sara."

He didn't answer. He just hung his head down.

Now he remained low on the ground. Elise thought it was in order to minimize the pain if the chains were pulled again.

"So, Candice was protecting Sara?" she asked.

Lazarus nodded. "I didn't want any of it to happen. I didn't want to hurt Sara either."

Elise smiled broadly. Then she turned and motioned to Sara.

"Come here, Sara. Let him look closely at your face."

Lazarus gazed upon her bruised face. Sara turned from his gaze as if he were a demon.

"Were you trying to kill her?" Elise asked.

"No!" Lazarus yelled. "I didn't mean to hurt her."

"Look at her," Elise said, gesturing to the bruises. "Look at her black eye. Seems like a pretty bad fight. I'd think anybody in that room would have tried to help her, especially our angel Candice."

"I told you, it was an accident. I didn't—"

"This!" Elise grabbed Lazarus's head and turned him

again toward Sara. Sara kept averting her eyes. "This! An accident?"

Then she threw his head to the floor again. She walked back up toward the window and gave a quick throw of her hand. "Pull his chains. Pull at him a few times. Let me hear him wail."

The guards shoved him to the ground. A couple of Officers lifted him up from behind, then threw him down and yanked at him again. When the guards were done torturing him, she cocked her head down at him from the top of the incline. "Who was holding the knife that killed Savant Harlow?" She wagged a finger at him. "And I warn you, I'm not gonna ask twice."

"I... I'm not sure."

"Wrong answer." She gestured to the Officers, but he tugged at his chains and screamed.

"Wait! I fell on her. I—"

"Why did you *FALL ON HER*!!!"

"Because... because we were fighting."

The idiot's honest. Better than Sara, anyway. His story matches the events completely with Rex's recording.

"When I fell, she must have held it," he continued. "She was waving it at me to get off her. When I fought her and tried to pin her, I must have fallen on the blade. That's... that's all I know."

Elise took a deep breath. Sara was crouched in a corner now, being held by two of the Officers. Sara covered her face in her arms as she cried.

"I'm sorry," Lazarus said. "I'm so sorry. None of it should have ever happened! I'm so sorry."

Elise looked back at him with wild eyes. She walked down slowly and stood right above him. "But it did, Lazarus. It did. You killed Candy Harlow, and to be honest, this trial is a complete sham. Truthfully, I don't give a damn as to what and how or whatever the hell happened. I don't even really care if you actually raped her."

She gestured for the Officers to lift him. They dragged him up like a marionette. Then she practically spat in his face.

"You fool. Your little accident cost me all the happiness in this fucked-up world, and for that, you ugly piece of shit, I will hurt you! I will hurt you far worse than you can imagine." Then she gently lifted up his chin and smiled a fake grin. "Before you are taken from this world, I will take your body and inflict as much pain on it as possible. I will make you feel all the pain I feel now, you fucking wad of shit."

She turned and walked back to the window. She heard the whimpering behind her as she folded her hands behind her back again. This time, it was too much. She spun around.

"Take him! Take him and burn him! Burn his flesh slowly in our lab. Burn him until his flesh melts from his face. But make sure it doesn't kill him. No. We wouldn't want that. No, that won't do at all. When he recovers, burn him some more. Do it again and again until he finally dies a slow miserable natural death!"

She was breathing heavily, and for a moment she had to steady herself. Lazarus was so shocked by the order that he finally stopped crying. Even Sara stopped whimpering.

"I'm gonna hurt you, you little prick!" Elise continued. "And then... it will be merciful, because maybe, just maybe, the pain will take away your guilt for killing your sweet mother —the only one who ever cared for you."

He said nothing, only nodded.

"Drag him to HQ lab!" Elise shouted to her Officers.

They bowed before her. She turned and walked up to the window again.

"We will give you a report when he dies, Mother," the Chief Officer said.

"Wait." Elise put her gloved hand up. She turned once more and looked at Lazarus with a wicked smile, walking slowly down the ramp to him once more. "Did you know, Lazarus, that three months ago I ordered Candy to kill you? I bet you didn't know that. I tried to force her. I arranged for you to stay at her home, thinking you would drive her as crazy as you drove me. She never did. She just suffered for you, like she did for the rest of us. Well, no longer, my boy. Now the only one who will suffer is you."

"Yes, Mother."

"I'm not your fucking mother." She turned to her soldiers. "Take him away."

30

THE END

CANDICE HARLOW'S FUNERAL WAS THE GREATEST FANFARE event that had crossed the city of Arkite in a century. Elise spared no expense for her love, arranging a motorcade for a mile with citizens forced to crowd along the sidewalks and cry over the death of their Chief Scientist and Chief Savant. Elise had Sara stand atop the front car float with her. They both wore black, with Sara for the first time wearing a copy of Team Mother's guillotine-like choker and black makeup.

Elise shed tears but stood at attention with a look of rage more than sorrow. It fit her. She also had to frequently help Sara stand as the poor girl continuously wiped her eyes with a white handkerchief and swooned. The mahogany coffin trailed behind them as they rode slowly along the road to Central Park.

Central Park was not a cemetery. There was no cemetery in the city. Citizens were cremated in Arkite. But for Candice, Elise had set up a plot of land for her mausoleum. It was to be placed in the park, exactly in the center of the city, directly under the opening of the Pyramid walls of Arkite. She and Sara knew how much Candice loved the green grass and trees of the park—the delicate fanciful arched bridges and meandering brooks. So, instead of a customary cremation, they would bury her as they used to do in ancient times.

The Officers marched in long black trench coats in single file on both sides of the large moving platform, protecting their Team Mother. Many of them held handkerchiefs for tears too, having been fortunate enough to have known their kind Chief Savant personally.

It was a pleasant midafternoon. The weather was temperate, not too hot and not too cold. That fit Candice, and Elise smiled at that.

By early evening, Elise rode back with Sara alone through the clouds to her penthouse. Then Elise invited her for a private meeting in her third floor "office."

It was dark in the house, with only the mood lights at the floor of the three-story apartment lighting the ramp. The two of them walked to the top floor. Then, as if the trial were still being held, Elise stared out of her window, chewing gum, her hands folded behind her back as Sara stood on the ramp below.

"I'm reporting for duty, Team Mother." Sara stood at attention. Elise smiled thinly.

Her heart was broken. So was Sara's. There was no energy left in them. Elise wondered if she would ever be whole again.

Elise walked over to a small table where she had arranged a bottle of red wine and two glasses. "I saved this for a special occasion," she said quietly. "But... I had hoped it would be more of a celebration." She uncorked the bottle and poured it into two glasses. "This is the oldest red wine in my cellar. Candice would have liked it. She always liked sharing red wine with me. Can you join me, Sara?"

"Of course, Mother."

Sara walked over to the green couch. She blew her nose and wiped her eyes with a white handkerchief.

Elise looked at Sara's face. Finally, the bruises and black

eye were fading. In time, Sara would be her beautiful self again. Then Elise looked at Sara's long blond hair and her pretty blue eyes. Her golden hair was tied in a ponytail. Her eyes were sapphire, exactly like Candice's.

"Did you know," Elise asked as she handed her a glass and sat beside her, "that you kinda look like her?"

"Yeah. Candice used to joke that she was looking in a mirror."

"It's almost like you were her sister," said Elise, running a hand through Sara's hair. "And you two liked each other so much."

"I once checked Magnacourt's database," Sara said. "Turns out we were cousins. The incubators made us with nearly matching gametes, but I'm younger, of course."

"Yeah."

Elise moved closer. She took another sip of her wine. It was lovely, the smoothest vintage she had ever tasted.

"I can't believe it, Mother," Sara said, choked up and on the verge of tears again. "I just can't believe it."

"Shh," Elise said, touching Sara's hair once more. "I know. Just don't think of it. Don't even mention it."

Sara smiled and nodded. She rubbed her sharp nose and turned toward the window. She stared out at the view with Elise.

"It is a great honor, Mother," Sara said, finally breaking the silence. She sat up straighter. "I'll do all I can, but I can't match her. Candice was—"

"Don't mention her anymore," said Elise, raising a hand. "Please. Don't."

"I'll do the best I can at the job."

"You'll do fine. I need help in the lab. You can finish the work and adapt it for the people."

"I'll do what I can."

"You'll do fine." Elise patted her leg. Then she jumped up and walked back to the window. There Elise stood sipping her wine for what seemed like forever. Occasionally, she heard the stir of her guest blowing her nose, but otherwise it was quiet behind her insulated window.

Below, the city was vibrant with life. There were flying cars and drones with glowing headlights circling along the pyramidal towers. And far below, on the streets, the citizenry had gone back to their mundane ways: ladies ran across streets, little girls chased each other under streetlamps, and everyday workers in boring gray suits from HQ emerged from nearby buildings to go home.

"Is it true?" Sara asked. "Did you propose to her?"

"What?" Elise turned. "I loved her—more than anyone in the world. That's all you need know... I suppose we were both lucky to have known her."

"I'm sorry for you, Elise." Sara looked deep in her eyes.

"Don't be," Elise said, her voice cracking. She gripped her leather-gloved hands tight and tore her eyes away from Sara's eyes: her blue eyes. Those eyes. Suddenly Elise couldn't stand those blue eyes. Not now. Sara's blue eyes and long golden hair were all too familiar. Whereas before it had comforted her, now it felt like a mockery, reminding her that she would never see Candice again.

It was too much. Tears began streaming down Elise's cheeks. It was the first time she had broken down so hard, and the first time in front of someone else. Sara reached up to comfort her, but she violently waved her away.

"I said, don't mention her," said Elise. Then she rushed to the table and threw her glass down, making her way quickly down the ramp. But by the first floor, Elise cocked her head back and said formally, "It would be nice to have company. You can stay the night, if you'd like, Savant Holmes. Please make yourself at home."

"I'd like that, Mother."

Sara couldn't sleep. Besides Elise's place being the nicest house ever, she could not stop thinking of her lover. And now she was gone.

The tears wouldn't stop. She looked at her wrist. It was three fifteen in the morning. She looked through the small window in the guest room. There was a toy sitting on the windowsill, a miniature sports car. She shuddered for a moment, realizing that she was sleeping in what had once been Lazarus's room.

She jumped up in her white nightgown. It was cold, and she folded her arms. She grabbed a robe on top of the bed and walked to the window.

Inside the robe—it was one of Candice's old robes—she found a packet of gum. She took out a piece and chewed. She hadn't had Mint in a week, and she needed it now more than ever. She knew it would keep her from sleeping, but she didn't care anymore.

"Are you all right, Savant Holmes?" asked Rex quietly. "It's very late. You should be in bed."

"Yeah, I'm fine. Just can't sleep."

"Well, Mint is not going to help."

"I know... hey, how did you know I was chewing?"

"I can hear your mouth, Sara."

"Oh."

Outside she could see the skyscrapers with many of their windows still shining yellow. So many people were up even at this ugly hour. There was a dense fog, and the light glowed about the windows. She looked beyond and could just barely see the shadow of the great pyramid wall surrounding the city.

I need rest. I have to get up early tomorrow and help Elise.

She yawned. "Rex? Are you still there?"

"I'm always here, Sara."

"How close was Candice with coding all gene variants into the mainframe?"

"Very. It is unfortunate that she died. She could have

completed her work and presented immortality to all four sectors in merely a handful of months. Now it could take much longer."

"Is that all? You're sad because Candy couldn't finish her work? Don't you feel anything for her? You worked with her every day for the past five years. You were closer to her than anyone."

Rex chuckled. It disturbed Sara, and a shiver ran down her spine. His laughter sounded just like Lazarus's.

"I don't feel anything," Rex said. "I have no emotion, Savant Holmes. I am a computer."

"Of course." She yawned. But her heart started beating faster. It was the Mint taking effect. "What remains to be sequenced?"

"You really should sleep, Savant. You've got a lot of work tomorrow morning. Why not worry about it when Elise takes you to HQ? Congratulations, by the way. I'm sure you will make an exemplary Savant for Magnacourt. And what an honor to be elevated to Lead Assistant to Mother."

"Please answer my question."

"Chromosome 23. Chromosome 23 is still being studied."

"The sex chromosome? That's all that's left? Why that one?"

"That is correct, Sara. Candice was close to completing the genetic modifications in all chromosomes but the last. She was likely concerned that research of the sex chromosome could lead to further XY research, which had previously cost the life of her best friend, Savant Bridgette Kelley. So she was being very cautious in sequencing it into the mainframe."

Sara nodded. "But... it can be researched without reproducing an XY, right?"

"Yes. But all citizens of Arkite are women. It is tricky. The blueprint was Lazarus—a man. And his structure can no longer be directly studied. The cellular structure of the last chromosome will have to be researched and modified to work for XX. That will take time."

"Well, there was Lazarus," Sara said with a shrug. "Perhaps we should create another complete specimen again?"

"No, Sara, it will take time," Rex said.

He chuckled again. As disturbing as that was, Sara found his words had altered too, becoming oddly smooth—clearer than she had ever heard a machine speak before, with no mechanical intonation whatsoever. Perhaps she was just tired and it was late.

"I'm quite sure, Sara." He added, "Elise will never sanction the creation of a man again."

THE END

ENJOY THE FURTHER ADVENTURES OF CANDICE AND ELISE IN THE CONCLUDING BOOK IN THIS TWO-BOOK DUOLOGY DYSTOPIAN SERIES: MOTHER SAVANT

2244. The all-female society of Arkite is on the brink of revolution. Supreme leader Elise Jackson has spent the last two years trying to repair her lover's damaged body and mind, but the Savant Council has no interest in squandering the city's resources for Elise's personal gain. Only the return of the Mother Savant can hope to maintain order.

ALSO BY A.L. HAWKE

THE NEXT BOOK IN THE SAVANT SERIES

- MOTHER SAVANT (BOOK 2)

PARANORMAL ROMANCE

- THE HAWTHORNE UNIVERSITY WITCH SERIES I-III
- THE HAWTHORNE UNIVERSITY WITCH SERIES 4-6
- THE HAWTHORNE UNIVERSITY WITCH HOLIDAY COLLECTION

- SHADES
- HAUNTING JOY
- PHANTOM MASQUERADE

- MY EVIL EYE
- THE GUARDIAN
- NECTAR OF AMBROSIA
- CORA

FANTASY: THE AZURE SERIES

- HARMONIA
- CORA: RISE OF THE FALLEN GODDESS
- AZURE BLUE
- CORAL RED
- PRINCESS SOJOURN

Books available at https://alhawke.com/books

PARTING WORDS

What did you think of *Candy Savant?* By placing a book review, you can inform others of your thoughts and help spread the word about my book.

Want more? Periodically I like to send news regarding current or new projects. If you'd like to be privy, I encourage you to sign up. Your information will remain private and you can cancel any time.

Sign up at www.alhawke.com or scan the following QR code:

Sign Up

ACKNOWLEDGMENTS

I owe a lot to the following people who shared my story. Thanks to my beta readers Rob C., George B., and John P. Your patient diligence over my writing obsession has finally paid off. See, here it is!

Huge thanks to my line editor Paul Witcover and copy editor Eliza Dee of Clio Editing Services. Some readers outside the writing world just don't realize how integral an editor's work is in shaping a novel. You've colored and enhanced my art.

And to Damon Za for book design and creating a really amazing cover.

ABOUT THE AUTHOR

A.L. Hawke is the author of the bestselling Hawthorne University Witch series. The author lives in Southern California torching the midnight candle over lovers against a backdrop of machines, nymphs, magic, spice and mayhem. A.L. Hawke writes fantasy and romance spanning four thousand years, from pre-civilization to contemporary and beyond.

Visit A.L. Hawke at www.alhawke.com

Email: contact@alhawke.com

www.ingramcontent.com/pod-product-compliance
Lightning Source LLC
Chambersburg PA
CBHW061553100726
47898CB00002B/352